FILTHY PLAYER

STACEY LYNN

Filthy Player
By
Stacey Lynn

Editing: Ellie at Love N. Books Author Services
Proofreading: Virginia Tesi Carey
Cover Design: Shanoff Designs

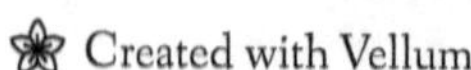 Created with Vellum

ONE

PAIGE

"You're late. Again."

I stared at my boss, Paulie, and tried not to flinch at not only his scowl but also the sweat already dotting his forehead.

"I know, and I'm really sorry, but my dad—"

"Enough excuses. If I heard one, I heard a million." His hand slashed through the air to silence my reason, not excuse. It's not like it was my fault my dad collapsed out of his wheelchair trying to get into his recliner and it took me twenty minutes to get him re-settled. I needed a weight lifting class.

I needed the money to pay for it first.

"Get to work," Paulie continued. "Annabelle called in sick tonight so we're down one waitress, and I heard the Riders might be coming in after their press conference."

"Great," I mumbled, at both the Raleigh Rough Riders football team coming in and the fact Annabelle was another no-show. I was late occasionally, but at least I showed. Annabelle was the least dependable waitress we had.

Least hard-working too, when she did show, and that bugged me more than her not showing.

"I'm warning you though, Paige," Paulie said, leaning in close enough I had to lean back. The man was overweight, with a gut that could bounce me into the wall five feet behind us. "This is your last chance. Be on time or don't come at all."

I wanted to remind him this was at least the tenth time Annabelle hadn't shown at all, only the third time I was late, but it wouldn't matter. Annabelle was his niece. He had to keep her on the payroll.

Me, on the other hand…

He huffed and puffed and shuffled away while I tied my black apron around my waist. When I started working at the Ride'Em Rough Saloon, a pretty trashy name for an American Grill but it worked because we were doors away from the Rough Riders stadium, every waitress assured me Paulie's bark was worse than his bite.

I hoped it was true.

Hours into my shift, I had boob sweat in my shirt, an impressive task considering my boobs were less than impressive. My hair was matted to the nape of my neck, and everyone in the city of Raleigh must have heard the Rough Riders were headed in after the press conference. They had one every year after pre-season, but before week one started. The place was so packed we had a line outside wrapping around the block.

On busy nights like that, Paulie hired bouncers who could give professional wrestlers a run for their money. The place was so crushed I wondered if one or more of them didn't show either.

My feet ached, my arches burned in the wedge sandals we were forced to wear with our cut-off denim shorts and tummy bearing, skin-tight teal shirts—the color of the Rough Riders— and I had had it.

Had it with men who thought they could brush their hand over my ass because I was wearing a uniform dictated to me.

Had it with drunken boys barely old enough to be legal hanging around, waiting for a glimpse of their heroes just because they could throw a pigskin thirty yards like well-aimed rockets.

I was born with Rough Rider love in my veins, but four hours into my shift, I had had it with them, too.

My dad loved football. Loved everything about the game and had been good enough to play for Purdue before he moved back to Raleigh to take over his dad's auto mechanic garage. My mom had wanted the football superstar she'd started dating in college, not the guy who sometimes had two pennies to rub together. When she decided she had enough of being married to an auto mechanic and not the luxurious life she'd grown up in and hoped she'd find with Dad, she took off back to her hometown in Michigan.

Apparently, she hadn't wanted me, either. I was four years old when she left. But no matter, Dad and I did just fine.

At least until he had a stroke a year ago, followed by another a few months later that left the right side of his body mostly paralyzed. He was finally getting some movement back, able to use a walker occasionally, but he still needed help taking care of himself and the house. On top of his paralysis, the strokes had affected his cognitive abilities and he didn't always make the best decisions.

Now, I was stuck not only managing the office at his garage but working for Paulie to make ends meet due to our astronomical medical bills.

I needed help, but there was no way I was asking for it. Nothing good ever came with asking for help, except strings that weren't worth the help given in the first place.

"Damn, Paige," Hannah said, sliding up to me and bouncing my hip with hers to ensure she had my attention. "You are one lucky bitch."

"Why, now?" I punched in more orders on the computer screen and didn't spare her a glance.

"You kidding me, right? Ray just sat the team at your open six-top. What I wouldn't give for a piece of that beautiful, Grade-A, prime piece of beef."

Her voice went soft and I laughed softly. Freaking Hannah. More stars in her eyes than sense in her brain, she was always trying to score a Rider. The problem? She tried too hard and sent off stage-five clinger vibes from the moment she stepped near. I'd seen more than one guy from the team back off, weariness in his eyes even though she was stacked with huge boobs and a slamming bod. She was also sweeter than my grandma's cherry pie. But she came off too strong, a bit too crazy, way too much fangirl in her breath.

"Freaking hell," I muttered. "You want them?"

"I wish. Beaux Hale is here. I swear last time they were in he was totally checking me out. But Paulie would can me if I ever waited on them again."

Paulie and his threats. It wasn't necessarily Hannah's fault she went all doe-eyed stupid at the sight of NFL players. Wasn't her fault those men put off so much testosterone a woman's libido jumped to attention at the mere sight of them. They wore their pheromones like I wore my independence... bright and shining like Times Square on New Years.

The men just had it.

I couldn't lie and say I was unaffected, but the last thing I needed in my life was a football player with more plays than morals.

"It wasn't that bad." I reached for a tray of orders and thanked the cooks.

"I spilled four bowls of tomato soup all over Oliver Powell, Paige."

I snorted. I couldn't help myself. It had been funny, and the famous Rough Rider's tight end always came across as a pretty uptight guy anyway. I didn't exactly feel bad for him getting doused with humble soup. Besides, someone else had bumped her and balancing heavy trays was difficult.

The guys he was with had laughed their asses off and no one had cared except for Paulie who was afraid he'd lose their business.

"Okay. So that was pretty bad, but I'll still give you all my tips if you take them for me. I'll make an excuse to Paulie if he notices."

I'd made hundreds in tips so far, and we needed it, but I was exhausted and serving a six-top of Rough Riders wasn't my idea of fun.

She rolled her eyes. "Like I'd do that to you. You need it."

See? Hannah was the best.

I didn't hide much but I wasn't an open book. Still, my dad had come in while I was working enough times for most of my co-workers to know his health wasn't the best and I was the one responsible for him.

"Do you know what you also need?"

I steadied my tray of burgers and glanced over my shoulder. "What?"

"You need to get laid." She grinned and practically bounced on her feet. "And oh look...a bunch of sexy men are at your table. I'm sure all the single ones would take you up on that."

"You're incorrigible," I said and walked away to the sound of Hannah's playful laughter.

The girl was nuts. She was also right. It'd been so long since I'd had sex I was beginning to think I forgot what dicks looked like.

But that didn't mean I was going to be taken by a Rough Rider.

No way.

No how.

Not ever.

~

"WELCOME TO RIDE'EM ROUGH, what can I get y'all to drink tonight?"

I tried to keep my voice firm and polite, a feat considering the mountain of men who surrounded the table in front of me.

Six Rough Riders, all big and strong, all grinning at me like I was their next meal.

It wasn't the first time I'd waited on some of the players, but it was never easy to stay calm in their presence.

I'd been a fan of the team since before I could speak, had the onesie I wore home from the hospital when I was born to prove it. Twenty-six years of watching the guys on television didn't prepare me for the visceral reaction my body had when I started working here over the summer.

It was also the first time I'd waited on Beaux Hale, even though he'd been in a handful of times. He was the starting quarterback and now he was seated next to me, close enough I could feel the heat of his body pouring off him through his shirt.

My gaze roamed the table and all eyes went to Beaux. Heaven help me, the man was undeniably sexy.

His eyes were blue, a thick pile of blond hair on top of his head. His cologne wafted off him in gentle, subtle waves I barely picked up over the scent of burgers and beer. He was also the only one in the group sporting a simple gray T-shirt instead of dress shirt and tie.

He totally rocked it.

By the smirk he gave me, he knew it.

"Two pitchers of whatever local IPA you have on tap."

"We have Vortex and Freak Nature." There went my voice. So much for strong. It wobbled harsher than our willow tree in the wind.

I usually didn't have a hard time being sane and normal around these men. They were guys like everyone else, they just made millions more than I'd ever see and wouldn't have to worry about taking care of their ailing parents.

Still, there had always been something about Beaux Hale that got to me in places I didn't quite hate.

Sacred, sensitive places.

"I don't know about the rest of these chumps," Beaux said, lowering his voice and leaning close, "but I like a little bit of freaky nature every now and then."

Oh goodness. I'd fan myself if it wouldn't make it too obvious. So much for my ability to stay unaffected by these guys. Hale was on a different plane than the rest.

I'd seen too much of him on Sportscenter and the covers of People and GQ. He was Raleigh's new hero, leading the team to their Super Bowl victory last season.

There were claims they were ready and able to do it again this year. They certainly had the talent.

I knew because I watched more ESPN with my dad than any other channel on television. And all summer long, the news since the draft and last year's win had been if the Rough Riders could come back for a two-peat.

So far, Vegas odds were pointing toward yes due to the fact they had just won all four of their pre-season games.

"Okay then," I said, and my voice had gone soft. Dreamy. Good grief, thirty seconds around the man and I'd turned into Hannah.

"Anything else?" I asked the table forcing my gaze to move from Beaux.

"I think we're good," one I didn't recognize, said.

"Oh," Kolby Jones, one of the team's wide receivers, said. "I think I'll have what Hale's having."

"No one's getting what I'm about to have." The firmness and richness of Beaux's voice startled me and I looked at him. "I don't share," he continued. His glare turned to the table before coming back to me. Then the glare evaporated, the blue eyes sparkled at me, and he winked.

Ruining my fantasies and snapping me back to reality.

Right. This man took a two-week long RV trip every summer and based on tabloids my dad had shared, because he shared everything Hale related, he'd had quite the summer. His adventures pictured him partying with various blondes and brunettes and a few redheads. Apparently the man didn't discriminate. All of them were dressed in barely there bikinis while Beaux's board shorts fell low on his hips, showing off a bare chest and a stomach that put washboards to shame.

He might have had an arm like a rocket and accuracy better than any Olympic archer, but this guy played the field of women faster than he threw a pass.

It was the last thing I needed.

"I'll be back with your drinks and to take your orders in a few minutes," I said, refusing to look at him. Around the table, men wore smirks as well as they wore their loosened ties.

No amount of tips was worth this stress. I'd give it to Hannah and work a double next weekend.

"What if I already know what I want?" Beaux asked, turning in his chair. One of his arms draped over the back of his chair, one rested on the table. Both of his hands were close enough he could brush his fingers over my thigh or against my ass.

My body shivered with anticipation before I scowled, his meaning clear.

"I'm pretty sure whatever you want isn't available."

I turned and hurried away to the bar and placed my order, refusing to look back, refusing to see if I had his attention.

I already knew I did.

I felt his eyes on my ass as I walked away so strongly it felt like his hands were already on me.

TWO

BEAUX

"Crash and burn, huh baby Hale? Man, that sucks. Probably doesn't happen much does it."

I shoved Kolby's elbow off the table, pushing him away from me.

"In your dreams. And who are you calling a baby?" But damn, he was right.

When was the last time I'd gotten such a quick brush-off? I'd seen the interest in our pretty waitress's eyes when she first saw me. It was impossible to miss the way her cheeks turned pink or how her breath went soft.

All of that happened about point two seconds before my dick hardened when she stepped close to me. She was fucking gorgeous and it wasn't the first time since I'd been in to Ride'Em Rough I noticed her.

She'd tried to hide it, but I'd had enough women throwing themselves at my feet over the last few years to recognize the signs.

I was also getting sick of it. This summer's vacation, one I took every year to blow off steam before I had to report back for pre-season training, had made me realize how tired I was getting of the fan-girling. The boobs thrust into my face, the autographs demanding to be signed, the constant touching my body like they had a right to it just because I was on television for three and a half hours every week.

Whatever happened to common decency?

I'd cut my trip early when I found myself missing my sister and the guys on my team who had become more like brothers than teammates more than usual.

Not that Shannon had missed me much. She'd fallen in love with Oliver Powell, our tight end and resident asshole team captain.

Fortunately, he'd fallen for her too. They were now engaged, planning their wedding for as soon as this season was done.

As much as I might have been tired of women shoving their boobs into my face, being so quickly rejected by a woman who blushed and went breathy in my presence was something new.

I kinda liked it.

Grinning, I rubbed my bottom lip and took a drink of my water while we waited for our drinks.

"I know what you're going to be dreaming of later tonight," Brian Matthews said. He was our center, and he and I were tight. Had to be considering I shoved my hands near his balls on every play of the game. He was my first in line protector and every time he saved me from a sack on a blitz, I owed him my life.

"Fuck off," I growled. God, I was strung tight. There was stress pressing down on me from all sides this season, more so than last, and the press conference earlier had cemented every-one's expectations for us. "Besides, there's no fun in the victory if there's no work in the fight."

Matthews fist-pumped me and nodded. "That's right, man."

The table erupted in a round of affirmations, but I didn't need them.

I didn't become the best quarterback in the NFL by luck. It was part skill, a whole hell of a lot of effort.

It helped that my body was built for speed and strength, something I'd worked on honing since I was twelve and had my first taste of a youth football championship.

I worked my ass off every day for what I wanted, never giving up, never giving in. If our pretty little waitress thought one rebuff would work on me, then she didn't know who she was talking to.

"Two pitchers of Freaky Nature." She stood on the opposite side of the table, as far away from me as she could get, and set down the pitchers. "Do you gentlemen know what you'd like to eat?"

I was beginning to. On further inspection, she wasn't only beautiful, she also seemed tired and worn down. Light purple circles were under her eyes, but it was the shining brown hair that swooped across her forehead in chunky bangs I was looking at. Slim fingers brushed them aside and I got the first peek of her eyes.

Beautiful almond-shaped, hazel eyes, chocolate hair, and shimmering pink lips.

Oh, yeah. I knew exactly what I wanted to eat.

"I'm ready," I crooned, my intent clear in the thickness of my voice.

Her eyes fluttered up and for a moment, I sat there, stunned at the depth I noticed in her eyes.

She wasn't worn out, she wasn't tired from a hard night's work. This woman was exhausted. She wore it as clear as my mom used to when I was a kid and she worked three jobs in order to keep a roof over our head and pay for my football fees.

I suddenly felt like a dick for coming on so strong. I wasn't the player or the arrogant prick some people thought me to be. I worked damn hard. I played harder. I was also raised by two women who'd kick my ass to hell and back if I treated a woman like trash.

"Double cheeseburger, hold the fries and a side salad with ranch, please," I said, tossing my menu to the center of the table.

I'd been teasing the woman, Paige, I now knew from the stitched-on name just above her left breast on her shirt. I hadn't seen it before. "And before any of these knuckleheads start arguing about splitting up the check later and making you work six times harder than you need to, it's all on me tonight."

"What the hell?" Kolby guffawed. "You're too cheap to pay for our crap."

"Not cheap. Frugal."

We'd had this argument before. Kolby thought I was a tight wad with my money because I didn't give a shit what I wore, barely ever bought anything new unless it was absolutely necessary. Hell, my entire team gave me crap about my old Ford pickup I'd had since high school.

Why the hell would I buy something new when the one I had still ran just fine?

Well, except for the strange sputtering it'd been making lately, but that was beside the point.

I came from shit, worked myself out of it, and no way in hell was I going back there.

One wrong hit and my career and endorsements could end before Christmas. I'd set myself up to live easy for the rest of my life. I never saw the point in throwing away millions on mansions and sports cars when if my career went, so did all that crap.

Kolby got it, despite the fact he did live in a mansion, but he had a daughter to take care of and a mom who lived with them. He needed a home.

I liked my brownstone just fine.

"Making it easier on Paige," I said. "It's busy and I was trying to help."

I glanced at her, saw her mouth drop open and her eyes flutter rapidly before she shook her head.

Her cheeks bloomed when she did. A pretty faint pink color I wanted to explore at other times, but now wasn't it.

I knew where she worked. I'd approach when she wasn't busting her ass.

"Order, assholes," I said, knocking my knuckles on the table. "We've got a meeting to get back to."

While the rest of the table ordered, I filled their glasses with beer. When they were done, I collected all the menus and handed them to Paige across the table, my arm long enough to reach so she didn't have to bend much.

"Thanks," she whispered, her eyes on me, a little bit glassy.

"Not a problem. Had a mom who waited tables. It's hard shit." I grinned intentionally, hoping like hell I looked sincere. I was.

She took the menus and gave another swipe of the table with her eyes. "Need anything else before I put your order in?"

Quinten opened his mouth.

"We're good," I said before he could speak. The guy was one of our best running backs. He was also picky as hell. I imagined him requesting six additional things to his order plus making it complicated. He could deal with whatever he got.

"Sounds good. I'll be back with your food as soon as it's ready."

"Thanks, Paige."

She blushed further and looked at her chest where her name was scrawled. She nodded once and walked away.

When she was gone, Kolby nudged me in the elbow like I'd done to him.

"The hell?"

"What?" I drank my beer. Smooth and sweet. Damn, I loved the local beers in Raleigh.

"You were nice to her."

"I want in her pants, dickface, I wasn't going to be rude."

A gasp hit me from behind the table and I cringed. Ah hell.

I turned and behind me was Paige. There was fury in her tired hazel eyes and a filled pitcher of ice water in her hand.

Then her hand lifted, and before I could move out of the way, it was dumped all over my head.

"Shit!" I ducked my head as ice fell down my shirt and all over my body.

"Never gonna happen, asshole." She twirled and stomped away.

"Aww fuck!" I was damn cold, dripping in ice and cold water that ran down my face and beneath my shirt, landing in a pool on my lap.

Around us, the entire restaurant had gone dead silent.

All except for my teammates, who were laughing so hard some had tears running down their cheeks.

"Go suck a bag of dicks," I said to all of them, shaking my hands in the faces of the men close enough to get wet.

Then I leaned over the table, shook my hair like a dog, splattering water all over the place and pushed back from the table.

I had my suit I had to wear earlier in my car. I hated wearing it, but at least it was dry.

"Mr. Hale, Mr. Hale, I'm so sorry. Please, let me help you."

An overweight man rushed toward me, white towels in his hand that couldn't hide the jumping of his large gut. "Please excuse my server," he said, shooting a glare in the direction where Paige had disappeared. "It appears we need more training."

I grabbed a towel out of his hand and wiped my face. "No big deal," I said. "Shit happens. Don't worry about it."

After what she heard me say, it's not like I didn't deserve it.

Hell, I even liked that she doused me. It showed she had guts and the ability to stand up for herself. My kind of woman.

"I'll take care of this immediately," he said, and by the look in his eyes, I knew how he was going to handle it.

"Honestly, man. It's not a problem. No harm, no foul. Besides, it's not like I haven't had an ice bath before." I laughed it off, using the towel to dry my arms and then I took the rest of the towels from his hand and tossed them on the table.

"Can you help and get this table cleaned up?" I asked the guys. One would do it. We weren't all entitled assholes like people wanted to believe. Rich yes, but not entitled. There wasn't a player I'd met yet who wasn't grateful for the opportunity to be playing ball for a living.

"You got it, Hale," Quinten said.

I turned back to the guy I assumed was the manager and lifted my hands. "See? No problem. If you'll excuse me, I'm going to get something dry on."

"I'll speak to your server about this while you're gone."

He hurried away before I could stop him.

My mom had lost more jobs than I could remember for reasons more minor than this.

Waitressing jobs were a dime and dozen, easy to find, easy to lose.

Damn.

I hurried out to my truck, shoved off my now soaking wet jeans and ripped off my shirt. Once re-dressed in the suit pants and dress shirt, I headed back inside.

I needed to find Paige and her manager before I owed her a hell of a lot more than an apology.

THREE

PAIGE

My hands were shoved into my hair, my eyes closed and I growled at the ceiling in a way that sounded feral and shocking to my own ears.

Damn him. Stupid men! For a split second when he'd mentioned his mom, I actually thought Beaux Hale might be a decent human being, despite his earlier sexual innuendo and flirting.

I'd thought he was so nice I'd grabbed the water pitcher from Hannah before I placed the football team's order.

It was rare in the service industry that people not only recognized how hard you worked but took steps to make that job a little bit easier. Splitting bills wasn't rocket science. It certainly wasn't brain surgery. It was the thought behind his actions that made my stomach flutter and my spine warm in a way it hadn't in a long time.

Yeah, I was independent and used to taking care of my dad and myself. But sometimes, occasionally, in the dark of night, what I really wanted was someone to come along, take my hand

and say, "Have a seat, honey. You've had a long day. I've got this."

This didn't have to be a big thing, it could have been unloading the dishwasher, taking out the trash, or grabbing the mail or the newspaper at the end of the driveway I always neglected.

This could be anything, and with Beaux's shining blue eyes on me, Hannah's reminder of my lack of a sex life, for a moment...one small, tiny, barely-there moment, I'd really liked the idea Beaux would be somebody like that for me, even if the small thing he was offering was saving me only a few minutes at my job.

But then he had to open his mouth. He was just as arrogant, just as cocky and self-serving as most of the men I'd come across in the last few years. More takers than givers, more likely to get off than ensure I did first, more likely to blow their load and begin wondering when I would leave before offering me a glass of water.

He was like the rest. Actually, he was worse. He knew it and clearly knew how to play the game. Flash a smile and a wink, offer up something nice, and just like all other strings, he tightened the noose and let it swing.

Ugh.

Stupid, stupid, stupid.

"What are you doing?" Hannah asked, rushing into the break room where I'd escaped to regain control of my emotions. "Are you insane? You just doused Beaux Hale of all people! What happened?"

"He's an asshole, that's what happened."

"No way." Her hands landed on her hips, and change jingled in her waist apron. "Not Beaux. Everything I've read about the guy says he super sweet. And you've read about his relationship with his sister."

"Having a sister doesn't mean he's not a jerk, Hannah." Stars in her eyes were shining bright like diamonds. Naive little girl. I swore she still believed in once upon a times and happily ever afters.

I'd thought I had found mine with Spencer, but I was wrong. We dated for two years and had lived together for one of them. Our relationship crumbled when my dad got sick and I moved home. After only two weeks of trying long-distance, he called and said it was over because I no longer had the time to invest into our relationship.

It was the first time a guy had left me because I couldn't give him my full attention due to helping my dad, but he wasn't the last. I'd tried dating since moving home, but in the end, those men also walked away when I couldn't give them the time they wanted.

Sorry, assholes and losers, my dad owned top spot. At least, he would until someone came along and realized that me taking care of him wasn't a burden, but an honor. How could I not when he'd given me everything he had and made me the woman I was today, busting his ass left and right at his garage so I could have the best of everything?

I turned to Hannah, hating to blow the light out of her excitement and told her what he said. When I was done, her pale green eyes were in danger of popping right out of their sockets.

"No way! He didn't!"

I nodded. "He most certainly did."

Saying it out loud stung worse than the reality that he was like everyone else. How ridiculous of me to think otherwise.

Good grief, I'd almost lost myself in his manners and charm. Was I really that hard up for a decent guy? I mean, I'd even been considering letting him in my pants if the opportunity presented itself until he told his whole table that was all he wanted from me.

Sorry, not sorry... I was raised with a small amount of decency. That meant not falling into a guy's pants just because he crooked two thick, callused fingers.

I had to stop thinking about it. Problem was, I knew Paulie wasn't going to let me.

"So, how bad is Paulie when he's really pissed?" I asked Hannah.

Her lips twisted and she made a face. "Well, I'm still here, so." She shrugged in that innocent, playful way of hers I loved so much. I pulled her to me and gave her a quick hug.

"Thanks for listening to me."

"Anytime, Paige."

I grinned. She grinned back.

"I should probably go find Paulie, huh?"

"Um. Well, when I saw him he was rushing to help Beaux."

"Great."

I walked around her and she called my name.

"What?"

"Well, I mean... would it really be bad to have him get in your pants anyway?" She smiled and her gaze did that hazy, glossing thing. "He was really sexy in a soaking wet shirt. Imagine how good he'd look out of it."

I laughed despite myself. "You're a nut, Hannah."

I opened the door and walked through as she yelled, "Yeah, but I'm a nut who gets laid!"

That girl. I was still shaking my head and laughing as I went in search of Paulie.

He was easy to find once I stepped out of the break room just off the hallway that led to the restrooms.

"What are you thinking girl?" he all but shouted, gaining the attention of several customers walking by us or seated at the nearby tables. "Beaux Hale? Of the Rough Riders? Did you have a brain fart tonight and forget who you were serving when you threw a pitcher of water all over him?"

"I'm really sorry, Paulie, I really am." I gave him the most apologetic expression I could muster. "I slipped."

"Slipped?" he blustered and repeated himself. "Slipped? You slipped? On what, your brain? You can't go dumping water on the Rough Rider's quarterback and not expect that to hit the news! No one will come anymore if the team stops coming."

I choked back a laugh and pressed my lips together. Pissed off Paulie was sort of entertaining. Unfortunately, I preferred him when he wasn't shouting at me, especially when I deserved it.

"She did," a deep voice said and all my humor instantly evaporated. "She did slip. Honestly sir, it was my fault."

Um. What?

Paulie turned and his jaw dropped as both of us stood, staring at Beaux. His hands were slid into suit pants and he was now wearing a dry and slightly wrinkled white dress shirt. Huh.

His hair was still a bit wet, and for a brief second, I almost felt bad for what I did to him. Then I remembered what he said and I glared at him.

"Excuse me, Mr. Hale?"

"Beaux, please." He lifted a hand and turned his stupid charming smile on Paulie. "She was right behind our table and I had jumped back, hitting her. Honestly, like I said earlier, it wasn't a problem, and like I just said, totally my fault. I didn't mean to bump into her, it just happened."

I scowled at him. He swooped the wind and anger out of Paulie's sails with one simple little lie. Now what did he want from me?

"That true?" Paulie asked, and his gaze flickered between

us. He was as doubtful as he should be, but not exactly like he could argue.

I shrugged. "I told you I slipped."

He huffed, his belly jiggling like a shopping mall Santa Claus. "Okay, then," he said and pointed a finger at me. "Last chance."

"I'll do better, Paulie. I promise."

"Damn straight you will, young lady." He walked away back to the restaurant's bar where he kept his eyes on the staff.

I tried to breathe, but everything was still stuck in my chest. When Paulie left, Beaux had moved until he was close enough to remind me how much I liked his cologne.

Stupid men.

"Thanks," I muttered, refusing to look at him. "I appreciate it."

"I'm sorry." His voice was a deep rumble, and I fought the urge to shiver. He was so tall, broad-shouldered with a narrow waist. He looked damn good in that shirt, too. The sincerity in his apology made me feel ridiculously silly things. Things like hope and lust.

Now I was the stupid one.

"For what?" I finally asked, trying to glare at him. "Saying it or me hearing it?"

"Both."

At least he was honest. "Fair enough. Forgiven. If you'll excuse me, I need to get back to work."

I stepped to the side and he swung an arm out, blocking my path. I could have moved around him, but I was curious. What else could he possibly say to me?

"You might think I'm a dick, but I'm not. What I said wasn't right, even if you didn't hear it. I'm not an asshole, Paige, even if I did act like it. I just got carried away with the guys, but I am sorry."

"No worries. I should have had more self-control. It's not like it's the worst thing I've heard working here."

"Yeah," he said, his voice going tight. "But you shouldn't have to, and that doesn't make what I said right either."

Wow. I hadn't expected that at all. Maybe the sexy man wasn't the prick I'd made him out to be.

"Like I said," I smiled this time, softening my words, "you're forgiven. Now if you'll excuse me." I gestured toward his outstretched arm that was currently inches from my bare stomach. He could pull me to him in a second, wrap his arms around me, press his lips to mine—and woah...

What?

I shook my head to clear the vision but unfortunately, like my manners and work ethic, it was ingrained somewhere deep, somewhere I knew I'd be replaying it later.

"I have orders ready to be delivered to tables," I said, staring at his hand. "I really do need to get back to work."

"Have a good night, Paige."

His arm fell and he walked away, leaving me staring at thick, muscled thighs and a perfectly firm backside tucked nicely into well-fitted black suit pants.

Maybe I should have listened to Hannah.

A night with Beaux would certainly be memorable and a great way to get over my dry spell.

And what kind of guy apologized in such a genuine way? No guy I'd ever met.

Whatever. I needed money, and I needed a job, and I needed to take care of my dad.

Nothing else mattered. Not for me.

AFTER I GRADUATED from the University of North

Carolina with a communications degree, I'd stayed in Charlotte to work for a local news station. I did a lot of fetching coffee, typing up taglines for the news screen, and making sure guests had everything they needed in their dressing rooms. Essentially, I'd been a poorly paid, glorified assistant. I didn't mind. The journalism and communications field was a tough one to break into. It could have taken me years to become a headline reporter, sitting behind the desk on the five and six o'clock news.

While I'd been prepared for the challenge, I also didn't regret quitting my job or moving home to take care of my dad. He'd insisted he didn't need it, and I'd insisted he was wrong.

Stubborn as a mule, he'd said to me.

Apple doesn't fall far from the tree, I'd replied.

While there wasn't regret, I definitely had days, mostly when I was sitting in the office of his garage, paying bills with money we didn't have, taking care of customers, that I missed the life I had.

Now, I was back on my own, taking care of everything and everyone by myself, and working in the garage, doing all the things my dad had taught me by the time I was fourteen to ensure I'd be able to take care of my car and myself. My days consisted of changing oil, re-aligning brakes, swapping out spark plugs, changing flat tires, and passing off the more difficult automotive tasks I couldn't handle to our mechanics.

It took me forever to scrub motor oil out from beneath my nails and I'd given up trying. It was easier to keep them clipped short than soak them in stale gasoline before I went to Ride'Em Rough.

There were also days, like that morning, when I couldn't stop thinking about the night before.

After I returned to Beaux's table, I'd delivered their food, refilled their water — all of them passing on more beer — and done my job without any further flirting. It wasn't until they left, though, that I'd gasped at the tip they'd given me.

Seven hundred dollars.

Seven hundred freaking dollars.

It was obscene. Two pitchers of beer, six burgers and fries, and a few salads weren't worth nearly that much.

By the time I'd rushed to the parking lot, elbowing and shoving slightly drunken customers out of the way, they were gone.

I wanted to thank them. They had no idea how much that helped me.

It could keep the creditors breathing down my neck out of my hair for several more weeks.

For once, I had some spare money to lighten our load a little bit, at least in one area.

And Beaux Hale played a part in all of it.

"Ugh. Damn it," I groaned and rubbed my shoulders. Waiting tables and then spending most of the day bent over the hood of an engine or slumped over a desk didn't bode well for my posture or my health.

An echo of an engine running sparked my attention and I looked at the neon, Budweiser wall clock. We didn't open for another twenty minutes but it wasn't uncommon for customers to show up early, generally with a distasteful disposition due to needing help with their car before their workday started.

Just what I needed. A grumpy customer to match my mood.

I went back to working, head down, so focused on shuffling money away from Peter to pay Paul that I jumped as the bell rang on the front door.

I looked up at the sound of the bell still ringing and a masculine, deep chuckle I'd heard only hours before.

Beaux Hale was standing in my dad's garage, looking just as shocked to see me, as I was to see him.

"What the heck?" I asked. "Are you stalking me now?"

"Not at all." His grin widened, he stepped forward. "But I can't say I'm disappointed at all."

My long-time neglected girl parts quivered and took notice.

Beaux's thick mop of blond hair was messy on top, shaggy, almost to the point of needing a haircut but still just this side of sexy and cool. He had a dirt smudge on his cheek that only made him sexier. A man with some dirt on him was much better than perfectly polished in my book.

Plus, he was wearing a gray, Rough Rider's T-Shirt, black athletic pants, and tennis shoes that looked like they needed to be replaced years ago.

Casual.

Unassuming.

Sexy as hell.

I was royally screwed.

FOUR
BEAUX

Well, well, well. Imagine that. The girl I hadn't been able to stop thinking about since we left Ride'Em Rough last night happened to be sitting in front of me, lips parted in an inviting way, almost calling me to press my lips against hers and slide my tongue inside.

The amount of attention my dick had gotten in the last ten hours to thoughts of Paige were so obscene I had left my house this morning thinking I might need a sexual appetite suppressant.

It was unnatural to be so stuck on a girl, jack off so many times and still want more.

And lucky, lucky me...I'd never been so grateful for Betsy, my rusted out Ford pickup, breaking down than I was in that moment.

I stepped up to the desk, grinning down at her. She hadn't moved a muscle except to tilt her head back, looking me straight in the eye as I walked closer.

"Paige Halloway, I assume, of Halloway Motors?"

Halloway Motors was the closest garage to where my truck

broke down. A quick look at the info on my phone had told me a Sam and Paige Halloway ran it. I'd smacked myself for thinking about the Paige I'd met the night before just because a similar woman's name was on my phone screen.

"Paige?"

She cleared her throat and pushed away from the desk. "Yeah. Sorry, you just took me by surprise. How can we help you?"

"We?" I looked around the garage. She'd said multiple times last night she wasn't available. I assumed it was because I was being a dick. Not because she was literally, unavailable. No ring on her left hand, though...trust me, I always checked. My back pulled tight. "Are you married?"

I saw the moment she debated lying. Eyes slid to the left, lips curled up on one corner.

"No." She shook her head. "Not married. This garage is my dad's, was his dad's before. Like I said, what can we help you with?"

"Not sure." I didn't know shit about trucks except that when my hood started smoking, it was most likely coolant leaking. Maybe. It'd also been making some strange clunking sound. Whatever. "Truck's been acting up the last couple weeks. Started smoking this morning on my way to practice and I dumped some water in it to get it here. Your garage was closest to where I was."

"Okay. Let's go take a look, then."

Her? "You?"

"Yeah." Eyebrows shot up with a vicious look in her eyes. So I sucked at hiding my surprise. "I'm going to take a look under your hood. Gotta problem with that?"

I had a few things she could check under my hood...or hers...or whatever. A pretty woman and a messed up morning made me stupid. "Uh. No. Not at all."

"Keys?" She held out her hand and took them when I offered them out, cupped in my hand so she had to touch me. One little touch was all I wanted. Just to see if the chemistry I thought was there was real.

Instead, she gripped them daintily between her finger and thumb.

Which said enough. She was afraid to touch me.

Considering I'd insulted her at one place of business, I had no intention of insulting her in another. I did want in those tight jeans she was currently sporting even if I was wise enough not to say it.

Didn't mean I didn't watch her ass swish and sway like she belonged on a runway while she walked a step ahead of me.

We headed outside, and as she hopped into my truck like she owned it, and then popped the hood, my dick grew harder with every second that passed.

Hot damn. My new favorite thing? A woman who knew her way around an engine, especially when she had to lift on her tiptoes and bend over to see inside.

Visions flashed in my mind. Multiple ones. Some so disturbingly and instantly vivid I stepped back and turned, adjusting myself so she couldn't see the obvious bulge growing inside my thin athletic pants.

Of all the damn days to run into Paige.

My phone rang in my hand and I pulled it up, immediately cursing. I'd forgotten to call to let someone know I was running late.

"Sorry," I said, even though she hadn't paid me a lick of attention since we reached my truck. "Mind if I take this?"

Her head, buried in my hood so all I could see was her wavy brown hair clipped back at her forehead, shook back and forth. "Not a problem. Do whatever you need."

There were multiple things I needed. One was her. With her greased up hands wrapped around my dick.

I cleared my throat and answered the call. "This is Beaux."

"Where the hell are you?" Powell barked in my ear.

"Fuck, sorry man. My truck broke down on the way to practice. I'm getting it looked at."

"And you didn't call anyone because...?"

His question trailed off. I despised it when Powell treated me like a little shit just because he was banging my sister, something that made me want to vomit just thinking about. I'd paid my dues with the team in the last year, proven my mettle on and off the field. Powell never resisted the opportunity to be a dick.

Even if we were friends now.

"Because I'm distracted, back off." Mostly it was the long legs fitted into tight jeans. An ass that made me think of things I'd never tried before, and hazel eyes that were now squinting at me. She flipped back to the hood and slammed it shut. "I'll call a car and get there in thirty minutes."

Powell barked something else at me but I hung up without listening. He was always a grumpy old man.

"Your truck should have been buried in a field about ten years ago," Paige said, wiping her hands on a towel she'd procured from somewhere. "We can look at it, fix it up, but my guess is it's worth more for parts at this point."

Damn. I knew it was coming. But I loved the old rusted thing despite all the ribbing I got for it. It even had the classic bench seat trucks didn't have anymore. That seat had a lot of memories for me. Naked ones.

Good ones.

I learned how to make a girl come before I did, in that truck. She was more precious than gold. The truck, not the girl who taught me.

What could I say? I was a sentimental schmuck.

"I figured you'd say that," I said, pulling up the Uber App. I needed to get to practice. Coach Pomville was most likely tallying the additional suicides he'd have me run for being late. I figured as many as it would take to puke up my breakfast. "Can you get it working enough while I'm at practice today so I can drive it to a dealership without a salesman laughing their ass off?"

The look she shot me told me no. "I can have some of the guys try."

"Thanks." I tapped the screen, ordered my Uber who was only a few minutes away, and slid my phone into my pocket. "You're not going to work on it?"

Paige shook her head. She had a smudge of grease near her temple. Sexy as hell. "No. I can do basics but your truck needs an overhaul. I could get the coolant taken care of so it doesn't blow up on you, but I'm not qualified enough to do the rest." She sighed and looked back to the shop before her gaze came back to me. "Mostly I work in the office, but we also don't open for a while. If you need a ride to the practice field, I can take you."

Wow. Unexpected.

"Yeah?"

"Well, you're not being a jerk today and you did apologize last night for being one. Plus, I have a favor." Her mouth twisted, like the idea of asking me for something made her a bit sick to her stomach.

I was all in. "Done. But you're not driving me to work. You got work to do here and I already ruined one night for you."

She glanced back at the car and then looked at the sky, shoulders slumping a bit. I hadn't realized how strung tight she was until she relaxed. Her face softened, and a shot hit my chest. My reaction to her was something I didn't expect, but God, she was beautiful.

"You know, you're not anything like I really imagined you were."

"Is that a compliment?"

"I suppose it might be." Her lips twisted like she didn't want to admit it. I couldn't stop from chuckling. Why did this woman dislike me? Instead of it turning me off, I was curious.

"Okay, then, how about this. You take care of my truck, I'll do your favor, and then tonight, you let me take you out for dinner."

"You don't even know what the favor is."

"Doesn't matter. I'll still do it, and I still want you across the table from me so I can keep proving how much of a non-asshole I am."

"You're sort of pushy, you know that?"

"I prefer 'determined' when I see something I want." I flicked my hand out. "What's the favor?"

She glanced toward the door to the garage and sighed again. "My dad's a fan—"

"Just your dad?" I teased.

She huffed, lips pressed into a pout and continued, ignoring me. "It's just, I was wondering, it doesn't have to be much, nothing big at all...but could you autograph—"

"Done." We had boatloads of crap in the marketing department I could grab. I'd take care of it and blow her mind with my generosity. And it wasn't just because I tried to do everything I could for fans, but because she was pretty when she blushed.

Even prettier as her eyes went soft when she mentioned her dad.

Spectacular as she gritted out her favor like asking for something from someone was worse than getting teeth pulled without Novocain.

"Yeah?" she asked. "That'd be really great. But dinner, I don't know."

The pretty little liar. Her blush told me she wanted it. "Tonight, whenever. You make the call, and it's not payback for the favor or you fixing my truck. I just want to share a meal with you."

"Why? Because you want in my pants?"

Her tone was snippy and her shoulders tightened. She'd handed me a loaded gun and hell if I was going to shoot myself with it.

I closed the five feet of space between us, making her step backward until she was almost plastered to my truck.

"I do want in your pants, Paige. Any American male who watches you for longer than two seconds probably wants the same. And I'll take my time getting there if I have to, so I'm not going to be a dick and lie, and I'm not being a dick by being honest. I'm just honest. But dinner is because you're pretty, and for some reason I can't explain, I want to know why you look so damn exhausted, why you just asking me for help made you look like you want to puke, and why you did it anyway. So basically, I just want to talk to you. Get to know you. I'm interested and I'm not going to hide that either. It's not my style."

"Wow." Her cheeks had turned pink while I was talking and by the time I was done, her lips were parted. "That's a lot to discuss at dinner."

"Then we'll tack on drinks and dessert at the end."

She smiled, blinding me with a soft and sweetness she hadn't yet shown. I took it like a present. Tucked it away so I could jerk off to it later. So maybe I was kind of an asshole.

Her shoulders rose and fell with a heavy breath, and she looked back to the garage. "I'll think about it. That's all I can promise."

"Done."

A black SUV pulled into the lot with the Uber tag in the windshield. I stepped back before I did something stupid like brush my fingers down her cheek and press my lips to hers. I didn't need to be slapped before practice.

"I'll be back at four. Will your dad be here then?"

"Um. He should be. Why?"

Because I wanted to see if she was as sweet and soft around him as she was when she thought about him. "So I can deliver some things to him in person."

"I can make sure he's here then, but you don't have to do that."

"I know. But I want to anyway."

She blinked rapidly, pretty brown lashes flickered on her cheeks. I'd surprised her. "Well, thanks then."

I grinned. "Thanks for your help, Paige, and I gotta tell you, I'm fucking thrilled I ran into you today. You give me a shot at dinner, you won't regret it."

The teeth disappeared behind her closed smile, but it was still sweet as hell.

Then I stepped away, grabbed my bags out of the back of my truck and headed to the Uber, climbed inside without looking back, but she was watching.

I could feel her gaze on me as the Uber driver pulled out of the lot. He recognized me and therefore, I spent the next twenty minutes hearing everything our team did wrong last year and how we were lucky to win the Super Bowl.

Awesome. A Monday morning quarterback on top of an already crappy morning.

But even he couldn't get me down.

Because I was going to get Paige out for dinner with me, and at that thought, nothing would pull me down.

FIVE

PAIGE

The last thing I needed was Beaux Hale walking into my life, and if that wasn't the last thing, the very last thing I needed was him being so darn nice to me.

It muddled everything I wanted to believe, that he was the guy he'd been at dinner before he apologized.

Instead, he kept his distance for the most part. He was polite, respectful, with only a small amount of flirting.

At least until he explained why he wanted to take me to dinner.

Was my exhaustion and stress so noticeable? Apparently it was because he brought it up and a quick check in the mirror after he left proved the bags under my eye true.

Darn. I'd even paid a fortune for concealer and foundation to hide all that and it still showed.

It still didn't mean I was going to go to dinner with him.

It'd be dumb.

It'd probably be fun.

I didn't have time for fun.

Needless to say, he left me so distracted that about halfway through the morning, I'd dropped enough cans of oil, the concerned glances I received from Lance and Mike, our main two mechanics, eventually turned to annoyance.

I debated calling Hannah for advice but didn't. Her advice would be something along the lines of, "Ride that buckin' Bronco until you're too sore to walk."

Which was more descriptive and visually appealing than helpful.

Eventually, I took an early lunch. I was a whole lot annoyed, a little bit turned on, and questioning if taking Hannah's assumed advice would really be such a bad thing.

What harm could a simple dinner bring? I'd get a free, decent meal, something I could desperately use, and I'd have conversation. It was the conversation Beaux wanted to have that made me uncertain.

After lunch, I went home and hung out with my dad for a while. Then I helped him out of his wheelchair and into the car, and we returned to the garage.

I barely had him settled back in his wheelchair when a black Cadillac Escalade pulled into the lot.

"What the hell?" I muttered as Beaux Hale climbed out of the gleaming SUV.

He wasn't the only one, either.

Close on his heels were Oliver Powell, Kolby Jones, and Danny Rudolph.

Holy mega load of pheromones.

"Christ on a cracker," my dad said, sitting in his chair at my side.

I looked down, unable to hide my excitement for him. Beaux didn't have to do this. Nothing like this. I'd expected a signed shirt, a photograph, hell, maybe a football. But with four guys from the Rough Riders showing up and walking through our parking lot carrying what looked like a large gift bag, I barely registered the work and blaring music from inside the garage screeching to a halt.

"The hell?" Mike asked. He rushed up and stopped at my dad's other side while wiping his grease monkey hands on a towel.

"I might have neglected to tell you the truck you're working on belongs to Beaux Hale."

Mike's eyes popped wide. "You shittin' me? That piece of crap?"

"Hey now," Beaux said, sidling up to our small, completely enamored group. "That's ol' Betsy you're talking about."

Mike, barely twenty-one, was a foster kid when he started working for my dad. As soon as he aged out of the system, he moved into the crummy apartment above the garage. He'd become like a brother to me over the years and was usually unflappable. Watching him stammer around this group of guys made me smile. "Sorry, man. It's just...wow...holy shit. You're Beaux Hale, and Oliver Powell, and —"

"Kolby Jones," Kolby cut in.

"Danny Rudolph," the last guy said, grinning. "We know our names. And you are?" He held out his hand and Mike's trembling one slid into it, cringing as he saw the oil on his palm.

"Mike. Mike Hannover. Damn glad to meet you guys."

The awestruck young man flashed his wide eyes to my dad as my dad introduced himself, barely keeping his composure. My dad wore his emotions on his sleeves, almost all of them always full of joy and love. In my entire lifetime, he'd raised his voice so few times I could count them on one hand. The worst being when I'd passed out at a high school party and didn't come home until the next morning. I was so hung over I practically crawled into the house at eight o'clock. Even then, my dad had been more worried than pissed.

It wasn't a surprise to see his excitement shining clear on

his face. If he could get up and jump to show his glee, he would. Damn the strokes that took away his ability.

"You must be Sam," Beaux said. "Your daughter Paige told me you were a big fan of ours, so the guys and I got together today after practice and got some things together for you."

Christ on a cracker was right. My dad clutched the handle of his wheelchair with one hand, the other one limp in his lap.

I looked away from the men and gritted my teeth. He was only fifty-five years old, had always worked out and taken care of his body. The strokes had destroyed his physical strength and I hated it. I hated seeing him turn into a man he'd never been and yet he handled it with such grace. Tears welled in my eyes and I forced them down.

This wasn't about my grief or my frustration.

"Damn," Dad said, as Beaux opened the bag. If they noticed he couldn't move his arm, they didn't say anything.

Oliver Powell reached in and the first thing he took out was a jersey with his name and number on the back.

"We all signed this. Didn't know who your favorite player was, so we went with mine because I'm pretty much the shit," Powell said, smirking at Beaux.

"Right, of course," he replied.

"No. This is good." Dad tried shaking the awe out of his expression but it was fruitless. He was in absolute heaven. "This is...shit, honey," he said. He clutched my hand with his good one and I held it firmly, looking down at him. The tears in his eyes mirrored my own blurry vision. "You did this for me?"

I squeezed his hand tighter. "You deserved it. It was just a simple favor I asked."

"One we were more than happy to give," Beaux said. He took out a football next, and a quick flip of it showed it covered in Sharpie marker. "It's not a game ball, but we used it at practice today. All of us signed it, including the coaches," he said, setting in my dad's lap. None of them had blinked at my dad's disability.

None had given me a look of pity.

They were just being nice. An onslaught of emotion slashed through me and I tried to hide it.

Beaux had done this for me, for my dad.

All to get into my pants? I was starting to doubt that was all he wanted. Seemed like a lot of work for little reward—for him, not me. With the way Beaux used his body not only on the field but standing in front of us, moving smoothly and confidently, his grin never slipping, I knew a night with him would be more rewarding than I could imagine.

And damn it. My heart was softening.

"We've got one more thing for you," Kolby said. He stepped forward with a white envelope in his hands. "Season tickets to the games."

"Holy crap!" Dad shouted. Forgetting about the jersey and the ball, he let go of my hand and reached for the envelope, clutching it in his hand. "You kidding me?" He looked at me and smiled wide. It'd been years since I'd seen him this happy. "What the hell did you say to them, girl?"

"Before you get too excited," Kolby went on, "those are tickets for my suite. I get it for my ma and daughter. Just thought you'd want some company, and I know Mya would. But if you think she'd be too much for you—"

"No problem. Love little ones. Been on Paige's butt to give me some grandkids of my own but she's too damn stubborn to listen to anyone. Told her I wasn't going to be around forever and she needed to give me that joy of seeing her holding her own newborn. Nothing better, man, holding life you created and been entrusted with it."

Kolby grinned with pride. "Definitely understand that."

Damn it. I'd flushed from head to toe when he mentioned

my name at first, but all that turned to grief I tried to keep buried and locked down tight as he continued speaking. Already overwhelmed, it was impossible to keep a lid on it.

I sniffed, swiped beneath my nose, and turned away, brushing tears off my cheeks.

"Aww. Damn. I'm sorry, girl."

"It's fine, Dad."

Next to me, Mike had slid to my side and he pulled me against him. I was falling apart in front of some of the best players in the country. How humiliating.

I couldn't stop it.

"It's all right," Mike said. "Give yourself a second."

I rested against his shoulder, nodded my head and waited until I could inhale deeply.

"Thank you," I said. I looked at all the guys. Most were trying not to make it obvious they had observed me fall apart. All except Beaux. He looked at me with knowing and understanding eyes so intently, my knees buckled. I grabbed onto Mike and faked a smile. "This is really nice of you. Too nice. It's too much."

"Nonsense." Dad patted the envelope on his lap proudly. "I've always said when someone gives you a gift, you let them have the joy of giving it to you. No such gift is too much if it's given selflessly."

"We're honored if you accept them. Any fan of ours we meet we try to do right by," Rudolph said. "We have the means to be generous and we like doing it. Beaux here, though, more than most."

"I would have got you your own box but Kolby said his ma likes company. There are tickets for four for you so you can bring anyone you want."

Dad squeezed my hand. "Know who I'll invite. Thanks."

"Me?" Mike said.

"Not on your life." My dad glared at him. "You still like those damn Patriots."

The players groaned but I rolled my eyes. This was an argument that grew old years ago.

"Aww, come on, Sam."

"We'll see." He nodded, head trembling a little bit and turned back to Beaux. "Can't thank you enough for this, honest, son. You've made an old and sick man thrilled today. But I also hear we got your truck in the back? What's wrong with it?"

"According to your daughter, my Betsy needs to be sent to the Ford graveyard."

"Yeah," Mike said. It was back to work talk in a flash. "She's not really wrong about that either. Your truck is worth more for parts than it is to fix. I mean, you can swing it obviously, but to be honest, you're looking on the downward slope of it lasting much longer unless you want to invest in a complete overhaul."

"Was afraid you'd say that. We've had a good run." His eyes slid to me and his grin went feral. There was no other way to explain it. Full bottom lip, thinner top one pulled into a smirk that said his kindness was over, and now he was coming to collect. "Hopefully that means Paige'll swing by the dealership with me tonight before we head to dinner, then."

"Ah." My dad shot me a look, eyebrows raised. Surprised and cautious at the same time. "So that's what the gifts are about? You trying to impress my daughter? Or me?"

Good Lord. Heat traveled down my spine. I kicked my dad's chair playfully. "Stop it, Dad."

"No, sir." Beaux shook his head. "We'd have done the same even if I didn't think your daughter was the most beautiful woman I'd ever seen."

Strangle him. I was going to wrap my hands around the quarterback's throat and throttle him until he lost all the blood in his brain. Which couldn't be much at the moment.

"Well, damn," Dad said, laughing. "You got balls, son." He took my hand. "You want to take her out, what are you waiting for?"

Beaux's look was just as intense as it'd been earlier as he looked at me. Watchful. Hopeful. Confident. He showed more emotions in his eyes than anyone I'd met and I barely knew him. He held nothing back. "I'm waiting for Paige to say yes."

SIX

BEAUX

If looks could kill, I'd have a knife sticking out of my chest from the heat flaring in Paige's pretty eyes.

I was pushing it, totally putting her in a corner that could turn her into a rabid dog or have her take a step, take a chance toward me. As soon as I saw her dad next to her in his wheelchair, the purple rims beneath her eyes made sense.

I didn't pity her. I couldn't pity someone like Paige who clearly had a lot on their plate and their biggest item was taking care of a family member. Shannon and I had lived that for almost all of our lives, Shannon taking on most of the brunt of it. When our mom died, mostly from sheer exhaustion and a too-late diagnosis on an infection, Shannon also made sure I didn't feel anything more than I had to.

She always had me focused on my dream, focused on making a better life for myself, getting out of our falling down home in Iowa and getting us out of there.

I loved her for it at the same time I'd always felt regret I hadn't been able to do more. But I was still a high school kid, spending most of my time on the field or hitting the books. It was Shannon who paid the bills and took on more responsibility than either of us should have had.

Now, though, was a completely different story and Rudolph was right. I'd intentionally brought some of the most generous, most grateful men I knew on the team to deliver the goods to Paige's dad. We'd all come from simple upbringings, worked our asses off and all of us gave as much as we could whenever we had the opportunity, especially toward our fans.

The suite Kolby gave them was nothing considering he'd already paid for it. I made a mental note to go buy a disabled parking pass for the underground, connected garage.

"So what do you say?" I asked Paige as she stood there glaring at me. Next to her, Mike, who was still holding her, shook her a little bit. "Want to help me pick up a new ride tonight?"

"Tonight?" her dad asked. "She can go now."

Paige glared at me, then her dad and shook her head. "Can't. I'm not caught up on work and I'm covered in grease."

The only thing she was covered in was a body made for a long night of fucking. Her jeans had a few dark spots on them, but I'd memorized the curves of her ass in them earlier. She was wearing a blue tank top with Halloway Motors stamped in a curve directly over her chest.

My gaze lingered there for a moment before I grinned at her.

"Work can wait," her dad said and reached for her hand. His trembled until she grabbed it. "When's the last time you had fun? More importantly, when's the last time you had a date?"

Behind me, the men choked back laughter.

Paige's ears turned the brightest shade of pink I'd seen on anything outside my sister's toenail polish.

I grinned shamelessly while she shot her dad the same

lethal look she'd given me. Apparently she'd mastered it long before I showed up in her life.

"I have to go home and shower."

"Cool." Her dad shrugged. "That'll give me time to chat with Mr. Hale here about his intentions with my daughter."

The guys behind me lost the control they had on their laughter and all three assholes slapped me on the shoulder. "Sounds like you have a ride, then, man," Powell said. "And speaking of rides, your sister—"

"Don't finish that thought," I growled at him. He never missed the opportunity to talk about Shannon. I turned back to Paige's dad. "Just dinner and a bit of car shopping, sir."

"Then you can tell me how it felt to stand on that podium last winter winning that ring that looks like it's weighing down your hand."

I liked this guy. He was a no-nonsense straight shooter with a protective streak for his daughter. "That okay with you?" I asked Paige.

"Looks like the decision's been made for me," she grumbled and kicked her dad's chair again.

"That's because you're too young to be making as many as you already are. Let your old man do something nice for you. Don't get the chances anymore."

"Damn you," she whispered, her voice hoarse.

"If you want," Mike said, "Sam and Mr. Hale can hang in the garage with me while I get it fixed enough to take it to a dealership. You can go home and come back when you're ready, Paige."

Her gaze swept around the group still standing around. My teammates were off to the side, no doubt hanging around to say their goodbyes and taking as many notes in order to give me as much shit as possible. Hell, it'd been a long time since I'd met a girl's dad, much less felt the need to impress him or the guy who was with him. Could have been her brother, but while they were close, they didn't treat each other the same way Shannon and I did. Close, but not close enough.

More questions to dig into during dinner.

"Paige?" I asked and her shoulders slumped.

A small, hesitant twitch of her lips before it evaporated said she wasn't as annoyed as she seemed. "I can be back in about forty-five minutes if you don't mind."

I lifted my hands and dropped them to my hips. "I've got all night."

A faint hue hit her cheeks. Damn, she was pretty when she blushed and sexy when she glared. I'd have my hands full with this woman.

Good thing I had big hands.

"So that's settled," Sam said. "Let's say goodbye to these boys and you and I can sit and chat while Mike finishes up your car."

I told the guys I'd see them tomorrow at practice and when Sam and Mike were distracted, I walked up to Paige. "I was kind of a dick, bringing up dinner in front of your dad."

"Yeah, you were."

"I'm not sorry this time. A man uses all the plays at his disposal when he has to."

"Spoken like a player," she said, and she wasn't talking about football.

"It's just dinner, Paige, and helping me buy a truck. I bought Betsy for five hundred dollars from a neighbor because it could get me to school, and that's all the shit I know about cars. Then as a thank you, I take you to dinner. We talk, hopefully I can get you to laugh, and I take you home. That's all that I'm looking for tonight."

"Really?" She tilted her head to the side and a chunk of her bangs that had fallen out of her clip dropped over one eye.

I smoothed it back, lingering at her ear before running it down her jaw. "Yeah. You want to give me more, that's your call, but I'm not playing you, and I wouldn't. I'm honest. Always."

"Okay, then. I should hurry to get ready."

"Dress casual. Not going anywhere fancy while I'm in this." I wiped my hands down my jeans and dress shirt. I'd thrown it all on after practice, hoping for her yes to dinner, but something told me Paige wouldn't be impressed with five-star restaurants and suits and ties. Which suited me just fine. I'd always prefer a good burger and beer to foie gras and champagne.

"All right, and thanks again for my dad. That was really cool."

"Be even cooler when you're in the box with him, wearing my number thirteen on a jersey and cheering for me."

Her cheeks burned and I told her I'd see her soon. I walked away before I pulled her in closer and kissed her like I wanted to.

Then I walked up to her dad, took the handles of his wheelchair and pushed him toward the garage.

Loud enough for Paige to hear, I asked, "So Sam, you got any embarrassing photos of your daughter lying around?"

I'd been nervous at home getting ready, debating what to wear and how to do my hair after I rushed through a shower. It wasn't that I was excited or nervous about going on a date with Beaux Hale, quarterback of the Rough Riders, Super Bowl Champions, necessarily. It was that I had a date at all.

It'd been over six months since I'd been out with anyone, and I hadn't had sex since Spencer broke up with me. I didn't have time with the other guys I'd gone out on a date with. They'd claimed I didn't have enough time to give them and walked away before we could ever make it that far.

Which not only still stung, but made me uninterested in dating anyone. If they couldn't understand the time my dad required, they weren't worth mine.

I still doubted Beaux would be any different when I arrived back at the garage.

Then my nerves spiked to DefCon freak out levels. And that was Beaux's fault.

He looked too damn good sitting in the office with my dad,

feet kicked up on the desk, beer in his hand and saying something while my dad threw his head back and laughed.

He looked at ease in our rundown garage's waiting room slash office. He looked like he was just a guy. Not a sports superstar, not plastered on the covers of magazines or headlining interviews on Sportscenter.

Seeing him appear to be just a normal guy, dressed to excite a woman's libido in well-worn jeans and a pale blue, striped dress shirt, well that did things to me.

As we climbed into the truck and started talking, I was beginning to think he was showing me exactly who he was—just a simple, laid-back guy from Iowa who threw a ball for a living. And I really liked everything he was showing me.

"Do you know what kind of truck you want?" I asked as we drove down the Interstate headed out toward Durham.

"Ford and black," Beaux replied. "That's all I really care about."

"Why a Ford?"

"Because Chevy's are shit," Beaux said simply.

"Nice." I laughed. It sounded exactly like something my dad would say and I turned to the window and watched the trees go by, the clouds roll in.

It felt like it stormed in Raleigh all the time during the summer. Huge gully-gushes that barreled over embankments and flooded roads.

We were supposed to get rain again tonight, and hopefully, it wouldn't be a bad one. I hated storms and the unpredictability in them.

He pulled in to the Cornerstone Ford and Jeep dealership halfway between Raleigh and Durham. He barely had time to help me out of the truck, when an excited salesman was strolling toward us.

"Hello there, good evening and welcome to Cornerstone, I'm Kyle Ballsman, how can I help you today?"

"Beaux, nice to meet you," he said and introduced me. While I shook Kyle's hand, Beaux scanned the parking lot, stopping on a shining black, Ford F-250 Crew Cab truck. The grill was an upgrade but other than that, we couldn't see anything about the truck.

"I'll take that one," Beaux said and turned back to the salesman. "Cash. How soon can we wrap this up?"

"What?" I exclaimed. He was...how could...why... what? "What are you doing?"

He looked at me and grinned. "Told you. I know what I want."

The heat in his eyes shocked me, forcing me back a step. My goodness he gave good innuendo. I wanted to lick it up like hot fudge off a spoon. Then my common sense kicked in.

"Would you like to take a look at it?" Kyle asked. His surprise was as evident as mine, but he wasn't about to lose a sale, either. "You're welcome to test drive it. It'll only take me a minute to get the keys."

Beaux shook his head. "Nope. I'm good."

"You don't even know if it has Bluetooth. Leather seats." I tried to come up with things he'd care about since he said he didn't know anything about trucks or engines. "How it rides. How many miles it has on it. If it's new or used. You don't know anything about it!"

So much for simple and normal! My heart was fluttering so quickly I feared it exploding.

Beaux pointed his thumb at me and looked at Kyle. "Does it have that crap?"

"Yes, sir. That truck is brand new and has been fully upgraded, the engine is—"

"Okay then." Beaux clapped his hands together and dropped them to his hips. "Let's get this taken care of."

He held his hand out for me to go in front of him, but I stood there, knowingly gaping at him. I'd never seen anything like this in my life. He didn't even know how much it cost.

"Maybe we should talk about this."

"We will. Over dinner."

I didn't know whether to slap him upside the head or think what he was doing was sweet.

Slap him. Definitely. But not in public. I'd wait until he was in his new stupid truck he'd tricked me into going to buy with him even though he didn't care at all about the darn thing.

Which was sort of sweet in itself. He truly didn't care what he drove. No pretentiousness in him other than paying for it in cash.

A memory of the cash my mom used to send me for birthdays after she left flickered to my mind but I pushed it away. Now wasn't the time to think about her.

Beaux shocked me further when we sat down, both of us on the other side of Kyle's desk while he went to get paperwork.

"His name is Ballsman," he snickered. "Poor man."

I laughed, unable to stop myself before it burst out. This guy was something else, definitely not right in the head. We were still smiling at each other, that heat I'd felt earlier swirling between us, enveloping us. It seduced me with the sweet scent of his cologne and the soft look in Beaux's eyes. It pulled me closer, made me feel something for the man in front of me. Things I had no business feeling, but could no longer remember why.

"Beaux," I said, my voice thick with something unidentifiable. Lust? Need?

"You do feel it." He leaned closer. "I've felt something

every time you've been working and I've seen you for months. Glad you're finally getting on the same page as me."

"What?"

"Don't come into Ride'Em Rough for the burgers, Paige. They're crap on a bun."

Oh my goodness. He'd just implied…He did. He said that. I had no response. I'd never waited on him until the other night, always passing it off.

And he kept coming back to see me?

"Why?"

"Because you're beautiful. You say thank you to everyone. You always smile even when I've caught you fighting a yawn. You laugh with the cooks and most of the other servers look to you like you're they're big sister. I like it."

Holy freaking cow.

"Plus," he smirked. "The wedge sandals and denim shorts you wear make your ass look fan-fucking-tastic."

I slapped his bicep before I could stop myself. "You're a jerk."

"Yeah." He took my hand and settled it in his and then on his thigh. His warm thigh. Hard and muscled. His hand curled around mine and held me tight to him. "But I think you're finally beginning to like it."

Kyle returned with paperwork before I could respond, which was good. Because what in the hell would I have said?

Beaux and Kyle went over the paperwork, while I sat back and watched. Beaux shocked me again when he didn't even try to get a better deal on the fifty-thousand-plus dollar truck.

We were back on the road an hour later. I soaked in the new car smell and fiddled with the controls on the radio and air vents.

"Why did you want me with you today if you didn't plan on asking for my advice?"

Without looking at me, one edge of Beaux's lip lifted and curved. "Because the first time I was in my truck, I wanted to have your fantastic ass sitting next to me."

"That's outrageous! You didn't even try to get a deal on it."

He flicked on his blinker and glanced at me as he turned a corner. "Why would I do that? I've got the cash to pay for it and a few grand is nothing to me. But the extra commission might make that guy's life a bit easier while he's providing for his family. Did you see that picture behind the desk? He's got like six kids."

I hadn't even noticed it. The fact Beaux did said volumes about him.

God. That did it. He really was the chivalrous and generous guy he claimed to be, or he was giving me an Emmy-worthy performance. Either way, I was falling for it, hook, line, and sinker.

"That's really nice of you."

"I'm a nice guy."

"Yeah, well, considering our first encounter, forgive me if I'm having a hard time reconciling the two together."

"Take as long as you need. I got all the time in the world to prove you wrong." He glanced at me again but this time his gaze swept my body.

I checked to make sure I hadn't turned on the heated leather seat feature.

EIGHT

BEAUX

When Paige came back to the garage, Sam and I had been kicking it in the main office. Paige's stamp was all over the place in a subtle but still feminine way. The small waiting room was picked up and tidy, cookies were laid out, coffeepot filled and hot.

The main desk had little splashes of color on it with neon Post-it notes and next to the area where I knew Paige sat was a small vase filled with three fresh flowers. Looked like fake colored daisies but the water in the vase was definitely real.

I'd had a decent time with her old man. He was quick to laugh, the straight shooter I pegged him to be. We talked about my last season with the Rough Riders, and he told me about his college days playing ball for Purdue. All surface level shit, but by the time Paige arrived dressed to kill in a short and frayed denim skirt that barely skimmed the bottom of her ass and a tank top that accentuated her assets up top, I had his approval.

He didn't say it, but I knew men like him. Good men with good hearts and strong minds. It was a shame his body was failing him.

I'd actually planned on taking longer at the dealership, but once Paige was in my truck, telling me about her jobs at the garage and the restaurant, all I could see were her tanned legs and all I could smell was the scent of her flowery perfume. My dick was so hard I had to keep shifting in my seat and drape an arm in my lap so she didn't see the bulge. Once we pulled into the Ford dealership, I just wanted the deal done so I could get her to dinner, keep her opening up and then take her home so I could finally kiss her.

Because I wasn't ending the night without our lips pressed and tongues tangled together and my hands tangled in her hair.

Now we were at IronOar Steakhouse, a casual restaurant where you picked your own cuts of meat when you walked in, grilled your own steak, and took whatever sides you were offered for the night.

It was a kick back with family, good friends, and a beer kind of place. I loved it. The wait staff and owners had recognized me the first time I'd come in with Shannon. When I came back the second time, they'd hung a photo of me with the wait staff so I had them take it down so I could sign it. Since then, I became a regular, stopping by almost once a week. No one gave me any extra attention.

I figured Paige would like that, too, and besides the smirk she gave me when she saw my photo on the wall when we arrived and requested our steaks, everyone had left us alone.

It helped that while it was Friday, we were still there before the main dinner rush.

Now, I was guiding us into deeper conversation.

"Your dad's a trip," I said. "He totally kicks ass."

We were snacking on peanuts, having a beer and eating our salads while we waited for them to deliver our steaks so we could go grill them. She took a drink from her Miller Lite, and her eyes slid to the left.

"Thanks. He's the best man I know."

"How'd he end up in a wheelchair?"

She sighed and the depth of her pain filled her face. "He's had two strokes." She set down her beer and wiped her hands together like she had to warm them. "The first one hit just over a year ago, the second one a few months later. That's the one that left him paralyzed. He's in therapy and slowly getting better, but some days are worse than others."

"And you quit your job at a television station to come home and help take care of him?"

Her brows rose and she tilted her head. "Are you sure you're not stalking me? Maybe checking my Facebook?"

"No." I hadn't even considered it. "Your dad and Mike are talkative guys."

"Figures." She pulled a face and took a moment before continuing. I had the suspicion she was debating how much of her life to give me. What she didn't know was that I was beginning to want it all from her. Every time she opened up about something, I fell harder. "It wasn't a choice. He's all I ever had until Mike came into our lives."

"How'd that happen?" I leaned forward and rested my forearms on the table. He was young and definitely wasn't related to them based on what I'd picked up through conversation, but that didn't mean he hadn't become their family.

Her nose scrunched into an adorable pout. "You ask a lot of questions."

"I told you I was going to." I shrugged shamelessly.

"Yeah, but..." her voice trailed and she lifted her hair off her neck, letting it drop back down like a silk curtain to her shoulders and beyond. "Okay. Mike was a foster kid. A good kid, though, just had some crappy life stuff happen but who doesn't, you know?"

"I do know."

For a brief moment, sadness filled her eyes. She knew about my mom and wasn't hiding it, but she didn't dwell, thank Christ. "Anyway, he came into my dad's office one day when he was only fifteen years old, said he needed a job and didn't know anything about cars, but he'd work hard. Dad spent the first month giving him the shit jobs. He cleaned the bathrooms, emptied oil buckets and swept the floors. Dad said it was to test his mettle. Mike showed up every day after school, stayed until we closed and didn't complain once. After that, he just sort of stuck."

"Your dad's a good man."

"The best." She grinned wide and easy. Now I knew how to get her talking...mention her old man. Simple as that.

"What about your mom?"

The smile fell. "She left when I was four. We're better off without her."

The chill in her voice set me on edge. "Yeah?"

"Yeah." She took another drink. "I mean, she wanted the guy she met in college, the football star. Dad never wanted to go pro, said he didn't have the talent to start and didn't want to bounce around pro teams playing back-up for his career, always moving. He wanted to have a family and settle."

"And your mom didn't?"

"Nope. Dad said she tried, but after they'd been in Raleigh for a few years, she turned resentful. Then she had me and really couldn't deal. He came home from work and her stuff was gone. She'd left me with the sitter without telling anyone where she was going."

"No shit?" The blasé way she spoke about her mom stunned me almost as much as a woman who would do that to her kids. You heard an awful lot of men taking off, my unknown dad being the perfect example. It always startled me more when it was a woman.

"Do you ever talk to her?"

She gave me a disgusted look. "I haven't had anything to do with her since I was seven. After she left, she got remarried to some rich guy in Michigan. Then she started sending a bunch of money, all the expensive toys a girl could ever want, but it sucked. All I wanted was a mom, and she didn't give a shit enough about me to even stay in the same state. I made my dad send it all back and told him to tell her I didn't want to see or hear from her again."

Jesus. If there was a worst mom in the world award, I knew who I'd choose as the winner. "I'm sorry," I said when Paige was still gritting her teeth. "I didn't mean to bring up a bad memory. That must have been hard."

"She was selfish enough to think she could buy me with money. And too selfish to see that before she left, even if we didn't have much, we had everything we needed in a family. I always figured I was better without her."

Damn. This woman. She blew my mind. Not only with her wisdom and her sexy pouty lips but her heart. She liked her simple life, and I loved that about her.

Paige would take what she got and make the most out of it. She'd squeeze the hell out of a pile of lemons and make the most delicious lemonade anyone had ever tasted.

Plus, there were similarities that only people like us who had lived it would understand. "We have more in common than I thought we would," I said, taking a heavy swig of my beer.

I was feeling too damn much. Too hot. Too tight. My dick was throbbing in my jeans making me bite back a groan.

"Because of your mom? What about your dad?"

Few people were brave enough to ask about my family.

Damn. I liked her. She didn't play games, didn't try to grab a leash and yank a man around. She just threw it out there, straight up. A girl who didn't play mind-fucking games was refreshing.

"I don't know who he is. Mom told me before she passed she was working at a hotel, had a weak moment of feeling alone, and there was some guy there doing some celebrity charity golf tournament. One night, he wham-bam-thank-you-ma'am'd her and nine months later," I sat back and lifted my arms and grinned, "perfection was born."

"You're so full of it." She laughed. It was low and husky like her voice. More porn-sex phone operator than peppy cheerleader.

My dick went hard again as I wondered what she'd sound like when I made her come.

"So, how about I go see what's taking our steaks so long and we get cooking?"

~

RAIN SPLATTERED the windshield so harshly it was diffi-cult to see the roads.

My new truck was getting quite the break-in as I drove through water-covered roads. Rain pinged against the metal truck it was difficult to speak over the noise.

Regardless, we were still talking. We'd stayed at IronOar Steakhouse long after I'd planned on getting Paige home, but once we'd gotten past the hard crap of her life, we'd briefly spoken about mine. I told her all about Shannon and how she took care of me growing up. I told her how I wanted to punch Powell in the face for being a dick to her when they started dating, and I begrudgingly admitted I actually did like the guy and he was good for Shannon.

She deserved to be happy and after a disastrous marriage of Powell's, so did he.

Still, most of the conversation was left light-hearted but deep. Paige told me about her jobs, that she worked at Ride'Em Rough at least four nights every week and sometimes picked up doubles on the weekends as long as she could find someone to help with her dad.

She worked hard, too hard for someone barely twenty-four should have to, but I admired the hell out of her for doing whatever she could to take care of her family.

It wasn't just because she reminded me of my mom or my sister, or that I liked her tight ass and her husky laughs when she gave them, but because the more she spoke, the deeper I fell.

I hadn't yet met a girl who made me think of settling down, and we were way too young in wherever this was going to think of something permanent, but I was a master at going with my gut.

With Paige sitting next to me, jumping every time thunder boomed, clutching my hand a little bit tighter, my gut was telling me this girl could be the one.

I'd played the field for the last decade not because I was afraid of settling down, but because I didn't have time to think about a serious relationship. Hell, I hadn't even really dated since high school. Hook-ups were easier, but I always made sure the woman I was with knew that going in.

I had been too focused on my game, my career, being the best, and fighting to stay there to even consider a relationship.

But now that I was settled and firmly entrenched in Raleigh, things were changing.

Unfortunately, finding a woman who wanted me more than they wanted the zeros on my paycheck were hard to find once I signed a multi-million dollar contract.

Money brought out crazy shit in people. It turned them

into monsters with dollar signs in their eyes. I learned early to stay far away from anyone who exhibited signs.

None of them came close to comparing to the ease of sitting next to a pretty girl in my brand new truck not even bothering to hide the fact she was afraid of a little thunderstorm.

"You don't like storms I take it?" She squeezed my hand again and thank God I was strong. My knuckles had cracked more than once since she'd tightened her grip.

"I don't like instability. It's never been my thing and I always think if the atmosphere can become so unstable, what hope does that give for the rest of us?" She laughed softly, tucking a chunk of her hair behind her ear and turning to me. The grin she shot me burned straight to my chest. The heat from our connected fingers following straight behind. "That sounds stupid doesn't it?"

"Not coming from a girl who didn't start off life having a lot of stability. Losing a parent, whether or not you become okay with it, changes you in ways that aren't ever fixed, Paige."

"Gosh, it's uncanny the way you understand me." Her smile turned soft and she brought up her other hand to cover her yawn as she rested her head on the seat of my car. "I'm sorry, it's late for me."

The GPS beeped, telling me to turn down her street. I focused on the road and pulled into her driveway, a short one that ended at a small carport so common in this area in smaller, older homes.

I must have been grinning because over another yawn, Paige asked, "What's so funny?"

"Carports." I shook my head. "So many things are different here and it still gets to me sometimes."

"Like car ports?"

"Yeah. And these storms y'all have all the time. Plus the

fact I just used y'all in a sentence. You southerners are rubbing off on me."

"Do you like living here?"

"Can't lie, living further north is all I've ever known. I miss the snow and the winters."

"What's it like?"

"Snow?"

"That. Minnesota. Iowa. How are they different?" She yawned again and I pulled my hand from hers and pressed it to her cheek.

"Twenty inches of snow and we live like it's a half-inch here. Nothing stops except a few hours to get the plows out. People either bunker down in the winter or spend it ice fishing, playing pond hockey, and in the summer, they live on their boats and their lakes. They're the nicest people I've ever met, just without the y'all's. I can also tell you're exhausted and the last thing I want is to keep you out later than you should be, so how about I get you inside and we finish this another time."

"Yeah?"

"Yeah. Which means you also have to give me your number."

She fished out her phone, a faint pink coloring her cheeks. Damn, I liked it. Gone was all the hesitation she'd had with me before dinner. Somehow during dinner, I'd picked through whatever had held her back from being out with me, probably because I hadn't been an ass.

"I gotta tell ya," she said around another yawn. Goddamn this girl needed more sleep. "It's only nine, but I feel like it's midnight. I swear, when I'm old, I'm totally going to rock the senior citizen life. Dinner at four-thirty, bath at six-thirty, in bed by seven-thirty. I'm ready for it."

I got stuck on the vision of her in a bath. Naked. Suds covering her breasts. Hair pulled up off her neck and some of it wet as it stuck to her skin. It would no doubt smell like peaches or strawberries, something sweet just like her.

I texted my own phone from hers and gave it back to her. "I've got a busy week. What's yours look like?"

She squinted for a moment. "Work all weekend at the restaurant. Next week during the day I'll be at the garage and then I've got Thursday and Sunday off from the grill."

"First game of the year is in Atlanta that Sunday." Damn. I wanted to see her, but now that the season was starting and since she worked so much, it'd be that much harder. We'd be swamped up until the plane took off Saturday, spending this week of practice preparing and finalizing the starting line-up. "We'll find our time to see each other soon. In the meantime, you want me, even if to say hi, call me."

She clutched her phone in her hand.

"Really?"

"Yeah really. Hold on." I hopped out of my truck and ran around the front. Damn this monster was big. I dodged slamming my hip against the bumper and threw open her door, ushering her out and under the carport before we were soaked. "Told you I wanted to see you. And I like everything I see, Paige. You want to see me again?"

"Yeah." She grinned softly, eyes lighting up even in the poor lighting by her house. "I guess I'd like that. Thanks for dinner."

"Thanks for coming with me, even if I had to strong-arm and trick you into it."

Our hands were clasped together and she tugged on mine, pulling herself closer. Head tilted back, lips parted, she licked her bottom lip. I bit back a groan. Goddamn. She wore seduction like she wore her confidence—understated, but sexy as fuck in its simplicity. "It would probably boost your ego if I told you I was thinking of saying yes anyway, but all that stuff you did for my dad really did seal the deal."

"Yeah." I slid my hand up her arm. I wanted to kiss her. Wanted to pull her into my arms and make out with her like a teenager. Hell, this felt like I was a teenager, dropping a girl off knowing her dad was inside — most likely with a loaded shotgun. This was the South. Everyone carried. I had no doubt Sam had a safe full of weapons he could destroy me with.

Good thing he liked me.

If I screwed his daughter against the side of his house on our first date that'd probably change.

"Thanks for not being a jerk, tonight, Beaux." She grinned again.

Screw it. One kiss wouldn't hurt. "I'll always be nice to you," I muttered, cupping her cheek and tilting my head. I moved slowly, let my intentions be known and was rewarded with a hazy look in her eyes giving me the all clear.

Ah yeah, she wanted me.

I gave it to her. Soft and slow, I brushed my lips over Paige's. She trembled in my arms as I savored the taste of her. Little flicks of my tongue against hers and she parted her lips, inviting me inside, but I took my time kissing her lips, memorizing the silkiness of her hair against my fingers, the weight of her body in my arms.

Her breath hitched, that little moan of hopeful pleasure I was waiting for hit my mouth. I slid my tongue inside. Our bodies melted together, her hands to my back, up and down, she held me, pressed her chest against mine. I forced my hips to stay still, not to rock my dick into her stomach, but the self-control hurt.

She met my tongue, tangled hers in mine and I took over, pushing it back into her mouth. We were moving before I knew it and stopped when I had her against the siding of her house. She let out at a gasp, surprised, and I pulled back.

Jesus Fuck. I really had almost screwed her against the side of her house.

"Holy hell," I mumbled. My grip on her head was firm, but not painful. "You're really damn good at that."

"You're not so bad yourself."

"I need to let you go before I do something that'll lose your dad's respect." Fuck if I wanted to though. I'd already spent a whole bunch of hours jacking off to the thought and the promise of Paige. Now that I'd had a small hint of that perfection, my dick craved the real thing.

"Thanks again for dinner."

"Thanks for coming with me. I'll see you soon, okay?"

I kissed her again and pulled back, both of us gasping for breath. I couldn't get enough of her. One small taste and I was drowning.

"Okay, Beaux."

I let go of her and stepped back. "Get some sleep. I mean it."

I turned, feeling like a victor at a gladiator match. Her matching smile was the last thing I saw as I pulled back down her drive and then her fingers went to her mouth, covering the taste of me on her lips, sealing me in.

NINE
PAIGE

Annabelle was another no-show on Thursday and Paulie called me to come in to work. Since it was my only night off, Beaux and I had plans to go out for dinner. I'd thought about telling Paulie I couldn't do it, but I'd received another physical therapy bill for my dad that morning.

We needed the money and since Thursday was the first NFL game of the season, Ride'Em Rough was sure to be packed, I told him I'd be there.

My fear had spiked when I called Beaux to cancel.

But when I talked to Beaux, while he'd sounded disappointed, he also hadn't sounded too upset. He at least hadn't given me the brush off despite the fact I hadn't seen him for a week. I'd been too busy with work and his schedule was packed while his team prepared for their first game.

He'd leave for Atlanta on Saturday morning, play a game Sunday, get back Sunday night. Who knew when I'd see him again.

Needless to say, despite the extra tips I was raking in, I wasn't in the greatest mood while I was at work. The

Tennessee Titans were playing and there were quite a few fans at Ride'Em Rough, shouting and drinking their weight in pitchers of beer. Some days I wondered if I'd ever be able to scrub the scent of stale beer off me.

In addition to the packed restaurant, the table that I was currently bussing left me with a measly five dollars for a seventy-five dollar bill. My already poor mood was disintegrating by the second.

I slammed my empty drink tray onto the stand and punched in orders for a table when Hannah came up next to me.

"So who pissed in your corn flakes this morning?"

"I don't know what you mean." *Punch. Punch. Punch.*

"I know that if you stopped scowling and started smiling at all your tables filled with men you might make the money you came in for tonight."

"Forget it, Hannah. It's just a crappy day."

Her hand went to my arm and she tugged me toward the back hallway. "Tell me what's going on. Is it your dad?"

I let her pull me, not wanting to cause a scene although no one was watching anything unless it was being broadcasted from one of our fifteen big screens. When we were in the hallway, I dropped the tray to my side.

"Talk."

I was starting to really like Beaux. For the last week, we'd talked almost every night. Some times we just talked about his practice or what my day had been like at the garage. But he'd made an effort to connect with me in some small way daily, and I was totally falling for him.

He consistently showed me he wasn't the jerk he'd been the first night at Ride'Em Rough.

But how many times could I cancel on him, when the

amount of time we could see each other was already so minimal, before he walked away, too?

I desperately needed someone to help me unravel the mess in my head.

"You have to promise me not to freak out," I said, making my voice as stern as possible. "And I mean it. No getting stars in your eyes. No excitement. Nothing."

"Okay," she drawled. Darn. Her eyes were already twinkling.

"I had a date last week and it went well."

"You did?"

I pointed a finger at her. "I said no excitement. No freak outs."

"Right." She nodded enthusiastically, not even trying to hide her smile. "No excitement."

I shook my head. It was pointless. "Okay, so Beaux came to the garage last week—"

She jolted back. "Beaux? Beaux Hale? Are you serious?"

"I'm warning you—"

"I know," she said and held up her hand. Her eyes stopped twinkling and narrowed. "Tell me everything."

I told her about Beaux coming to the garage, the gifts he gave my dad, four of the team members showing up with him, and then dinner and drinks. I told her about everything but the kiss.

Some things were just for me.

By the time I was almost done, her brows had almost disappeared into her hairline, her eyes barely in her sockets, and her jaw almost touching the floor.

"You're dating Beaux?" She shook her head like she couldn't believe it.

"I wouldn't say dating, Hannah." I shrugged. I didn't even know what we were. He was making it clear he was interested.

I definitely was. Time together was a barrier I didn't know how to conquer. "We only went to dinner once."

"So why you'd come in to work if you wanted to see him? If Beaux wanted to date me or spend time with me, or whatever" —she flicked out her hand —"I'd do everything I could to be with him."

"Because I have a mountain of bills to pay."

"But it's Beaux." Her voice took on a wispy tone. She didn't understand.

Frustration spiked in my veins. "And before Beaux there was Spencer. And John and Colton. All of them left when I couldn't give the time they wanted, Hannah. I have other responsibilities, and my dad will always come first."

Damn it. My nose stung and the back of my throat burned. Thinking of all the rejection I faced was humiliating.

I shouldn't have started something with Beaux.

"Maybe Beaux will be different," she said, and she still had that wistful expression on her face. "I mean, he seems like such a great guy."

"He is," I said.

He was.

He was playful and funny. He made me laugh until my stomach hurt. He was fiercely protective of Shannon and hilariously ridiculous in the way he made vomit sounds every time he talked about Shannon and Oliver Powell. He was also intense when he talked about football, totally focused. And he never failed to ask about my dad or Mike. "But you know, I always thought Spencer was a great guy too, the best, and look how that turned out."

I'd thought I loved him and he'd stomped all over it. And while I was over him, knew I had moved on from him, it didn't mean his rejection and the subsequent ones hadn't left their scars.

"Who's Spencer?"

I jumped at the sound of Beaux's voice and spun on my feet. He was there, standing behind me wearing jeans and a Nike T-shirt, and a hat pulled down low on his head.

Blond wisps of his hair stuck out from beneath the hat and that, along with the surprise of seeing him and the scowl on his face, sent my heart racing.

He was so damn sexy. "Hey," I said, my voice breathy. "What are you doing here?"

He slid his hands into the pockets of his jeans. "You had to cancel and I wanted to see you. Was hoping I could talk you into hanging out for awhile after your shift."

He what? I stared at him. Next to me, Hannah sighed. She nudged me with her elbow and snapped me back to the fact that Beaux had wanted to see me so he made a way to see me.

If swooning was still a thing, I would have done it.

"Wow. Well, that's nice of you."

He flashed me a lopsided grin. "I told you. I'm a nice guy."

He had. He'd also proved it. My cheeks ached from the smile splitting my face. "I'd like that. But it's another hour until I'm off."

"I know. I figured I'd grab some dinner and a couple drinks while I wait." He walked toward me, rested his hand on my hip and before I'd adjusted to his presence so close to me, he pressed his lips to my temple. "It's good to see you. And maybe later, you'll clue me in on Spencer?"

He pulled back and gazed down at me. Blond brows arched on his head beneath a frayed and faded red ball cap, there was a question in his eyes.

"An ex," I said, waving him off. "Not a big deal."

"Sounded like it."

Damn it. Of all the things I wanted to discuss with Beaux, Spencer was definitely not one of them. I also knew he was determined, and because of that, he wouldn't let up until I told him.

"Later," I said. "We'll talk later."

"Good. Now get to work. I have a surprise for you when you're done."

He turned and walked away. I was still so shocked by his presence and his sweetness, and the fact he'd wanted to see me so badly he'd come to hang out where I worked, it was moments before I remembered Hannah was still standing next to me. Like me, she was watching Beaux walk away, but there wasn't the sweet goofy expression in her eyes she usually had. Her body was pulled tight, her chin jutted out, and a frown wrinkled her brow.

"Hannah?"

"Hmm?" She turned to me. "What?"

"You okay?"

"Yeah." She nodded once and her playfulness returned. "Of course I am. Told you Beaux was a nice guy."

I followed her out of the hallway and was stopped by Ray who told me I had a new four top to take waters to.

I WIPED off the last drink tray and placed it on the stack, tossing my cloth back into the wash bucket behind the bar.

My feet ached, my arches were killing me, but my apron was weighed down in tips as well as the count I'd taken from the credit card receipts. Hannah had been right. After Beaux showed up, I couldn't stop smiling. My tips increased exponentially.

I would have been able to do all the tasks required of me before clocking out, but when I took my trays over to where

Beaux was still sitting at the bar, only a glass of ice water in front of him, we started talking while I worked.

"I think I'm done," I said, untying my apron and tossing it onto the bar.

"What do you need to do to leave?" He pushed his glass toward the edge of the bar and Joey grabbed it from him with a thanks.

While I'd been busy working on the other side of the restaurant, I'd kept my eye on Beaux. Even with his faded and frayed red ball cap on, dozens of people recognized him. He'd spent most of the night alternating between signing autographs and eating his burger.

He'd always been smiling, and more than once I'd caught that smile directed at me.

"You still have energy to go out?" I asked. I was thrumming with a mixture of exhaustion and anticipation. I wanted to see him, but he had practice in the morning. "We don't have to."

"Didn't sit here all night drinking gallons of water and having a shit burger to end up spending the night alone." His grin hit me in places, sweet places. Somehow, Beaux's smile was a beacon, a light to all the stress I carried.

He smiled at me and it all melted away—while other things overheated.

"Okay. I have to grab my things from the break room and I'll be off." I turned to Joey and slid him my apron. "Hey, Joey, can you cash me out please?"

"Sure thing, Paige." He winked at me and I laughed. Joey was almost forty, divorced with kids old enough to be starting middle school. A boy and girl twins, they often came in on the weekends he had them if he couldn't get off work. I'd hung out with Bella and Bryan on more than one occasion. Sweet kids. That wasn't unexpected since Joey was a nice guy, and even managed to co-parent his kids with his ex-wife with a grace that was sweet enough to be make believe.

He was also a huge flirt and winked at everyone.

Next to me, Beaux pushed off his spot at the bar. "I'll wait for you out front. Don't take long," he whispered in my ear, hand on my hip like he'd done earlier.

My body gave the same trembling reaction.

He walked away and I hurried to the back, throwing on a change of clothes before heading back out to the bar.

Hannah was there, grabbing drinks for her last table.

"You headed out with Beaux?" she asked.

"Yes." I bit down on my lip so hard it stung. "I can't wait."

"Have fun." She flashed me a tight smile and hurried off.

Weird. She must have been stressed if she didn't tease me about giving her the juicy details.

"Here are your tips," Joey said when I returned to the bar. "Looks like you had a great night."

"I did." I didn't count the stack of cash he handed me, but it was definitely thicker than normal. I shoved it into my purse. "Thanks for all your help."

"No problem. Take care tonight."

"I will. See you tomorrow?"

He shook his head. "Nope. Got the kids this weekend. I'll be back on Monday."

I grinned and waved. "See you then. Tell them I said hello!"

"You got it."

I headed toward the door to the restaurant, unable to stop smiling when I thought of Beaux.

Even before I met Beaux, one of my largest concerns had been the chance of finding a guy who understood my priorities would always have my dad at the top of the list. I'd been burned enough to know it wasn't easy, and after the last time I'd been rejected, I'd given up on dating at all.

So far, Beaux hadn't only shown me that he understood my priorities, but he was okay with them. I might not have done it intentionally, but I suspected that for the last week, I'd been getting to know Beaux while keeping my arms up, forcing distance between us.

His actions tonight told me that distance might not be necessary with him.

My arms were getting tired from forcing it.

At some point, I had to let someone in, didn't I? Why not risk it with a guy who made me smile and seemed to understand how much time I had to give?

I didn't have long to think about it because as soon as I stepped outside, the beautiful sight in front of me wiped my concerns from my brain.

Beaux was there, standing in front of his giant black truck, arms crossed over his chest, hat bill pulled low, and jeans low on his hips. His T-shirt showed off the dips and ridges of his stomach so fiercely my girlie parts quivered. One of his feet was up on his grill, the other planted on the pavement.

It wasn't just his body and the way he was standing that skewered through me like a hot summer night.

It was his smile. It was directed at me, and it told me all the things he wanted to do to me as soon as he got me alone.

TEN

BEAUX

Several times over the week I'd gotten the strange sensation that while Paige enjoyed being with me, she wasn't really giving me all of her. It was too soon to push it, we could take our time, but I'd never exactly been a patient guy when it came to something I wanted.

I was trying with her though, because not only did she mean something to me, I could tell she needed it. She was probably the only person I knew whose life was busier than mine, and that meant whatever we were doing wasn't a sprint, but a marathon.

But I still sensed her hesitancy in sharing her life with me. Even the small way she shut down when I overheard her talking about her ex earlier showed it.

Paige lived her life with a wall around her so high I couldn't even see the top of it.

And sometimes, I didn't know if I was fruitlessly pounding my head against that brick wall, or punching through, getting closer to shattering it.

As Paige stepped outside and her face lit up when she saw

me standing against my truck waiting for her, I hoped like hell it was the second.

"You need more lights in this parking lot," I said, dropping my foot from the grill of my truck as she came close. "It's dark and unsafe out here."

She scanned the parking lot and shrugged. "We've never had any problems."

Her car was parked out back with the rest of the workers, but other than a light near the dumpster, most of the lights in the parking lot were out.

"You walk out here alone?"

"Sometimes. Sometimes one of the guys walks me out."

Grabbing her hand, I pulled her to me until her chest collided with mine.

"If you're with me, people will recognize you. I travel a lot. When I'm gone, I want to know you're safe and that lot out back where you park is dark. I don't want to be staring down a line of three hundred pound assholes, worried about you, or wondering if you're getting shanked on your way to your car."

"Wow." She laughed and her hand slid to my chest. "That's quite the imagination."

"I just want you safe," I repeated, threading my hand through her hair. My thumb brushed against the bangs that had escaped her clip like she usually wore it. "Talk to your manager about the lights or I will."

"Bossy when it's late, aren't you?"

Her tone had a bite to it, slightly defensive, a bit breathy. I liked the combination. Strong and vulnerable, a little needy. Yeah. Hopefully I'd punch through that brick wall around her soon.

"I prefer concerned, but if bossy is what it takes, I'm okay with that."

She twisted her neck and looked at the back lot. "I see your point, though. I'll talk to Paulie." Her nose scrunched. "Or, wait. He's cranky. I'll tell the bouncers or have Joey talk to him."

"Thank you." I pulled her flush against me, trapping her hand on my chest between us. Then I slanted my head, tilted her chin up, and pressed my lips to hers. "I just want to know you're taken care of when I'm not here to do it, okay?"

"That's the sweetest thing anyone's ever said to me." Her grin went soft. It was a look that made my heart swell and want to pummel someone at the same time.

She deserved someone being nice to her. The fact she hadn't had it, pissed me off.

It also made me think of Spencer, but we had time to get into him.

"Can we go now?" Paige asked, "or is there anything else you'd like to go alpha-male bossy over."

"We can go." I held her hand while I opened her door and then shut it. Her grin was still in place when I climbed into the driver's seat and pulled out of the parking lot.

"Do you want to tell me where you're taking me?"

"Nope, but it's not far." I switched off my rap playlist so it wasn't blaring through the speakers. "How was work tonight. Seemed busy."

"Slammed. I haven't worked there during a football season yet but if tonight's any indication of how the next few months are going to go, I can't complain. Tips are amazing."

I understood that. My mom had loved waitressing jobs when she could get them and she never worked at a place as busy as Ride'Em. I still didn't like that this girl was working just as hard as my mom used to.

If I thought she wouldn't cut off my dick if I offered her money, I'd give her millions so she and her dad could rest easy.

"I bet," I said instead. "Do you like working there? Or have you thought about looking for jobs in your field?"

As an athlete, and someone frequently in the media, I had a love-hate relationship with people who chose that as their line of work. The line between news and gossip was easily blurred.

"No." She wiped her hands down her jeans, something she'd changed into before coming out. Now dressed in white jeans with small patches of frayed material and a navy blue tank top, she looked not only ready for a date but much classier than her typical Ride'Em Rough uniform. "I've thought about it, but it's a tough field to get into unless you have contacts and if I did that, I wouldn't be able to help my dad at the garage."

"What about Mike? He seems capable."

"Yeah," she laughed, "at fixing cars, but he'd lose it if I asked him to do the ordering or payroll. Besides, that's my family's garage. It's not only my responsibility, I like being there, sitting in an office my dad has used since before I was born, and my granddad used before him." She shrugged, head falling to the headrest and turned to me. "It's just a car garage, but we do a lot of great work with custom vintage cars. I grew up with that and it's hard to let it go."

"Then I hope you can figure out how to keep it all without having that happen."

I could give her anything she asked for and financially, it'd mean nothing to me. Hell, I wouldn't even feel it in my bank balance. I also knew I'd barely been able to get her to go out with me. Offering to help wouldn't go over well.

There was punching through a brick wall and there was going full speed ahead like a man on a death mission.

I wasn't ready to burn into a ball of flames quite yet.

Besides, my mom always said you had to pick your battles and this one could wait for another day.

I guided us to safer topics, mostly talking about practice

when she asked and some of the guys on the team as I drove us through Raleigh to a little park near my house. I didn't go there often, but it was quiet and dark. It also was sort of romantic, but that wasn't what I was aiming for totally.

I just wanted to give Paige some peace and quiet for a while.

~

IT DIDN'T TAKE LONG to get to the park and when I pulled into the parking lot, car lights shining toward the pond out in the distance, Paige turned to me with sleepy eyes.

Damn. She'd worked a long, hard shift and she was tired. Yet she still came with me. That meant something good, right?

"Are we parking?" she asked, a glimmer in her hazel eyes.

"Well, you did make me give up the truck I lost my virginity in and I haven't christened this one yet."

Her eyes popped wide open, cheeks flushing. "Are you...what...no..."

"Relax." I laughed and grabbed her hand. She tried to pull away but I yanked her closer, moving in until I was bent over the armrest. "I'm messing with you. I like this place and I come here when I need quiet. That's all I wanted to share with you tonight."

"Okay." The breathiness of her voice shot straight to my dick.

"Besides, the first time I have your sweet little naked body in my hands it's going to be in my bed, not straddling me over this seat."

Her jaw dropped and I turned, hopping out of the car before she could protest. I'd play it slow and easy while keeping her on edge at the same time. This girl would never doubt how much I wanted her, or how good I'd be for her if she gave me an honest chance to show her.

Out of the truck, I flung open the back door and grabbed the cooler filled with wine and snacks. When I decided to surprise her at work, this was the first place that came to mind, and I figured she'd like a glass of wine after a long night of work. Inside the cab, Paige was still sitting there. Eyes wide open, lips still parted, a furious blush staining her cheeks.

"Paige?"

"Uh, yeah?" She shook her head. Hot damn. She wanted what I was offering up.

"Are you thinking about what I just said?"

"No. Of course not."

"Sure you're not. Come on. Park closes soon. You going to come on out or am I coming back in there?"

"Out." She jumped. "I'm coming out."

Wise decision. I didn't have a problem taking her in my truck, but I did want her in my bed. Spread out so I could roam my hands over every inch of her soft skin.

She climbed out of the truck and I beeped the locks, meeting her at the front. Grabbing her hand, I threaded our fingers together.

The heat from her palm spread to mine, up my arm. I liked touching this girl. She made me feel like I was eighteen all over again and horny all the time. This was one of the best parts of being with a woman. Each new discovery of how we connected, what made them tick, what made them smile. What made them come...that was my favorite.

They were puzzles and each one cut differently. Paige was by far the most complicated.

Or, she was the first I cared about to stick around to try and solve all the pieces.

I guided her down the path, lights sparse the further we

moved into the park, and I took my time, neither of us really speaking.

I'd found this park one night when I was out running. I didn't want to run around the city or drive to a track and run laps like a hamster on a wheel.

Instead, I'd plugged in my GPS, found this place and I'd run for what felt like hours. Exhausted, I'd plopped down on the grass near the small pond and rested. I stayed there for hours more, doing nothing but thinking. Relaxing. I didn't run plays through my head. I didn't think about my volunteer schedule that was crazy busy during the off-season. I hadn't thought of anything important, and when I needed a break from life, I always ended up there.

"You ever been here?" I asked. We were only twenty minutes from where she grew up.

"Yeah," she said, her voice whispering like we were afraid of disrupting nature. We were surrounded by the still of the night, punctuated with the buzz of cicadas.

"When?"

A grin lifted her lips and she pointed back toward a playground we'd already passed. "I had my first kiss back under that jungle gym."

My head snapped toward the jungle gym. The playground was old and not updated, still had the dome of metal bars from when I was a kid. "Seriously? You let some guy take advantage of you in a public park?" My expression went aghast.

"Who says he took advantage of me? Maybe I was the one doing all the taking."

Holy hell. It was the first time she'd so brazenly flirted with me, bumping her hip into mine and squeezing my hand. Felt like a gold medal won after years of brutal training and time investment.

Yeah. I liked this girl.

"Nice to know I'm with an experienced woman, then. At least one of us has it."

She pulled to an abrupt stop and she turned to me. Even in the dim shine of the poorly lit path, I could tell her face had paled. "What? But you said earlier in the truck..."

"Holy shit! I'm not a virgin!" I shouted. I tugged my hand from hers and covered my face, laughing my ass off. "That's what you thought I meant? You're a nut."

"Well, what am I supposed to think when you talk about being experienced?"

"Jeez, woman. Get your head out of the gutter. I'm not always thinking about sex." She flashed me a look and I quickly amended my statement. I raised my hands. "Okay. When I'm around you, I'm pretty much always thinking about sex, but that time, I wasn't talking about it honestly."

A blush hit her cheeks. Hard and fast. "Do you always say what you think?"

"Yes."

"Have you ever heard of a social filter?"

"Please. Do I look like the kind of guy who cares what people say about me?" I flung my arms out, might have puffed out my chest like a peacock strutting. Her eyes roamed my body, slowly, as if she was already inspecting every inch of me while I was naked. "Need a closer look?" I asked when she didn't speak.

A sliver of her tongue poked out and wiped her bottom lip. She turned back toward the pond. "Nope."

"Sure you don't."

She flashed me a look over her shoulder and winked. "Need and want are different things, Beaux Hale."

"Woman," he growled and charged at me. Beaux had flung a blanket and cooler over his shoulder when we started walking but as he charged me, the blanket flew off his shoulder and the cooler slapped his thigh.

I screamed and started running but I was no match for him. Three steps and I was flung up in the air and one of Beaux's arms was behind my back, the other under my knees.

"Can't tease me like that and not expect retribution." He spun around and headed back to the blanket. "Grab the blanket."

I tried to wiggle out of his hold but he gripped me tighter, lifting my legs high. I scrambled and grabbed his shoulder.

"Can't grab the blanket while you're tearing through my shirt."

"I can't get the blanket when you're holding me."

His eyes glimmered. "I lift weights more than three times heavier than you. Let go of my shoulder before you tear my tendons with your nails and get the blanket."

He swung me like he was going to toss me and I lost my grip.

"Beaux!" I screamed as I tried to reach the ground but he lifted me higher in the air. I was dangling, upside down, my knees hooked only by his forearm. "Put me down!"

"Get the blanket before I drop you."

He was laughing. The force of his laugh vibrated through my legs up to my center. And I stopped squealing and tried to look at him. He was so damn beautiful. Not a manly enough name for him but he wasn't handsome, either.

He was a force of power and confidence all on his own.

I was swimming upside down, falling for this guy.

"You wouldn't."

His arm dropped and I screamed his name again. This time though, the blanket brushed against my fingertips and I clawed at it, gripping it in my fingers. Then I was up, his hand at my back and I was thrown over his shoulder, along with the blanket, covering me.

"Put me down."

"No way."

We were both laughing, his shoulders shaking from it. All the blood rushed to my face.

Awesome. I'd look like an eggplant when he put me on my feet.

"Put me down now or you're not even getting a kiss from me, Beaux Hale, and I was planning on giving you a lot more than that."

He pulled to a stop.

"What are you going to give me?"

All of me. I wisely, and barely, held the errant thought back. If I told Beaux I wanted him to do all the things to me he'd teased me about, I'd be naked and beneath him in five seconds flat. "You'll just have to wait to find out."

It was all the talk of sex. That's what was making me act like some brazen little hussy, flirting and throwing myself at him.

But I was tired of holding back. I was tired of putting my life on hold, tired physically. I wanted to reach for something that was mine. I didn't lie when I said I liked working at the garage. It was my second home and I wanted it to stay in business more than I wanted to be a reporter.

When I was with Beaux, I didn't stress about anything. He gave me the freedom and escape from responsibilities while strengthening me for the next day at the same time.

Beaux Hale, quarterback of a Super Bowl winning team, summertime RV partier...all around nice guy.

Who would have thought?

I tossed the blanket over my head and braced my hands on his lower back, pushing myself up. "Can I walk?"

"No. I sort of like having your ass right next to my face." He turned his head, and playfully bit the back of my thigh.

"Ouch."

"It didn't hurt, but if it did, I'll kiss it and make it better."

I couldn't suppress my shiver. My whole body lit up at the idea. His words, the image of me, legs spread, his mouth at my thighs...my ass...more pleasurable places. I moaned, unable to stop myself at the thought of his mess of blond hair between my legs.

"Jesus, Paige." He stopped and set me down. "That turn you on? I felt your whole body shake."

"Maybe." My hands slid to his shirt, fingertips dug into his pecs. Good grief. This man. His eyes were narrowed on me, a few sprinkled lights in the background hiding the color of his blues I knew were piercing based on the heat rolling off him.

His whole body had tightened, chest moved erratically up and down as he breathed harshly.

"I didn't bring you here to screw you on a blanket, but you're making it awfully difficult not to think about it."

I pressed my chest toward him, slid my hand up, up, and up toward his neck, pulling him down to me. "Can plans change?"

I had never been this bold. Get me around Beaux and I wasn't lost in the size of his wallet or his contract, but everything that he was showing himself to be.

He studied me intensely, blinking slowly and then shaking his head. "Not yet. I have other plans for you."

Disappointment swirled inside me, making me tremble with untended to desire but I inhaled a deep breath and moved toward where he laid the blanket on the grass.

In front of us was a pond, the sounds of nature echoing and shimmering across the water and all around us. Frogs croaked, cicadas purred, and crickets chirped all in a rhythm of their own but beautiful in the stillness.

I wasn't a huge nature person, but as Beaux settled next to me on the blanket and unloaded the cooler, I could have stayed there forever.

Visions of camping and bonfires and cold beer slid into my mind. We'd be on lounge chairs in the middle of nowhere, nothing to do but talk and laugh, maybe a few stolen kisses.

"Here," he said, jolting me out of the fantasy. He handed me a glass of white wine in a plastic cup and poured one for himself. "Can I tell you what I am inexperienced with?"

I barely suppressed choking on my wine. "Sure."

"It's not, sex, Paige." He smiled, white teeth sparkling in the setting darkness.

"I didn't say it was," I said innocently.

"I can practically hear your dirty thoughts. But what I was going to say earlier was dating."

"Dating?"

He had one leg stretched out straight, the other bent, knee

high and Converse shoe planted on the blanket. His arm holding his wineglass dangled in his large hand, arm settled on his knee. Looking out at the water, he pushed back his hair. "Yeah. I gotta be honest here. I have no clue what in the hell I'm doing. I haven't had a date in who knows how long."

My grip tightened on my glass. He didn't date. He did, most likely, go around screwing random women, but why wouldn't he? He was in his twenties, single, and a multi-millionaire who drew notice wherever he went.

"I'm not sure why you're telling me this," I mumbled and took a hefty swallow of my drink.

"Because I want to be honest with you. And because I like you. I don't want you sitting here thinking I've fucked every chick who walked up to me, but I don't want you thinking I do this shit all the time, either."

The urge to ask why me burned on my tongue, but I washed it away with more wine. "Well, wow. I mean, I'm not sure I'm up for this kind of pressure." I nudged his shoulder with mine and stayed close. He was warm. Smelled fantastic. And his hard, muscled body felt like a boulder. "I mean, what if I turn you off dating forever?"

He laughed. It was low and rumbly and before I knew it, he'd set down his glass of wine, reached for me and yanked me onto his lap.

"Hey," he said, once he had me settled facing him.

"Hey, you." I set down my glass of wine before I dropped it. Our faces were inches apart and I was sitting on his lap. Straddling him. His knees were bracing my back behind me. I was cocooned in all things Beaux.

I was falling for him. His honesty, his looks, his sincerity. Everything about this guy screamed too good to be true but I didn't care.

If I was going to crash and burn, I wanted to enjoy the fall.

I slid my hands into his hair and clasped my hands together at the back of his neck. "Since we're confessing things here, I have to say that I think your ass looks really good in your uniform, I've always wanted to run my hands through your hair when it's sweaty after a game, and I'm a really big fan of yours, Beaux Hale."

"Yeah?" His shoulders shook with laughter and his head tipped to the side. His hands at my hips slid down to my backside and he squeezed. "I think your ass is pretty fantastic too. Why didn't you tell me you were a fan?"

I shrugged. "I didn't want it to go to your head."

Speaking of, one of his heads was becoming more pronounced the longer I sat on him. I'd felt it immediately, but the longer we were connected, the harder he became. I dug my fingers into the back of his neck to keep from rocking against him.

Good Lord, this guy was impressive. It'd been so long since I'd had sex, good sex at least, the kind that left your hips sore and you remembering every moment for days with a little secretive grin on your lips even strangers knew you'd been laid recently. I'd forgotten how good all of this felt.

The temptation. Desire. The anticipation of that moment when everything clicked together, when you connected with another person.

My pulse thundered and as we laughed, grinning like fools, I couldn't wait anymore.

I had to have him.

"Beaux," I whispered, my voice gone needy and thick.

"I confess I really want to kiss you," he rumbled, shoving his face into my throat, "and I'm afraid I won't be able to stop."

"Then don't. I'm with you, one hundred percent."

TWELVE

PAIGE

"Fuck, Paige," he groaned.

I couldn't believe I was doing this. I wasn't someone who threw themselves at men. I certainly didn't straddle their laps in a park, but Beaux was different.

He was playful and sweet, and around him, it appeared my inhibitions took a flying leap into the pond.

He pressed his lips against the side of my throat and my body lit with anticipation. His full, warm lips against me, the slightest hint of stubble scraped my sensitive flesh as he moved higher until our mouths were inches from each other.

He gazed at me like he was trying to pry into my soul and my eyes fluttered close, unable to handle the inspection.

"You're beautiful," he whispered, leaning in.

A shiver wracked my spine and I clung to him, fingertips pressing to the back of his neck, and into his hair right before he moved in, lips sealing us together.

A fire ignited deep inside my stomach.

He slid his tongue against my lips, seeking entrance and I

allowed it, parting for him and as I tasted him, the mix of man and sweet white wine, I was gone.

I was swimming in the ocean, free falling, skydiving without a tandem partner. Beaux's kisses sent me swirling into the eye of a hurricane and I couldn't care what happened once I landed. Everything inside my body soared to life, heated, cooled. I held him against me, my hands in his hair, his shoulders.

I clung to his biceps like I'd fall without him but he held me just as tightly. Our mouths fused together, tasted each other, and I reveled in the moment until I was shamelessly moving against him. The friction of our denim, the pressure of his hands on me, guiding me and helping me, shot delicious sparks up my spine, and I groaned into his mouth.

"So good," I whimpered, my breathing erratic, my chest tight like it could explode.

I was lost in his pleasure. The only sounds I could now hear were my needy little whimpers and his harsh breathing.

"Fuck," he groaned and flipped us over. My legs opened immediately, taking his weight and then we were together again, fully clothed.

I didn't care. I lost all track of time while we made out like teenagers. I wanted this.

Wanted him.

"Beaux—"

"I know—"

"Do you—"

"I feel it, Paige."

God. We were finishing sentences and thoughts, and I pulled away from him, catching my breath with my hands clinging at his shirt. Lifting. Tugging. He moved off me to discard it and then he was back, his hot hand pushing beneath my tank top.

"I'm not fucking you here," he said, lips pressing kisses to my throat. He reached my bra, his thumb slid over my nipple, and my entire body trembled from the friction.

"Please." I had never begged. I'd do anything to get him to continue doing what he was doing.

"I need to see you come, though. Need to see you light up for me, you okay with that?"

Only an idiot would say no, and I had always been a four point oh student. "Please."

He pulled me toward him, draping my thighs over his while he bent down and pulled the cups of my bra down. Cool air assaulted my breasts right before hot heat from his mouth covered them. He tortured me with his mouth and his tongue while his hand went to my jeans.

A button popped.

A zipper slid down.

I was already so close, my release making me shake with the need to take over but I fought it back, tried to sear every one of his touches, every delicious moment of this night into my memory banks. Yet, I couldn't stop moving.

I was greedy, so damn greedy that when he tugged down my jeans, I helped him, shoving them down as far as they could go.

"God, you're gorgeous," Beaux said. "And you taste like heaven."

I laughed, gripped his shoulders. "I want to kiss you."

He didn't make me wait. He arched above me, settling some of his weight off my body and then his hand was there, pressing that sweet spot beneath my panties.

It was glorious.

His forehead hit mine.

"So damn wet. I can't wait until I can see all of you."

"Yes," I gasped and arched into him. My spine burned like

I'd been electrocuted. This was too much. Too fast and too strong and too powerful. The threat of my orgasm hitting me so fiercely terrified me and yet I wasn't moving away.

"Oh shit," I panted. I couldn't stay still, I couldn't kiss him, couldn't breathe him in. I wanted to pull his body to mine, fuse us together and my Lord...when did I think such crazy and asinine things?

It didn't matter.

"Come for me," Beaux ordered, and then his mouth was on mine again. He continued his ministrations, playing my body perfectly and I couldn't hold back.

I cried out, pleasure coursing through me I'd never felt before.

"Shit, shit, shit." My words became vowels, consonants too much effort as I clung to him. His shoulders, his back, his arms. I grabbed every small piece of him I could, and it only fueled my desire for more of him.

"Beautiful," Beaux crooned, bringing me down from sweet orgasmic bliss. "You're so damn beautiful when you come, Paige. God, I want you."

I wanted him too. Barely catching my breath, I was still panting, still running my hands along his arms to his back. "I might need a minute to recover."

He pulled back, cocky grin reappearing. "That good huh? The best, maybe?"

It had been. I smiled, leaned up and pressed my lips to his. "I want to take care of you."

"No way." He shook his head and leaned off me, fixing my bra and my shirt as he spoke. "Can't. I get busted for public indecency and I'm fucked, and not in the good way." As if he just realized it, he looked up, scanned the area. "Thank God no one saw us doing that."

A flicker of reality with him niggled at the edges of my

mind and I pushed it back. Reality was for tomorrow or later tonight when I was alone and missing him—because I would miss him. Fantasy and now was all we had.

I pressed my hand to my chest. "I can't calm my heart. It's racing."

"Like I said the other day, it's because I'm the best."

"And arrogant."

"Funny and sweet."

"Cocky."

"Humble and kind."

"Okay." I shoved him off me, our grins as wide as could be. "Enough. I get it. You're the best. Happy now?"

His smile fell. Gently, he brushed my hair off my face with his thumb, cupping my cheek. "I think I am."

The power in his statement made me gulp down my fears. I was trying to keep this light. Open up and give him parts of me I usually kept tucked away.

He was making it so damn difficult to not hand over all my hidden places.

"I need my wine."

Chuckling, he sat us up. Then he dumped out my wine and as he refilled the glass, I dug in my purse for my phone.

"Oh no." I jumped up as I stared at the screen. Four missed calls. Two voicemails. I didn't listen to them. "I have to go home now, Beaux. Now."

"What is it?"

"My dad."

My heart raced for a different reason. I pulled up Mike's number and hit send, one hand tugging my hair. Damn it!

"What is it?" I said as soon as Mike said hello.

"Paige? Where are you? Jesus, Elsa and I have both been calling you."

"I know. What is it?" I didn't have time for this. "Beaux!" I snapped. "I need to go."

He must have sensed the panic in my voice because he had everything loaded, blanket tossed over his arm.

"It's dad," Mike said. "He'll be okay. Just know that he's going to be fine, but Elsa found him outside tonight. He was wandering we guess."

Crap crap crap! This wasn't happening. Damn it. I should have been there.

"Elsa found him? I thought she was with him!" She'd told me she would watch him tonight. Where had she gone? "How bad?"

"He's in the emergency room. I'm here, waiting, and I haven't seen him. Elsa said he was bleeding pretty bad. A few cuts. I don't know much else, she was pretty upset."

"Shit!" I cursed and started running. Beaux was hot on my heels, the thumping of his feet keeping pace with me. "I'll be there as soon as I can. Which hospital?"

He rattled off the name and I shoved my phone into my purse.

"Raleigh Regional, Beaux. I have to go."

"What happened?"

"My dad is hurt." I glared at him. He was taking too long. Hurrying as fast as me but damn it. I shouldn't have done this. One night. I took one night for myself and this was what happened.

By the time we hopped into my truck and I'd set the GPS for the hospital, Paige had already shut down. I saw the moment it happened, when she realized while she was off enjoying herself, her dad was somewhere else, injured.

The moment she glared at me, her walls had slammed back up.

I got it. I did. I understood the guilt and the responsibility.

Didn't mean I liked it and it didn't mean it didn't tick me off.

Fuck. I had one night of her. One night where all she gave me were smiles and her body and her playfulness and I was hooked.

No way in hell was she taking it back now.

She was sitting next to me, arms crossed over her chest. The gesture was obvious. Another back-the-hell-away from me stance and I gave her that play, my mind on the end zone, not the fifty-yard line. When we pulled up close to the hospital, only a few turns left until I knew she'd hop out of my truck before I came to a stop, I couldn't take the silence anymore.

"You know this isn't your fault, Paige. There's nothing for you to feel guilty about because you went out and had some fun."

Her eyes slid to me, a glare so chilled I felt it in my balls.

I sighed and pulled into the parking lot. Emergency in red and white flashed like seconds on a game clock. "Let me park and I'll wait with you."

"You've done enough, thanks."

I slammed on my brakes. Thank fuck there wasn't another car behind us. She yanked forward in her seat and fell back, the seat belt locking immediately.

"What the hell!"

"Don't," I growled. "Don't fucking tarnish what we had tonight. Don't do that to us. I get you're mad. I get you're blaming yourself, and most of all I get why you feel so damn guilty. You forget I've been where you are, Paige. Don't fucking forget I spent most of my teenage years watching my mom die. I fucking get it. But don't for one damn second think you get to take what happened between us tonight away from me, or you. I won't let you."

Tears spilled from her eyes before I was done lashing out.

For a moment, I thought she was going to soften, but she rolled her shoulders back and wiped tears off her cheeks. "You don't have a say in it. I need to get to my dad."

She flung open the door. I reached for her other hand but she pulled it from my grip. "Paige—"

"I told you the first night we met I wasn't available, Beaux, and this is why. My dad will always come first, and he needs my help and attention more than I need to be getting off in a field."

"That's not all that was and you know it. And you don't have to do this alone."

"I'm not alone. I have my dad." Tears were falling from her

cheeks and she viciously swiped them away, shaking her head. "He's all I have, Beaux."

God. Her pain was as evident as her anger and guilt.

She had me. All she had to do was reach out and take it.

There was no way she'd listen to me, not as upset as she was and blaming herself.

She hopped out of the truck. "Thanks for the ride."

She slammed the door before I could respond.

It sounded eerily like my head crashing into a brick wall.

FOURTEEN
PAIGE

I rushed into the emergency room already regretting the way I talked to Beaux. Too bad I had other, more important things on my mind.

Every word he threw at me was true. Tonight had been incredible.

I felt mounds of guilt that were piling higher than Mt. Everest. My dad had gotten hurt and I wasn't there. The entire reason I moved home was to take care of him. And where was I? Out getting off like a teenager with no responsibilities.

Crap!

I hurried to the nurse's station, out of breath and panting as the woman behind the desk looked up. "Paige Halloway. My father, Sam, was brought in by ambulance earlier."

Her finger clicked on a keyboard. With an emotionless voice, she stated, "He's in bay five currently. If you take a seat, I'll have someone come out and give you an update as soon as I can."

"No." My head shook so violently my hair stuck to my wet

cheeks. "That's not good enough. I need to know what happened."

"Ma'am—"

"Paige." I whipped my head and there was Mike. He was already reaching me, arms outstretched and I fell into them. "He'll be okay. Come sit with me."

"I need to know."

"He fell. He's hurt. That's all we know so far. But he's strong and he'll be okay."

I let Mike usher me into the sitting room, his chair closest to the doors heading to the back as if he knew that's where I'd need to be. As close to my dad as possible.

"I wasn't there."

"It's okay that you weren't."

It wasn't. Nothing about this was. Not me freaking out on Beaux—again. Not me shirking my responsibilities for even a few hours.

I shook my head against his shoulder. "Tell me everything you know."

He sighed, pressed his lips to the top of my head and squeezed me tighter. "Not much. Elsa said she'd gotten him ready for bed and thought he was settled so she went home to let her dogs outside. She went out later to bring her dog in for the night and saw him collapsed on your lawn. All she got from him as she was calling nine-one-one was that he'd gone out for a walk and fallen."

Damn it. He knew better than to go walking alone. His balance wasn't that great and it'd been dark. Unfortunately the stroke hadn't just left him slightly paralyzed, but had affected some of his mental abilities. He didn't always make the best choices. He and I went for a walk almost every day. I'd just assumed since I was working he wouldn't go without me.

That's not even true. As soon as Beaux showed up at the

restaurant, I hadn't thought of my dad at all. Not even to call him to tell him I'd be home late.

"Maybe he just twisted his ankle," Mike said. His effort to calm me was useless. "They're probably just checking him over, being careful, but you know Sam. He's probably in the back right now demanding his release and for everyone to stop all the hullabaloo over him."

"Okay." I squeezed Mike tighter and lied through my teeth. I didn't believe a word he said, and wouldn't until I saw my dad. "You're right. He'll be fine."

"That's the spirit. Now, tell me about your night. I'm assuming since you're not dressed in your uniform you went out after work?"

"I don't want to talk about it."

"Bet you had fun," Mike said, totally ignoring me. "And that's okay, Paige. Your dad hates it that you're here taking care of him and not living like you're supposed to."

"I can't, not when I know I can leave him and things like this could happen."

"They could happen even if he was healthy."

"Stop trying to be so smart," I said, poking him in the side of his stomach. His quiet laugh echoed in my ear. "You sound like my dad."

"Yeah, well he's the smartest man I've ever met and you know exactly what he's going to say to you once you see him and start with this guilt trip you don't need to be carrying. He's going to say you're too damn young to be taking care of him and all he wants is for you to experience the life you were supposed to have. That's what he's going to say."

God. What was it with men throwing all this in my face? He was my dad. My responsibility. Mike repeating almost the same thing Beaux had said didn't help, either. They might have understood. Hell, logically I agreed with them.

It didn't help me emotionally.

"You sound like Beaux." I should have kept my mouth shut.

"Yeah? Is that who you were with tonight?"

"I said I don't want to talk about it."

Mike sighed and hugged me tighter to him. I pulled back from his embrace and wiped my cheeks. My dad would hate knowing I was crying over him. I had to be strong. "Bet you don't want to talk about it," he murmured. "I bet that's a yes, too, then. Look at you, hot shot...out with the quarterback of the football team. He bring you here? Awfully late for a girl like you to be out."

He shot me a smirk and I rolled my eyes. Mike played the big brother card perfectly, even if we weren't related and he was years younger than me.

"I was a bitch to him," I admitted reluctantly.

"Eh. He's got big shoulders. Strikes me as the kind of guy who can handle it."

Perhaps. But tonight very well could have been my third strike, too. How many times would a guy come back when he was constantly pushed away? At some point, he wasn't going to think crazy was cute, and tonight's behavior could have permanently blown my chances.

Which was really for the best.

Tonight proved I didn't have the time for a relationship anyway.

So, why, as Mike and I settled into silence, did I palm my phone in my hand, debating whether or not to text him an apology?

He deserved one, but more, he deserved an explanation why I was such a mess.

Before I could pull up the message app and send something to him, a woman dressed in scrubs came out of the emergency and scanned the waiting room.

"Paige Halloway?"

∼

A BROKEN FREAKING LEG. After spending hours in the emergency room Thursday night, my dad had been taken back for surgery to have pins placed in his leg. He'd be in a cast and would re-start physical therapy as soon as he was strong enough. At least we already had a wheelchair for him in the mean time. I was able to get the story from him once the doctor had taken Mike and I back.

On a walk around the block using his walker, he'd stumbled over a crooked sidewalk a few houses down and fallen into a shallow hole right next to the cement. He'd broken his leg, laid there in pain and then somehow managed to drag himself back toward home, collapsing in our yard when he couldn't walk any further.

Thank God for Elsa. Who knew when I would have found him? That thought only made my guilt heavier.

Beaux still deserved an apology from me, and he'd get one, but I was too busy and too tired while I spent most of the weekend in the hospital with my dad.

But it didn't feel good to ignore the text from Beaux I'd gotten on Friday night asking how my dad was.

That was all he said. How is your dad?

No hello. No call me. Nothing personal. I deserved it, completely, but it still stung.

I hadn't bothered to answer. He had to have sent the text on his way to Atlanta. He needed to focus on the game, not on me.

Now it was Sunday, and Dad and I were home from the hospital. I'd called Paulie and told him I needed two weeks off work until Dad was more mobile again. He'd argued, threatened and told me this was my last chance, and after he begrudgingly told me he hoped my dad was okay, he hung up.

I was really starting to like my boss.

We were settling in. I'd helped Dad out of his wheelchair and into his recliner, propping up his casted foot on a pillow to keep it elevated and then handed him the remote knowing exactly what he was going to turn on.

"Stop fussing over me," he said when I draped a blanket over his lap. It was almost ninety degrees outside, but I still wanted to make sure he didn't catch a chill.

"No."

"You're driving me crazy, girl."

"Right back atcha." I kissed his forehead and smiled. "Stop being so grouchy. I want to take care of you."

I walked away and went back to the kitchen, grabbing his pain pills and going through all the instructions the hospital had given us. All of it was common sense, I just had to make sure I didn't overdose my dad or get him addicted to the painkillers.

I took a few more minutes and made us lunch, trying to ignore the broadcaster's voice on the television coming from the family room. He was talking about the Rough Riders, how great of a pre-season they'd already had and how good they looked for the upcoming season.

But as soon as he mentioned Beaux's name, my ears perked up.

I couldn't get away from him. It only made me feel like shit for not even responding to his text. I'd been raised to be independent, but I hadn't been raised to be a complete bitch, and he hadn't deserved any of the stuff I'd thrown at him since I met him...except for maybe the water.

I smiled at the memory and made a decision. I'd call him later, like the grown-up I was and apologize, again, over the phone. Then I'd gently let him know that I was too busy, had too much on my plate to handle a relationship.

We'd end things friendly. And that would be it.

It was the best, smartest, decision I could make. At least that way, my heart wouldn't end up hurt when he walked away from me like Spencer did.

So why did it feel like I'd been punched the gut at the idea of not seeing Beaux again? Because I liked him. A lot. I'd have to move on from that, too.

I finished up lunch and loaded up our plates, taking them to my dad on a serving tray and setting everything he needed within reach.

"Thanks, Paige," my dad said.

"No problem. Anything for you, Dad."

He gave me a look, one that didn't exactly look thrilled with my statement and turned back to the television.

I settled on the couch, wishing I could ignore the game, but there was no escaping it. As soon as the Rough Riders took the field and the game kicked off, I was entranced. Every time I saw Beaux on the screen, I thought back to how I'd admitted how much I loved his butt in his uniform. When he ripped off his helmet at halftime, the Rough Riders down fourteen to zero on a team they should have been easily beating, and scrubbed his hand through his hair, I wanted it to be my fingers running through his silky mop.

And when a reporter stopped him, frustration evident all over his face, I wanted to be the one to smooth away his stress lines.

All of it only made the ache in my chest more intense until I felt like it was being squeezed to pieces.

Stepping away from Beaux might be the smartest decision to make, but once again, logic and emotions were battling inside of me, causing a churning storm I had no idea how to settle.

FIFTEEN

BEAUX

I had fifteen minutes to get my head on straight. Fifteen minutes to try, again, to wipe away the way Paige had slammed the door in my face and hurried away from me like the time we'd spent together had meant absolutely nothing to each other.

Fifteen minutes to scrub away the memory of her that was seared into the deepest recesses of my brain.

Fifteen minutes to get over the fact she hadn't returned a simple fucking text asking how her dad was.

I'd tried for the last two days and it hadn't worked, but now I was playing like crap. I was making sloppy plays, slow in the pocket, hesitating when I usually envisioned the play before it ever happened. Hell, I'd even managed to get myself sacked.

We were getting our asses kicked, and I had no one to blame but myself.

I was sitting on the bench, knees spread, head in my hands. Damn Paige Halloway. She'd invaded my brain and I couldn't shake her. Now was not the fucking time to be strung up on some girl who'd made it clear, time and time again, she wanted nothing to do with me.

Move the fuck on, Hale.

"What the hell is going on?" Coach Pomville asked. "Hale?"

I lifted my head. "Yeah, coach?"

"Coach." He sneered the word like I'd cursed at him. "If I'm the fucking coach, why the hell aren't you listening to me out there?"

"Off night. I'll do better next half."

I meant every damn word. I'd take the blame on this loss, but after looking so good in pre-season we were looking like fools out there.

He glared at me for a minute, and I took it. Absorbed it. Let his anger and frustrations fuel my focus. This was the season opener. I didn't have time to be screwed up over a chick.

I didn't let women screw with my head.

"Defense," Pomville barked. He grabbed their attention and I muted out his instructions to them.

Oliver Powell sat down next to me.

"Don't start with me," I groaned, scrubbing my hands through my hair.

"Pussy can fuck a guy up, you know?" He laughed as he said it and bumped my shoulder.

I did not need the visual of the words pussy and fuck coming from my sister's fiancé. "Don't make me vomit either."

He punched my thigh. "Just sayin', never seen you like this. It's like your first training camp all over again. Remember those fun days?"

"When you got in my face and screamed at me every two minutes? How could I forget?"

He snorted. "Yeah, but you've come a long way since then,

and since I did so damn well making you the best quarterback in the league, I'm going to give you some more advice."

I arched a brow at him. "You made me the best quarterback?"

Powell ignored me. Self-righteous asshole. "Leave it here, Beaux, in this locker room. Deal with it later. You got thirty minutes and then you can go back to trying to fix whatever the hell is screwing up your head, and from what Shannon said, it's a woman. There's not shit you can do about it now. Focus on the ball, do what you were born to do, and win us this fucking game. Everyone is fucking looking to you, more so this year than last. You let us down and you're going to be the fool."

He didn't say anything I hadn't thought. He didn't say anything I didn't already know. But Powell was one of the most experienced guys on my team and he took it upon himself to be a father-figure...sometimes, a super large prick of a father figure, but one all the same.

It helped. Sometimes, even a grown man needed a damn pep talk, someone in his corner. My jaw hurt from clenching my teeth so hard and I popped it twice. "Right. I'm on it."

"I know. I only play with the best, which is why I worked you so hard last year."

"To make me the best?"

He ignored my sarcastic tone and grinned. "See? I think we're finally beginning to understand each other."

I shoved him as he stood, making him lose his balance. He collapsed right into Quinten who pushed Powell to his feet.

I shook my head, grinning at the smirk on Powell's face before he snagged his helmet off the floor and sauntered away.

"He help?" Quinten asked.

"Yeah."

"Good. You got this."

I fist pumped him. "Yeah, we got this."

Thirty minutes.

I had the game. A comeback from fourteen points was nothing.

I would do it.

And when the game was done, and I was back in Raleigh, I was fucking calling Paige.

Then I'd deal with her, too.

I TURNED on my phone as soon as I slid into my truck in the valet parking garage.

We'd won the game. We came back, won twenty-one to fourteen. I played a second half that felt like instinct and not work, the ball sliding from my fingers on every pass, perfectly aimed for my target. The defense held Atlanta to less than sixty yards in the second half and had kept them from getting close to even kicking a field goal.

We ended the game feeling good, playing like we were trained and paid to do, like we loved to do, but I had other things on my mind as we dressed, boarded a bus and went straight to the plane. Three hours after the game ended and I was back in Raleigh.

I had one more play in mind for the night.

My phone pinged with incoming texts as soon as it was powered on and I quickly scanned the few from Shannon.

OMG you suck. What's wrong with you.

Get your crap together.

My sister. So supportive. Those were all during the first half. I was used to her running commentary and since I hadn't blown the game, I shook my head and kept scrolling.

Better, dipstick.

Amazing pass!

PS — Did you see how good Oliver looked in those pants tonight? Scrumptious.

Supportive and disgusting. I shook my head and went to her last text.

Woo-hoo! Knew you could do it baby bro.

I flipped through a few texts from Shannon's best friend, Melissa, congratulating me along with a handful more from guys I played with in college.

Then two more showed up. My breath caught as I saw Paige's name on the screen.

Great game.

Home from hospital with my dad. He had surgery.

Shit. My chest burned with worry. I'd gone so far as to call the hospital on Friday when I didn't hear back from Paige but they wouldn't tell me anything. I'd considered driving to the garage and seeing if I could find out information there, but then I picked my balls back up.

I was falling for a girl who slammed a door in my face. No way was I showing up at a garage with a bunch of men looking like a pussy.

Another text came after that and it took me a minute to process it.

Can we talk?

Oh. We were talking.

I pulled into the nearest parking lot and pressed the phone icon, dialing Paige's number.

Pick up. Pick up.

Good God. I was desperate for the sound of her voice falling from her sweet lips.

"Hey," Paige said, her voice quiet and breathy. "Good game tonight."

"Is that why you called me tonight Paige? To talk about the game?" I couldn't keep the coolness out of my tone. My fingers were tapping the steering wheel so hard I could punch a hole through the wheel.

"Well, no." Her voice went softer. "I called to apologize, about...well...I wanted to say sorry for the other night."

"I'm coming over."

"No," she half-whispered, half-shouted. "My dad's sleeping, and I think it's best if you don't, Beaux, really. I just wanted to talk."

Fuck that. She was giving me a sliver of an opening and I was sliding in.

"I'll be there in twenty minutes, and you better answer your door."

"Beaux—"

"Don't worry, Paige, I can be quiet."

I hung up on a breathy little gasp from her and tossed the phone into my cup holder. I expected a string of texts telling me not to come, giving me the brush off. Something.

I got nothing from her, which made me grin as I pulled back into traffic and hopped on the interstate, taking me straight to her.

We had things to talk about. Problems to figure out.

If I was getting to know Paige at all, she'd already concocted a list of reasons to keep me away.

Hell if I was listening to them.

I pulled up onto Paige's street twenty-three minutes later, slowing down so the roar of my truck didn't wake anyone even though it was only nine o'clock. But the neighborhood, while well-maintained, was still older and I already knew there was one elderly neighbor, Elsa, who lived nearby.

When I pulled up to Paige's house, I slowed to a stop at the curb and hopped out of my truck, quietly closing the door.

She was sitting on her front porch, a glass of what looked like tea in her hands. She was rocking on a wooden swing, covered in the shade, feet pulled up on the swing, tan legs on full display with the short sweat shorts she was wearing.

Her brown hair was pulled into a mess on the top of her head, bits and pieces fraying around her temples and sides, and as I got closer, I could tell she wasn't wearing any makeup.

She'd never looked more beautiful to me. She was always dressed casually when I saw her, but there was something about that picture, her lazily rocking back and forth, sipping what I assumed was sweet tea that hit me straight in the chest.

Visions of doing the same with her, night after night after a long day of work or a day off traveling, enjoying the quiet.

Doing nothing but being together and knowing it was the best thing to do.

That burn in my chest ignited all over again and I leapt up the stairs, settling myself against the railing.

"Hey," I said, as I watched her gaze roam over my body, my eyes, my chest, dipping low quickly and snapping back up.

"Hey."

"So you watched the game tonight?"

She sipped her tea and nodded. "We always do."

"How is he?" I nodded toward the house. I didn't need to specify I was asking about Sam.

She blew out her breath and brushed hair off her nape. "He broke his leg. Fell in a small hole off the sidewalk."

"That doesn't tell me if he's okay."

"He's fine. Or he will be. He had surgery and…"

She bit her bottom lip, chin quivering.

I moved and pulled her next to me, rocking the swing and

careful not to spill her drink. As soon as I pulled her into my arms, her head hit my chest and her shoulders shook.

"God, it was so damn scary, Beaux."

"Had to be."

I didn't ask her more. I was perfectly content to bear her stress and her worry while she fought back tears and took deep shuddering breaths that made her entire body tremble.

When she'd calmed, she pushed against my stomach. I let her go reluctantly.

"I didn't call to talk to you so I could cry on your shoulder," she said, reaching for her tea.

I took it from her hand and set it on the railing behind us. "Then why did you?"

SIXTEEN
PAIGE

It was do or die time and all I wanted to do was crawl back into Beaux's lap and ignore the reality I was facing.

With his crystal blue eyes on me, hair done and swept nicely to the side, and dressed in his suit, he was devastatingly sexy.

He must have come to me straight from the airport, and that thought shot a piercing pain to my chest.

Beaux was a great guy, and I was going to shove him away from me even though it was the last thing I wanted. I had to in order to preserve my own heart.

"You going to say anything," Beaux asked, a beautiful smirk twisting his full lips. "Or are you going to keep staring at me?"

I wanted to keep staring, to memorize the hard line of his jaw, the perfect point of his top lip, the thick lashes that rimmed his eyes.

Instead, I sucked in a breath and let it all out. "I called to apologize. I was rude to you, again, and I don't like that when you've been nothing but nice to me."

"Nice?" Two perfect brows rose on his forehead. His tone went icy with the word and I tried to pull away.

He didn't let me go. Instead, he shoved his arm to my lower back and pulled me so I was once again in his lap.

The forceful jerk of the swing made me cling to him.

"Well, yeah," I said when I'd gathered my wits. It was difficult. He was too consuming. Too beautiful. Too effortlessly, genuinely kind. "And I enjoy the time we spent together, but nothing more with us can happen."

It was the speech I'd research ad nauseam all afternoon.

"No?" His head tilted to the side. One corner of his lips hitched up. "You don't think?"

I shook my head. Leave it to Beaux to find me ending things with him funny. "Well, yes, I do think. You're busy right now, and I appreciate the nights I've had with you, Beaux, honestly, but I don't have the time right now. Not with my dad needing extra help, the bills from the hospital are going to start pouring in and I'm going to have to pick up extra shifts. I have too many responsibilities to consider a relationship with you."

By the time I was done talking, he was full on grinning. His hand was at the side of my neck, thumb brushing beneath my jaw.

I fought a tremble at his gentle, intimate touch, and failed.

"Beaux—" my tone lacked the warning I intended.

"All I just heard was that you appreciate me, enjoyed our time together, and I'm a nice guy."

I frowned. "And?"

"And nowhere in that list did you list the reason that you don't like me or don't want to be with me."

I couldn't say those things. Not directly to him. I wasn't a liar by nature, but he wasn't understanding me, either.

"I don't have the time."

"And I don't give a shit. We'll make the time. We'll figure it out, but if you're not pushing me away because you think I'm an asshole or you're not attracted to me — and don't even think about lying and saying you aren't because I still remember the way you lit up for me last week — then you're not ending this, and you're definitely not going to do it using your father as an excuse."

"I'm not."

"You are." His hand on my neck tightened. His humor evaporated until I felt the icy chill of his serious gaze. Good Lord, this must have been his game face. If I saw him on the field looking this intense, I'd pee my pants. "And I'm not letting you. More so, I bet if I went in and told Sam, he won't let you use him as an excuse, either."

My hackles rose. The stupid, bossy man. "Maybe neither of you have a say in it, either. It's my life and mine to choose to live how I want."

"Yeah?" he challenged. "Then when are you going to start living it?"

His question was a slap to the face and anger from his accusation simmered in my veins. "Beaux—"

This time my warning was exactly as I intended but he interrupted me.

"So, here's what we're going to do. You're going to let someone step up and help you out. You got me, the team, Mike, and the guys at the garage. You have neighbors that will help him out. You're going to take some time off the restaurant so you can be with your dad at night, and then, you're going to trust me to take care of the rest."

I shook my head. He couldn't step in and do this. "I can't not work, Beaux."

"Trust me." His hands framed my cheeks, holding me steady. "I want to help you, Paige. Just let me."

"Why? Why would you do that?" No one else ever had and

I'd known this guy for mere weeks.

"Because," his grin went wicked again, "I like you, and I'm not afraid to say it. I didn't just enjoy our time together, I fucking loved it. I want more of it. And if you're ending things because we don't have a lot of time, that's not a good reason for me to stop seeing where this could go between us."

I fought the urge to melt against him. Breaking it off with him was the right thing to do.

Listening to him felt better.

I slid my hand to his chest and up to his shoulder. His muscles tensed beneath the jacket of his suit. The man was pretty hard to say no to, especially when saying yes sounded like so much more fun.

I brushed my fingers over the knot of his loosened black tie and tugged. "You know, you're making it very hard to break things off with you."

He tipped my chin up until our gazes met. Narrowed blue eyes hit me with the force of hurricane right before he leaned in closer. "Then don't."

His lips brushed against mine; stealing all my rehearsed arguments. God help me if I was becoming a mushy little girl who wanted a man to take care of her, but the hope of such a promise was too large to ignore. He kissed me again and I was gone, lost in him, the hardness of his body, the strength of his soul, the scent of his cologne and the taste of his mouth.

"Okay," I whispered, brushing my lips against his.

I could kiss him until the sun rose and not regret a single moment of lost sleep.

"Good. Now stop fighting me, let me fucking help you, and kiss me again."

I complied instantly. I surrendered to my desire to lean on him and melt into him and I shifted my body until our chests aligned. I reveled in the feel of his heart beating against my chest, the calluses on his palm scraping my cheeks, the warmth of his lips as we kissed for minutes, hours.

"Come on," Beaux said, and he grabbed my backside, hefting me to his hips as he stood. "I'm fucking wiped."

My eyes popped open. "You can't stay here."

"Thought you weren't going to fight me anymore." He kissed my nose and walked toward my front door.

"But, my dad, and ... us... and you..." I'd never brought a man home, not overnight anyway. I was pretty certain my dad would be the kind of guy to sleep with a shotgun next to him and one eye open if I did.

I explained it to Beaux as he had his hand on the doorknob. "Trust me, Paige. He's not going to shoot me, and I'm not going to disrespect the guy in his own home, anyway."

"Oh." It made sense. I couldn't stop the spring of disappointment. Beaux must have caught it in my tone because he kissed me again as he pulled open the door.

"Nice to know you wanted it, though."

"I didn't."

"Sure."

"You're pretty irritating when you don't listen to me."

"I think you love it."

Crazy thing was, I was beginning to think the same thing.

He set me on my feet once we were inside. "I've got a bag in the truck I'm going to go grab. Do what you need to do while I'm gone, okay?"

"Sure, Beaux."

"You're pretty beautiful when you listen to me."

"Irritating," I hissed, mindful my dad was lightly snoring from his spot on the recliner just down the hall and around the corner.

"Lovely." He winked and kissed my nose before sauntering out to his truck.

While he was gone, I ran to the kitchen and grabbed a couple more pain pills and a fresh glass of water. After setting them on his side table, I rearranged the blanket and gently pressed my hand to his forehead.

He was warm, but not hot. He'd slept off and on the entire day, but hadn't once complained about the pain in his leg. It would come though, and then my failing dad would act like it was nothing.

All to protect me.

I sighed as I kissed his cheek and whispered my good night to him. He didn't twitch a single muscle and his breathing never faltered. The pain pills knocked him out cold.

It was then I knew Beaux was absolutely right.

It killed my dad I'd given up so much for him. He hated that he'd become my main focus. Reality was, there would come a day and he wouldn't be here.

Down to the depths of my soul, I knew the only thing that would make him disappointed in me was if I lived a life that was only half alive, not taking hold of every opportunity thrown my way.

It would kill him quicker if I became something less than what he always wanted for me. Considering there was a guy nearby who could possibly help make my life happier, a little bit easier, Dad would want me to reach for it, hold it and grab onto it with both hands and never let go.

"I'll do better, Dad. I promise." I brushed a finger down his arm, reassured he was sleeping soundly and as pain-free as possible. I hurried back to the front door, reaching it the same time Beaux returned with a small black bag in his hand.

I WOKE up the next morning to the obnoxious beeping of my phone's alarm and reached over, tapping the snooze button.

Stretching, I blinked the sleep from my eyes and catalogued a list as long as my arm of everything I needed to accomplish that day. Call me obsessive, but I enjoyed beginning my day making a to-do list. It woke me up, got me moving even if most days I wanted to curl back into the covers.

It wasn't until I was on point five of my list—call a nursing agency for my dad for daytime help—an errant thought ran through my mind.

Last night, Beaux had shown up at my house and hadn't left.

"What the heck?" I whispered and rolled to my side. On the opposite side of the bed, the sheets were a mess, thrown back and clearly showing someone had already climbed out of them.

When we'd come upstairs last night, we'd taken turns using the hall bathroom. When it was Beaux's turn, I'd thrown on an old college T-shirt and a pair of yoga shorts, sleeping in way more than I usually did but I wasn't giving Beaux any ideas, not with my dad directly below us, despite what Beaux had promised.

We'd climbed into bed, he'd curled me into his side and we'd talked about his game and all the traveling he did. Eventually both of us had drifted off to sleep.

It'd been sweet. Absolutely perfect. The best night I'd spent with a guy in a bed in a long time and that was pretty miraculous considering we hadn't even made out.

But he hadn't stayed.

My heart dropped in my stomach and I sat up, clenching the covers to my chest. I scanned the room looking for any sign of his presence, but the black bag Beaux had brought in and set inside the door to my bedroom was also gone. So was his suit.

Disappointment ate at me and I brushed back my hair, letting it fall to my neck, thinking. He had practice that day, I knew that, but he hadn't mentioned having to leave early, and my alarm was set for six o'clock exactly. The sun was barely rising and he'd disappeared in the night.

"Awesome," I muttered, and threw off the covers.

I needed a shower, get dressed, and a carafe full of coffee before heading into the garage. Hustling through my bedroom, I grabbed all the clothes I'd need and then took a quick shower. The whole time I was getting ready, which didn't take long since I wore minimal makeup and didn't bother blow drying my hair when I went to the garage, I hoped for the best.

Perhaps I'd missed a text. Or a note.

He'd call me later, I was certain of it. No guy would put in the effort Beaux had done for me, made the promises he'd made last night, and rip them away.

"He's not Spencer," I assured myself.

So far, Beaux had proven he was the exact opposite. And if I wasn't going to end things with him, if I was going to let him in, then I also had to start trusting him.

He'd shown me he was worth it.

I clipped my bangs back at my temple like I usually did and gave myself another perusal in the mirror.

When I was done, I tossed everything onto my bedroom floor. I wasn't messy, not a neat freak. I cleaned my room between shifts at the garage and the restaurant, the only time I had a few free hours and on my days off from the restaurant, and I cleaned the whole house. Not that it got that dirty with just dad and I, but I'd done it ever since I was old enough to use cleaning supplies.

My dad never noticed dust and clutter and toothpaste gobs on the counter. When I became a teenager and heard my friends talk about their brothers, I became certain those kinds of oversights were ingrained in male DNA.

But my mood didn't change through my morning routine. I sucked in a breath, trying to put on a happy face as I hurried down the stairs to take care of my dad and make sure he had everything he needed before I left for work.

Only I didn't get as far as the kitchen because at the bottom of the stairs, I froze.

Beaux was sitting on the couch, facing my dad, coffee cup in both men's hands and they were talking quietly, nodding and smiling. For the first time since my dad's injury, he didn't have a glassy look in his eyes from either the pain or the pills to take it away.

The black bag was next to the couch, suit draped over the armrest, and he was casually sitting there in gray athletic shorts and a black shirt that stretched so tight over his muscles and chest, the seams were in danger of popping.

Beaux had stayed, and from the looks of it, he'd taken care of my dad. He was dressed in different clothes, his face looked washed up, hair combed, and he was sipping coffee from his favorite mug.

I really needed to stop underestimating Beaux Hale.

A warmth flickered through me and I shivered. This guy. Everything he was showing me was too good to be true but absolutely perfect.

"Good morning," I said, my gaze flipping back and forth to them when neither noticed me.

"Hey," Beaux said, standing from the couch and headed my way. "How'd you sleep?"

I glanced at my dad who was now intently staring into his coffee. "Um. Good."

Beaux walked up to me, smiling. "I didn't want to wake you. I don't sleep much after game nights."

My cheeks burned. Good grief, was this what teenage girls felt like when they brought boyfriends home? It'd been so long I couldn't remember. Everything he said made me more embarrassed. "Uh. Thanks."

He chuckled again as if he understood. In addition to being a superstar quarterback, the man had to be telepathic.

He took my hand and pulled me toward the kitchen. "I made coffee this morning too, but your dad tells me it sucks."

"Too freaking weak. You young'uns. You're all weak. Weak coffee, weak running, weak tackling—"

"Easy tiger," Beaux said. "I've already heard your opinions on last night's game. Keep critiquing and I might begin to take it personally."

"See?" my dad called, but his voice was thick with humor. "You're all weak today."

I was laughing by the time I reached the kitchen. "You didn't have to come with me."

"I did if I wanted to kiss you."

His lips hit mine and my ass hit the counter behind me before I could blink. Heaven. His body surrounded mine and he took over, took what he wanted, and I was so damn grateful he'd helped my dad I could have cried tears of joy.

I threw all my thanks into that kiss and when Beaux pulled back, his gaze flickering between my eyes, I could barely breathe.

"Good morning," he murmured, sliding his fingers through my still wet hair. "I really like the way you look when you're sleeping."

I looked at his shoulder, more embarrassed. "Beaux—"

"Coffee first. We got a lot to talk about today and I've already got most of it done, so you need to catch up."

That sounded ominous. "What did you do?"

"Coffee. Your dad says you can't count to two in the morning before your first cup you're so out of it."

"Lovely," I muttered, but I couldn't argue. More than one roommate and boyfriend had called me a zombie over the years.

And since his words left me nervous, fortification in caffeinated form was definitely necessary.

SEVENTEEN
BEAUX

Leaving Paige sleeping was one of the hardest things I'd ever done. I woke up hard, my dick knowing exactly what it wanted, and it'd been a power struggle not to wake her up with my mouth on her nipple and my fingers teasing her in other places. Damn, she was pretty when she was sleeping though. All that brown hair all over her pillow, her cheeks pressed to her hands beneath her. She'd snuggled up to me during the night and I woke up with her legs plastered to mine, sweating like a demon, but all of it felt damn good.

I couldn't remember the last time I'd woken with a woman lying all over me. Paige was different than the rest. It didn't matter why and it wasn't something specific I could put my finger on. I just knew I really liked everything about her, even when she was pissing me off with her running.

It might have made me a glutton for punishment, but I still understood where she was coming from. That didn't mean I was going to let her keep doing it.

The fact my dick got hard whenever she was nearby told

me everything I needed to know. He hadn't let me down yet and I was certain the big guy had a mind of his own.

So I'd taken my bag and gotten dressed and cleaned up in the hall bath, being as quiet as possible. When I'd hit the main floor, I'd gone to the kitchen and started some coffee and by the time I was done, Sam was waking up, groaning every time he shifted.

It'd taken a while to talk him into letting me help get him dressed and cleaned up, but considering I could carry him up the stairs and he couldn't walk on crutches yet, there wasn't much point in arguing. His pride had taken a hit, I knew that.

I also knew that by the time I'd convinced him to let me hire him a home health nurse, he'd take the hit to his pride if it meant making things easier on Paige.

Now, with her standing in front of me, eyes brightening with every sip of coffee she took, I was certain I'd made the right decision.

Still a bit sleepy, dressed in her Halloway Garage shirt and cut-off jean shorts, minimal makeup, she was the girl who could sling back beers with the guys, spend the night in a tent or under the stars and she wouldn't need anything fancy. I'd give it to her if she needed it, but everything about her spoke to me on a visceral level.

"You had enough yet?" I asked when she was pouring cup number two. She plopped in a dash of milk and re-settled her hip against the kitchen counter.

"Enough that I'll be able to remember what you said, yeah."

"Okay." I prepared myself for the verbal assault she would surely lash out at me and took a seat next to her.

"Your dad and I talked this morning," I started, and her grip tightened on her coffee mug. "We made some decisions."

Her chin jutted out in an adorable way. "You and my dad made decisions."

"Yup." I grinned and took a drink from my own mug. "I'm hiring a home health nurse for him. She can help with physical therapy, getting him cleaned up...giving you some time to relax."

Two brows rose on her forehead. "You hired him a home health nurse."

"Already made the calls."

Her quiet stillness concerned me. I was used to buckets of ice water on my head and verbal lashings. Paige hadn't yet shown me what it meant when she was frozen and silent.

She brought the mug to her lips. "Okay."

Not what I was expecting. "Kay?"

"I mean, you've already done it, and frankly I need the best care for my dad. I can't be around him as much as I need to and I don't have the money to pay for it, but I had already decided upstairs I needed to do it. It kills me you're paying for it, but if he's okay with it, he's still mentally there enough to make his own medical decisions."

It seemed like a trick. "Yeah? I'm going to be honest, I expected more of a fight."

With a heavy exhale, she asked, "Did you help my dad this morning?"

"I spent a lot of years helping my mom." It wasn't a direct answer, but it was enough of an explanation, she understood.

"And he was okay with it?"

"As much as he could be." He'd actually called me a rich prick at first, accused me of just wanting to spend more time with his daughter. I'd said yes to both and he'd laughed.

She was silent for several moments, draining her second cup of coffee. "I told myself this morning when I was upstairs getting ready and I thought you'd left, that it was time I stopped underestimating how good of a guy you were."

Now that's the kind of news I wanted to hear. "Yeah?"

Another pause. She looked into her mug.

As she took her time, my back pulled tight and I walked closer. "Paige?"

Her cheeks puffed and she exhaled a harsh breath. Lifting her head, she scraped her teeth over her top lip. "I had this boyfriend."

"Spencer." I hadn't forgotten about him. Crossing my arms, I waited for her to continue.

"We'd been dating for a couple years when my dad had his first stroke. When I decided to move home, he'd promised me we'd make a long distance relationship work." She turned and refilled her coffee. Every second she delayed talking made my pulse ratchet up. When she had taken another sip, she continued. "Two weeks later, after I'd told him I couldn't go back to Charlotte one weekend he broke up with me."

"Paige—"

"He's a jerk. I know that now."

"He's not a jerk. He's a dick, and not worth your time."

She laughed once, but it was cold and flat. "Like I said, I know that now." She squeezed her eyes closed and when she opened them, sadness filled her hazel eyes. "He isn't the only guy who's not wanted anything to do with me once they realize I don't have the time they think they're entitled to."

She'd laid a minefield, but it helped me understand where she was at, why it'd upset her so much that she was with me when her dad was hurt. Why she approached us with a wall between us.

The sound of bricks crumbling to the floor between us echoed in my ears.

"I'm not them, Paige. You forget I know what you're going through. I don't think less of you because you're busy caring for someone you love. I admire the hell out of you for it."

Tears swam in her eyes but she blinked them back, nodding

rapidly. "That's why I decided this morning that I was going to trust you."

Jesus. She slayed me.

My hands went to her cheeks and I pressed my lips to hers. I poured everything I felt for and her confession into the kiss. When I pulled back, my chest burned.

"Thank you," I said, my voice rough, thick and filled with need for her.

She licked her lips and opened her eyes. "I'm not happy you're paying for my dad's nurse. I always thought that help came with strings attached, but if there aren't—"

"Oh, there are strings. It means you spend more time with me, and I get what I want from you."

Her head tilted toward her shoulder. "And what do you want from me?"

Everything, popped into my mind and I barely forced it back. I slid my hand to her hip and brushed my lips against her ear.

She trembled, leaning into me while a puff of breath rushed from her lips. "Whatever you'll give me, Paige. And trust me, I'll be happy to take it."

EIGHTEEN
PAIGE

I waited around Monday morning until Elsa could come over and hang with my dad until his new home health care nurse showed up. Then I lost myself in eight hours of work where I did at least a dozen oil changes and then helped out with a new commission for a 1964 Camaro. A rusted and dulled orange color with thick black racing stripes that ran from the front all the way to the back, it looked like a disaster when it arrived on a flat bed trailer. The rust all around the wheel rims and missing two tires were the least of our restoration problems. In four to six weeks, it would be a thing of beauty.

I called and talked to Melanie, the nurse, a half-dozen times and every time we spoke she assured me with a sweet tilt in her voice that everything was fine and she and my dad were just settling in and getting to know each other.

Everything Beaux had done made me more indebted to him. Not that I expected him to hold it over me. He was quickly showing me he was the kind of man to provide and protect and be a partner in all things big or small. Sure, he did it in a way that was way more bossy than I would normally be attracted to, but I'd also grown up with my dad, a man's man through and through, being the only guy I knew. And in some ways, Beaux reminded me of him. Strong and resilient, confident with a hint of well-deserved arrogance.

When I closed my eyes while I sat in the office and thought about Beaux, I could imagine this was exactly the kind of guy my dad would want for me. It had nothing to do with the multi-million dollar contract attached to Beaux's name.

It was his kindness and his patience and his easy smiles and his intensity and pure focus whenever I was in the room.

It was his undeniable sexiness that made my knees wobble every time he flashed his blue eyes on me.

Good Lord. I was falling for him, and for once, I didn't want to step on the brakes.

I talked to Beaux last night on the phone. He called me after he got home from practice and the first thing he'd asked was how the nurse was working out and how Dad was feeling.

My heart turned to a pile of mush.

So when he told me—commanded, not asked—I was coming to his place tonight after work to have dinner, I had absolutely no way to refuse him.

I didn't have a single excuse and for the first time since I could remember, I didn't want to spend the time thinking of one.

Now it was Tuesday, and I was walking up the three small steps to his brownstone.

In my purse was a clean pair of underwear and a toothbrush, because if he expected me to pay up for his help with my body, I was primed and ready to go.

He'd already proven to me he wanted more than a quick one night fling.

I scraped a hand through my hair while my heart palpitated at an alarming rate.

"Dinner," I told myself. "He'd only said dinner."

I rang the bell and almost immediately heard footsteps echoing on the other side of the door. Quick and firm, they sounded hurried, and then the lock was undone, the door opened.

In Beaux's typical, casual fashion, he was wearing a pair of faded, ripped jeans and a teal Rough Riders T-shirt. His hair was swept to the side and styled in that sexy and popular way of his. His jaw was clean of scruff giving me a perfect view of his sharp, defined jaw and beautiful full lips. I couldn't do anything except stand there, on his stoop, mesmerized by the magnificent sight of him.

At six foot five, almost a full foot taller than me, he was a mountain of a man.

I loved his size.

"You coming in?" Beaux said, one hand on the door the other on the frame. "Or do you want to keep staring at me."

"Yes."

He laughed and reached out. His hand slid to my back, hot against the cool silky cream top I was wearing, and he yanked me inside.

I fell to his chest and then his other hand was at my jaw, thumb sweeping, driving me breathless.

"Have a good day?" he asked, murmuring and moving down toward me. His eyes dropped to my mouth.

I wet them on instinct and tilted my head up, seeking his mouth. "Yes."

I didn't have to ask and I didn't have to wait long. His nose glided against mine and then his lips brushed over mine. He tasted sweet, with a hint of garlic telling me he'd been cooking dinner, which surprised and pleased me.

I'd assumed we'd order in. But his house smelled divine and I took it all in as my hands pushed into his hair, I arched into his body, and then my back was against a wall. He'd pinned me and yet I never felt freer.

"God you smell good," he said, shoving his face into my neck. "And you taste even better. I just want to stand here and ravish you."

It sounded like the perfect way to spend the night. "Yes."

His breath warmed my throat as he laughed and he pulled back, kissing my nose. "After we eat. Need you to have some energy for later."

He winked and stepped back, gripping my hand and leading me into the kitchen.

HIS HOME WAS AN IMMACULATE, narrow brownstone. The front room led into a dining room and then a kitchen. Beaux's had an addition on the back with an extra large living space and I knew upstairs there'd most likely be three bedrooms and two bathrooms. They were typical of the Raleigh downtown area, some well over a hundred years old and decrepit, but Beaux's had been modernized and updated over the years.

White quartz countertops and stainless steel appliances filled his kitchen and when we reached it, he pulled out a barstool. He demanded I sit while he finished grilling chicken and what smelled like lamb burgers on his gas stove top, added a side of asparagus, and then fixed up a salad filled with a variety of different lettuce. While he worked, he filled a glass of wine and slid it toward me and grabbed himself a bottled water.

Had to hand it to the guy, he had serious skills in the kitchen.

I moaned for what had to be the fifth time since I'd started eating. "How did you become such a good cook?"

"Have to eat twice as much as the average person and I

need it to fuel me, not just fill me. In college, we had a nutritionist. I learned what I needed to eat, learned I liked doing it, and then I kept trying new crap."

He always made everything he was talented at sound so simple. Perhaps he was that gifted at everything he tried.

I'd be jealous if it hadn't so far turned out in my favor.

"How was your practice today?" I asked. The team hadn't played great on Sunday and last night he'd said practice had been rough.

"Good. We've got some new guys on the defensive line and some timing kinks to work out, but we'll get there."

"Of course you will."

"Yeah? You have that much faith in me?"

Yeah. I was beginning to think I did. "No," I teased, laughing at the face he made. "I have faith in your tight end."

"Powell? He's your thing?" He held up a hand, covering his eyes. I laughed so hard tears were forming in my eyes. "Gah! Never mind. Don't tell me. That dude's marrying my sister and I don't even want to think of you wanting him, too."

"I don't want him, you ninny." I tossed a tomato from my salad at him. "But he's more serious. More determined. From everything I've heard he'll probably retire soon and I'm sure he wants one more ring."

"Eh." Beaux shrugged. "Once you have one it's not important."

Liar, liar pants on fire. "Really?"

He skewered me with a look and shoved a fork full of chicken into his mouth. After he swallowed, he winked. "Fuck no."

We finished our dinner, talking about family, he told me about Shannon and the jewelry store she opened in the warehouse district. It was more successful than any of her wildest dreams, even though she was still certain part of her success had to do with being engaged to Oliver.

After dinner was done, I tried insisting he let me clean up but he filled my glass of wine back up and pointed toward the living room. "Go turn on the television. It's your night off so relax."

I hesitated. I always helped. Then I remembered just weeks ago I was thinking of how nice it would be to have a partner, someone to lessen my load, and notice when I needed a break.

He kept pointing. "Go."

Fine. He wanted to wash dishes. I'd let him wash dishes. I hated doing them.

My next surprise came when I saw the two, at least seven-foot tall built-ins flanking his extra large television.

Filled with books.

I scanned the shelves. He had everything from courtroom dramas, murder mysteries, and thrillers to non-fiction autobiographies and self-improvement books. I was just finishing a sip of wine when Beaux entered the room.

"You read all these?"

"Plane rides get boring after awhile and you can only play so many games of Candy Crush or Casino Royale. Have to do something to not be bored out of my skull."

"They have these devices these days, you know." I made a sweeping gesture with my hand toward the shelves. "All these books fit on one small little tablet and you can read them there."

He had at some point opened a beer and he brought it to his lips. "I like the feel of paper. Hate reading on my phone. Shannon bought me a Kindle a couple years ago and I never got used to it."

"You are full of surprises."

"Yeah." He set down his beer and walked toward me. No,

not walked. He prowled, slow and steady. I'd become his target and I didn't for a second doubt his aim. "Want to see what other surprises I have for you?"

I did. I really, really did. I'd been a brat to him several times. He'd been nothing but kind to me.

He was the first attractive guy I'd been with in a long time and it wasn't just physical, we connected on a level I didn't understand. Perhaps it was our common, simpler backgrounds.

Perhaps it was the crazy thing called chemistry I never really fully believed in.

Whatever it was, I set my glass down on the coffee table and rested my hands on Beaux's shoulders. "Yes. Show me more surprises."

This was our second date. Felt more like our fifth if you included all the times I'd seen her.

We were well past the point of me hiding exactly what I wanted from her, what I wanted to give her, what I wanted to do to her. Not that I'd done such a bang up job of keeping it a secret from her since the moment we met at the restaurant, but slow was no longer in my vocabulary or on my agenda.

I had her for the night, and I had an early team meeting. I planned to use every single second I had available to my complete advantage, so when Paige said yes, I took her hand in my mine, guided her toward the stairs, and led her straight to my room, only taking a quick detour to show her the bathroom in case she needed it.

I went to the other bathroom, rinsed the taste of chicken and garlic off my breath and was entering my bedroom when Paige was coming out of the master bath.

She paused, gaze taking in the room, which wasn't really much. I loved my house, loved how Shannon had helped me decorate it. A lot of white and gray, a lot of straight lines, and a lot more macho artwork and worthless knickknacks than I cared about on the shelves downstairs, but it all looked good and that was all I cared about.

My bedroom, though, was my domain. All over one of my bedroom walls were photographs and framed newspaper articles of my teams and my accomplishments over the years. I didn't keep them to give myself a big head.

I kept them to remind me of where I came from. How I could lose it all if I wasn't the guy I was trying to be.

I kept them framed and displayed so every morning I woke up, even if I didn't feel like hauling my ass to the gym or wanted to do nothing but drink a case of beer and lay around, I had motivation to go out and continue striving to be better.

Still, I hadn't brought a woman to my home since I moved to Raleigh, and the fact that Paige was staring at that wall looking awed, made me self-conscious.

I wasn't used to people questioning me unless I already knew the answer I planned to give them. With Paige, I was learning that not everything could be scripted.

Women didn't come with a playbook you could memorize with enough study sessions.

She turned to me as I stepped into the room. "You're impressive."

I gripped my T-shirt at the back of my neck and ripped it off my head, moving toward her and flinging the shirt to the floor. "Am I?"

Her eyes dropped, trailed my body and her bottom lip disappeared between her teeth. "Um."

"Yeah, that's what I thought." I reached for her and my hands went to her hips. She was wearing short, navy blue shorts and an off-white top but all I could think about was everything beneath it.

I'd had my hands on her before. Felt like it'd been forever, but that night at the park was a bit wild, way too rushed, and I needed her stripped and exposed to me. All of her — her heart and her body.

"Look at me." Her gaze came straight to mine. "I'm going to undress you and you're going to get on the bed. And then you're not going to come until I say you can."

I shot her a warning look, one daring her to argue with me but instead, she reached up to her hair and removed the clip that was there holding back her bangs. Chunks of her chocolate colored hair fell forward and she brushed it back, tossing her clip onto my nightstand.

"Then you should probably get started."

Her body was trembling beneath my hands as I slid them up the sides of her body. My thumbs brushed over her breasts, teasing her. But I didn't remove my gaze from hers. I wanted to see every reaction she gave me, every little panted breath and I wanted to see her eyes go hazy as I turned her on.

"Ready?"

She nodded. Barely. "Only as long as I can undress you, too."

"We'll see," I whispered, moving in so our bodies were pushed together. She smelled like springtime and flowers. A light perfume scent that drove me crazy as soon as I pressed my lips to hers. I parted her lips with my tongue and slid inside, tasting the cavern of her mouth while she clung to me, hands at my sides, chilled fingers pressing against my ribs.

My skin burned with need to have her, my dick hard as a rock. She pressed into me, and I was done.

The mewled sounds she made, the neediness in her breath spurned me on. I slid my hands to the hem of her shirt, pushed it up and only pulled away to remove it from her and then my hands were at her back, unfastening her bra. I didn't pay attention to color. Satin, lace, cotton...made no damn difference to me. I wanted us flesh to flesh, heat to heat.

My hands went to the button of her shorts and she reached for my jeans.

Mine were unzipped.

I pushed down her shorts, along with her underwear.

Then I was kicking off my jeans and she was stepping out of her shorts. Clothes were a puddle on the floor and my hands were at her waist, lifting her and guiding her to my bed. I shoved back the sheets, pushed aside the pillows and settled her right where I wanted her.

On my bed. Naked. Splayed out and completely bare. It was all my fantasies over the last month come to real life.

"Damn," I said, running my hand down the center of her chest. I kneeled back on my knees, draped her legs over mine.

She was tan. Lean. Beautiful small breasts because I didn't care about size. Just that I wanted her and I wanted to know every inch of her skin.

"You're beautiful," I said, watching her reaction. My hand spanned her stomach, moved to her hips.

Goose bumps flared on her sensitive skin but it was her face that turned me on more. Flushed cheeks. Parted lips. Half-lidded eyes. She licked her lips, arched into me.

I pushed her hips into the mattress and leaned over her. "Stay still."

"I can't."

"You'll try if you want to come soon."

I sealed my command with a kiss, ravishing her mouth before I pulled her hands down to her sides and held them in mine.

Beneath me, she spasmed and trembled, muscles tightening while I explored her throat, her chest. I flicked her nipples with my tongue, sucked them into my mouth, and her body went taut from the strain of trying to listen.

"Beaux," she whimpered. "Please. Please."

"God, you're beautiful. So creamy and sweet everywhere." I was at her stomach, doing exactly what I wanted, tasting every inch of her while I had her confined and restrained. She was splayed open, draped over my thighs and with my hands on her wrists holding her still, she looked so damn fucking vulnerable, my dick was rock hard with the need to slide inside of her.

I forced myself to wait and trailed my tongue down the center of her stomach, moving to her hips, tasting her soft, so fucking soft, and sensitive skin.

She bucked against me wildly, the scent of her almost overwhelming my need to take this slow.

"God damn. So fucking perfect." I moved further down, draped her legs over my shoulders and pushed her wide open and for a moment, I did nothing but stare at her. I looked up at her face to see she was watching me, cheeks flushed, eyes half-closed, lips parted.

Spectacular.

"You going to watch while I eat you?" I asked.

"Give me my hands, I want to touch you."

"I like you restrained. Makes everything more powerful."

"If it's any more powerful, I'm going to have a heart attack."

Challenge accepted. I grinned. "Let's see if I can do that."

"Beaux—"

But the rest of her words were lost because I slid my tongue through her center, humming against her pussy and flicking her folds, finding her clit. Swollen and hot, it throbbed against my tongue, showing me how close she already was.

Fucking delicious. She tasted like her perfume, sweet and so damn delicious I'd just found my new daily dessert.

Her hips thrust up, meeting me while I devoured her. I

teased her clit, pushed my tongue inside her, and none of it was enough. I needed more. All of her. Her walls pulsed and trembled, her thighs were quivering, but fuck I wanted to draw this out, make it the best she ever had.

Her pleasured sounds echoed in my ears. *Yes. Yes. So close. Damn. Please. More. Beaux. Please.*

All that begging, so damn beautiful coming from her, I stopped wasting time.

I let go of one of her hands and pushed two fingers into her. Fuck, she was tight. Hot. So damn wet, my fingers glistened as I eased them in and out of her.

I focused my mouth on her clit, swirling and flicking, finding the rhythm that made her claw at the sheets and I pulled back, just enough to watch her.

"Come, Paige. Give it to me."

"Yes!" she shouted. I dipped back down to her clit, fucking her relentlessly with my fingers and as soon as I sucked her clit into my mouth, biting gently, she came apart, shattered into what sounded like a thousand pieces, her pussy clamping around my fingers.

Fuck, I couldn't wait for that to be my dick.

She was still quaking from aftershocks when I moved to the bedside. I shoved off my underwear, grabbed a condom from the side table and was tearing it open with my teeth when I climbed back on to her.

"Holy shit," she whispered, brushing her hair off her face and smiling lazily at me. "That was insane."

I rolled the condom on, squeezing the tip of my cock. I was so damn close to coming I needed some pain to take the edge off.

"We're not done yet, either."

I winked and then my hands went to her hips, flipping her

over and pulling her up. "Grab the headboard," I said. "I need to explore the rest of you."

Her head fell, and she looked at me over her shoulder. "I don't know if I can take much more."

"You can. I have faith." To prove it, I leaned down and ran my tongue up her spine. I brushed her hair over her shoulder to give me an unhindered view of her and it was there I saw a small little birthmark at the edge of her right shoulder.

I kissed her there, eyes on her as she shivered and arched back against me.

"Ready?" I asked, bending over her and running my dick through her still drenched folds.

Fuck. This was going to be hard and fast. No way was I going slowly once I was in her. I wanted my hands on her ass, on her hips.

"Yeah," she whispered. She was still panting. Eyes barely able to stay open.

I'd let her rest soon.

"Hold on tight, then, honey. I'm going to sink inside you and lose all control."

She dropped her head and her fingers tightened around the top slat of my headboard.

I went back to kissing her shoulders, her quivering arms as she held on. I pushed my dick through her center again, gathering her moisture and then I was sliding my hands down her hips, lining myself up.

And I fucking slammed home so harshly her back bowed and her head threw back, brown sheets of hair flying all over the place.

"Beaux!" she cried out.

I shoved deep inside her, bottoming out and my balls slapping against her. "Fuck. Yes."

"Move," she groaned when I stayed there, her cunt clenching and pulsing around my thickness, like she'd never been so full. I gave her another moment to adjust to my size and pulled out.

The need to release burned in my spine, heating my lower back, but I still forced myself to focus on her.

With one hand I held on to her hip, and the other moved to her front, back to her still swollen bundle of nerves, and then I moved.

I propelled my hips against her, the sounds of flesh slapping and her moans and my grunts filled the room.

It was perfect. She gave herself to me freely, so damn wildly and unhindered. She was the kind of woman who would allow me to do whatever I wanted with her body.

I'd had weeks of planning fantasies. They rushed through my mind, burned into my brain while I thrust into her, until I felt her orgasm begin to take her over.

I pulled out.

"Beaux!" I flipped her to her back and then I was over her, needing to see her face when she came. I needed her to see what she was doing to me. I pushed back inside of her, gripping her hip, falling to an elbow, so damn close to her.

Her legs went to my hips and she rocked against me, taking as much as she was giving, and hell if a woman chasing her own orgasms wasn't the sweetest thing ever.

"Come," I grunted, "Come with me, Paige."

I adjusted, hit her in her sweet spot, and her hands came to my arms. Nails dug in, clinging to me while she orgasmed and I moved, hips slapping hers once. Twice. Three more times before the tightness of her gripped my cock and refused to let go.

I settled balls deep inside of her and shoved my face into her throat, groaning her name as I came deep inside of her.

My heart was thumping against his bedsheets and my knuckles ached from clawing at them. I knew Beaux would surpass any expectations I had of him in bed, but nothing could have prepared me for that.

I was sated. I wanted to do it all over again and again. I'd be sore in the morning but holy cow that was absolutely totally worth it.

His large, warm hand came down and brushed my hair off my face, tucking it behind my ear. He'd gotten up to use the restroom and clean up. "You doing okay?"

"Yeah." I gave him a lazy smile and rolled to my side. From the moment Beaux set me on his bed and settled his intensity on pleasing me, I'd lost all self-conscious thoughts about my body.

He'd liked what he saw so I didn't bother covering up.

"You wore me out," I told him, my hand drifting to his abs. He was still naked and my gaze went straight to his length. Thick and heavy even now, I couldn't help but admire him. "It's been awhile."

"I figured that out when you lit up for me as soon as I got my mouth on you."

"What?" I jerked up, propping myself up with a hand on the bed.

He dropped his head, shoulders shaking from laughing. "I'm not complaining, Paige."

I huffed and wiggled closer to him. "Well, I was going to give you all the credit for that, but now I don't think I will."

"Right. You just came three times. I'll take the credit whether or not you want to give it."

It hadn't been three. Just two, really long and fantastic orgasms I'd never forget. "You're arrogant."

He kissed the top of my head and wrapped an arm around me, holding me tight against him. "You like it."

My eyes closed as I breathed in his scent. Gosh, this guy. I waffled between wanting to jump him and strangle him at all hours, but I think I liked that, too.

Things with Beaux would never be boring.

"Yeah. I like it."

"And you like me."

I grinned up at him. "More now than the first night we met."

He threw his head back and laughed, rolling us so I was on top of him. My legs fell over his narrow hips, and I dropped closer, so we were chest to chest.

My body shivered. He drew reactions from me that couldn't be helped.

"We need to get you cleaned up."

"Uh-huh." I played with his hair, my body arching into him. With every brush of my sex against him, I felt him harden. "Yeah. I need to wash up."

"Then we'll shower," he said. He moved his knees as if to move us, but I pressed against his chest.

"Later," I whispered, brushing my lips over his jaw, over to his mouth. "I want more of you first."

"Good God woman, you're going to break me."

He'd probably break me, but I liked knowing he was just as affected by me if not more so. He also quit arguing. Our mouths fused together and we grinned against each other until my slickness rubbed against his tip.

"Condom," he groaned and rolled me off him. "Hold on, crazy."

I laughed against his throat before releasing him. I wasn't crazy. Not in this sense. I was always a one and done kind of girl, and typically had no problems climaxing. But this was different. More animalistic need than chemistry or desire.

Something deep inside me urged a connection with Beaux and while I had him, I was taking everything from him I could.

Sheathed, he returned to me. His hands wrapped around my thighs and he spread me open.

Then he was there, at my entrance. Pushing in. I watched, forcing my eyes to keep from rolling back into my head at the absolutely, unfathomable pleasure his size filled me with.

"Beaux," I whispered, tipping my head back. "God, you feel good."

"Yeah," he grunted, pulling out and pushing in. He teased me until he was fully inside me, settled to the root of him and it was glorious.

I pressed my fingers to the back of his neck and angled my head and he kissed me.

Then he moved. Dropping to his elbows, he shoved his hands into mine. I'd never imagined being restrained during sex, but I really liked that when Beaux was in me, he held my hands. It was confining, but intimate, as if he needed every single inch of us connected.

We clung together while we moved. Gone was the frenetic

pace of earlier. This was two bodies molding together, fused in the closest, most intimate way possible. My fingers dug into the backs of his hands. I could only touch him where allowed, but it was all I needed.

This.

This moment.

This blissful, beautiful, moment where all I saw and felt was Beaux and all I heard were our sighs and grunts.

They filled the room like mystical music. A symphonic sound that reverberated in my ears and echoed down, deep within me.

"Beaux," I cried out, arching into him. My mouth was at his shoulder, breath panting, heart feeling like I was soaring.

It was too much.

"Come, Paige." He thrust deep inside of me, making me cry out. My ankles tightened on his back, slippery from his sweat-lined flesh. "Fucking come."

His grunts grew frantic along with his pace and my lower back was burning with my impending release.

I clawed his hands and sank my teeth into his shoulder, crying out against the onslaught as everything exploded into a cacophony of sounds and ecstatic pleasure.

"Beaux—"

"Yes," he groaned and slammed in deep. He came as my orgasm rolled through me. Our hearts pounded against each other's chests and he collapsed onto me, giving me all his weight.

When he released my hands, I wrapped them around his back, clinging to him like I couldn't get enough.

"Shit," I breathed, my chest pained from the exertion and content at the same time. An odd mixture of adrenaline and pleasure coursed through me and made my body tremble as the aftershocks subsided.

I was still catching my breath as he slowly pulled out and looked down at me.

"Beautiful. You're absolutely fantastic."

"So are you."

I pressed my hand to his cheek. He turned and kissed my palm. His eyes were fixed on me like they'd been so often over the last several hours, not examining; memorizing.

I melted further into the sheets. His softened look, his messy hair, and his gentle way of treasuring me after being so wild and crazed threatened to undo me.

"We need to clean up," he said.

"Yeah." My breath was a mere whisper as if sounds would be too harsh in the aftermath of what we'd experienced.

"I also feel like we've had this conversation before."

"And look where it got us." I grinned.

His eyes lit with the brightest blue and he dipped down to me. "Yeah. Look what it got me."

Beautiful. I shivered from the depth of his emotion he poured out with a look.

"I'll use the restroom. Be right back."

He offered me a brief kiss, one I greedily took, and then I kept my eyes on him, turning to watch him stroll into the bathroom.

He came back with a wet cloth and he wiped me, the warmth from it and the gesture sent goose bumps skittering down my skin.

"Good?" he asked.

"Yeah. I'm good."

"Then use the restroom and get back in bed. I'll go close up the house." He opened a dresser drawer and tugged on a deliciously perfect fitting pair of boxer briefs.

I scooped up the T-shirt from the floor he'd discarded earlier and went to the bathroom.

When I was done, I sat back down on his bed, crisscross style and stared at the frames he had on his wall.

I'd been drawn to them earlier. They showed Beaux at various ages. There was an article titled, "Sophomore Quarterback Headlines at State. Gets The Win for Lincoln." On the front page of the sports section of the Des Moines Register was Beaux, sitting on the shoulders of his teammates as they carried him off the field. He had his helmet in his hand, high above his head and his same hair was flopping and flying.

He was younger then, his face still more boy than man, but it was clear even then he'd grow up to be handsome as all get out.

Then the articles and a few endorsement photos filled the rest of the space. College, his year as a backup quarterback in Minnesota before he was transferred. There was even one of him wearing nothing and holding a football over his groin for an Under Armour Ad.

I kept going back to the photo of him in high school. It showed pure thrill, the pure love of the game and as I tracked the rest of the ads and articles, absolutely nothing had changed.

This wasn't a job.

This wasn't about the money.

He freaking loved the hell out of the sport he was playing.

"Here," Beaux said, yanking me out of my admiration. "Call your dad."

My eyes darted to his to see him holding my phone in his hand.

I pulled it from his hand. "Is everything okay?"

I looked down at the screen but there weren't any missed calls.

"Don't know," he grinned. "I just know you'll sleep better if you check in before you go to bed, and I'm fucking wiped."

"Someone wear you out?"

"Yes." He kissed the top of my head and moved toward the bathroom. "And I'm not complaining."

He was right. I hadn't spent the night away from my dad since I moved back home.

Fortunately, it only rang once before Melanie answered, "Halloway Residence."

"Hi, Melanie, it's Paige."

"Oh, hi! Are you calling to talk to your dad? I've just helped him get to bed for the night but I can go get him."

"No." A breath I didn't realize I was holding escaped, releasing pressure from my chest. "No, it's okay. I was just calling to see how he's doing."

"Well, we watched six hours of Lethal Weapon movies today."

"So, good then." If he wasn't watching ESPN, something with Mel Gibson in it was usually on.

"He's fine, Paige. I gave him his meds a few hours ago, but mostly he napped and we watched movies. Truly, he's one of the easiest patients I've ever had."

"Easy?"

Her light laugh tinkled through the phone. "Okay. He's a bit grumpy, and a whole lot stubborn, but that's to be expected. I can handle him, I assure you."

"Thank you," I said, just as Beaux came out of the bathroom. He walked up to the bed and climbed on, pulling me onto his lap as he moved. "I really appreciate your help. I should be back tomorrow morning."

"No rush. I'm here for the long haul. And if there's anything else you need, I can always help with light cooking or cleaning if you need."

"Oh, that's not—"

"It's my job, Paige. And truly, you're helping me keep busy when your father's sleeping."

Goodness. How did this become my life? Help for my dad and help around the house? Beaux wrapped his arms around my waist and I relaxed into his strong, warm embrace.

"Thank you. I still appreciate it. We'll see you tomorrow, okay?"

"Sounds good. Enjoy yourself tonight."

Heat hit my cheeks and chest. She hadn't implied anything, but it produced vivid flashbacks I never wanted erased.

"Good night, Melanie."

She returned the goodbye and I set my phone on the nightstand.

"I don't have any way to thank you or pay you back for helping with my dad," I said to Beaux. My vision went blurry as I spoke and I pressed my eyes closed. "There are no words."

"Don't need 'em. I'm happy to help. And don't forget it's part selfish on my part, too."

It didn't matter. If this was Beaux being selfish, he was still more selfless than anyone I'd ever met.

"Still, thank you. It means a lot to me."

"I'm not your ex, Paige, and someday you'll start believing it. I have no desire to walk away from you."

It was uncanny how much he understood me. He knew my fears, my uncertainties before I did. I shoved my face into the crook of his neck and shoulder to hide my emotions.

His hand slid up and down my back, soothing me. How did I get so damn lucky?

"Ready for bed?" he asked.

I shook my head against his shoulder. "I need to brush my teeth. It's in my purse downstairs."

He pushed me away from him and pointed to his dresser where my purse was sitting. "I brought your purse up when I saw your phone next to it. Have at it and hurry back."

I did what I was told and by the time I returned, Beaux had

fixed the covers and pillows we'd destroyed earlier and was already in bed.

We snuggled up together, spoke quietly as he flicked through a few news channels, and I was out, completely out, within moments, with Beaux's arm around me, my thigh draped over his, and feeling more rested and relaxed than I had in years.

The man was a superhero.

I'd had almost two weeks of bliss. I went to the garage in the morning, helped the mechanics on jobs so they could focus on the '64 Camaro. We were searching for parts so in between oil changes and fluid re-fillings and car cleanings, I was spending most of the time searching vendors and vintage junkyards for all original pieces.

So far, it was slow going, but we were committed.

After the workday was done, I was able to go home and spend the rest of the evening with my dad. I spent a handful of nights with Beaux, but the others I stayed at home with my dad and his nurse, Melanie.

With my dad recovering nicely, his pain lessening by the day, he was awake for longer periods. After he went to bed at night, I was finally able to relax for the first time since moving home.

I needed it. Twice I fell asleep on the couch at nine o'clock and didn't wake up until six when my alarm went off. Once, I'd poured a glass of wine and fell asleep before I ever took a sip. I hadn't realized how run down I'd become until I was given the time to do nothing.

I poured my appreciation into my time with Beaux. We did dinner on Wednesday. I went over there later on Thursday after dad was in bed, and Friday and Saturday we didn't see each other.

Now, Melanie and I were helping my dad into his wheel-chair and guiding him to the suite Kolby had provided, all with the assistance of two security guards courtesy of Beaux.

My mouth had dropped when we'd parked in the underground parking garage connected to the stadium and John and Ryan had introduced themselves to us. They'd said Beaux had requested them to escort us for the day, courtesy of stadium security.

That wasn't my first clue being with Beaux was life-changing in more than one way, but it was one of the most jolting.

Being with Beaux required security?

We were taken to a private elevator to the floor of our suite and then another life-changing realization hit me as we stepped into the suite.

It was a suite the size of Rhode Island.

My breath stalled as soon as we entered. The stadium had recently undergone massive renovations and the suites had definitely been included.

We'd arrived early to ensure plenty of time to get my dad settled and Kolby's mom, Charlayne, and his daughter, Mya were nowhere in sight.

"Holy cannoli," Melanie whispered, her eyes wide open and awed as we entered.

"Now this is what I'm talking about!" Dad exclaimed. "My kind of way to watch the game."

I was more than impressed. I was floored. Black leather

chairs. Three tall bar-height tables. There was a small kitchen area where a waiter, someone at our beck and call for drinks and food, stood waiting dressed in all black with a white towel tossed over his shoulder.

"Good afternoon," he said. "Name's Shane. Anything you need today, let me know."

"I need a good slap to the face of reality," Melanie said.

I snickered. In the two weeks since she'd been at our place, I'd found out Melanie wasn't just a really great and patient nurse, she was hilarious and sweet. I didn't possibly think there were really people in the world as gentle and kind and good as her.

She also came from one of the most normal sounding families I'd ever heard of. She had a sister and a brother, parents who were married for forty-nine years. They still got together once a week for family dinners.

When I stayed home on Friday, Melanie and I opened a bottle of wine and had an impromptu girl's night in.

It was the exact kind of night I missed from living in Charlotte and one I'd desperately needed.

"I'll slap you," I offered Melanie.

She giggled and settled my dad right behind the top row of chairs. "This okay?" she asked, locking the wheel and getting Dad's attention.

"Perfect. Thanks, Melanie."

She patted his hand and came to my side. I was standing back, surveying the field but it only took moments for me to recognize Beaux out on the field as the team warmed up.

It helped he was the one throwing the ball and I knew his number. Even without that, it would have been easy to spot him. Besides being one of the tallest guys out there, I'd spent the last week memorizing his body, running my hands over every accentuated muscle.

"Careful," Melanie whispered, "I think you might be drooling."

I shook my head. "I can't help it."

She clapped her hands together and nudged me with her hip. "Which one do I get?"

Apparently Melanie was just as taken with the idea of dating a Rough Rider as I was starting to be.

"Don't know," I murmured. "I don't know who's single besides Kolby."

A door opened behind us and the sweetest little voice I'd ever heard cried out, "Yook, Namma! Dere people here!"

Melanie and I both turned as Mya skipped into the room. She was wearing a teal skirt and white shirt with the Rough Rider's logo on it. On her back, which I saw as she twirled and danced straight up to us, was Kolby's name and number.

"Hi," I said, crouching down her level. "You must be Mya."

"I yam," she almost shouted. "Who are you?"

"I'm a friend of Beaux's. Your dad said we could watch the games this year with you. Is that okay?"

I looked from her to a beautiful African American woman who had entered behind her and arched a brow in question for her as well.

"Kolby said what he'd done," she said. Her smile was friendly as she approached. "I'm Charlayne, Kolby's mom, but everyone calls me Char."

"It's nice to meet you, I'm Paige, and this is my dad, Sam, and his nurse and our friend Melanie."

We made the introductions all while Mya bounced to each of us, shouting more hellos and then she skipped off to where Shane stood.

"Chocowate milk, pease, Mister Shane!"

"Already have it ready," he said. He grinned at her, I was certain all of us were. Mya was a sweet little bundle of energy.

It was no wonder why Kolby said she'd enjoy the game with more people around here.

"That girl is either hopped up on sugar while she's here or bored to tears. It's nice to have some company," Char said, getting my attention from Mya who was slurping chocolate milk out of a straw and handing it back to Shane requesting more. "I'd tell her no more, but it's pretty much the only time Kolby allows her to have sweets."

"Strict dad?"

"Ha! Doting dad, but he's got a sweet tooth unlike I've ever seen in a grown man. During the season he refuses to allow anything unhealthy into his body. When it comes to sweets, he has the self-control of a mosquito."

I laughed at the image of Kolby Jones not having self-control. "I suppose it's done him well, he's looking great this year. Thanks for letting us join you guys, too. It was really nice of the guys to do this for my dad."

"Child," she said and set her hand on my arm. "All of us go through hard times. Trust me, I seen 'em all, lived through most of 'em. And when times are harder, ain't nothing better than people at your back to hold you up. Sounds to me like you got that now if you didn't before."

A lump lodged in my throat at her poignant but blunt words. "Right."

"Now I don't know about you, but along with Kolby's ban on sugar, he's also banned alcohol. This here's one of the few times I can imbibe in some wine and not get scolded by my grown son. You want something with me?"

"I'd love some. Melanie?" I asked, turning to her, but she was already at the bar. Elbows propped on it, she was leaning over it, talking to Shane.

Oh Lord.

"Great," I muttered. "All I need is her flirting with the bartender."

"Shit," Charlayne said. "If I were thirty years younger, I'd be doing the same thing. That man is fine."

I kissed my dad on the cheek and took his request for some water, all while he grumbled about not being able to have a beer due to his meds. Charlayne and I met up with Melanie still hitting on Shane, flipping her pretty platinum hair over her shoulder and making it known a drink wasn't all that was on her request list.

Then we settled in for the game, talking and cheering and laughing, all while my dad fought to stay awake. I felt bad for him, was worried we were overdoing it, but when he nodded off shortly after halftime began, I forced myself to stop.

Melanie knew what he could handle, and he didn't seem bothered by our noise, mostly Mya's as she entertained us all game long with her cheers and dances.

And since the Rough Riders pulled out a win over the Saints twenty-four to eight, we all left in high spirits.

We parted ways at the elevator with John escorting Melanie and Dad back to the car. I followed Char and Mya along with Ryan down to the player's tunnel beneath the stadium so I could go home with Beaux.

TWENTY-TWO
BEAUX

Games were a mixture of exhaustion and adrenaline rush. I usually left the game trying to decide if I needed a four-hour nap or run a marathon.

With Paige sitting next to me in the car, reciting every single play I made plus laughing about Mya's silly antics and relaying the information that not only was Melanie flirting with the bartender, but she'd also demanded a list of all the single players under the age of thirty, I wasn't thinking about a nap.

I definitely wanted a marathon—in the form of sex. In multiple rooms of my house.

Definitely multiple positions.

That, I was more than ready for.

Unfortunately, my big sister was trying to play cock blocker and I hadn't yet warned Paige.

I pulled down the back alley of my brownstone and parked my truck in the garage.

Paige rested her head against the headrest and turned to me. "Have I said thank you, yet?"

"About a million times. I'd prefer to not hear it anymore. But you can keep showing me your gratitude."

"Always," she mumbled, opening the door and hopping down. "Always with the sex with you."

I followed her out. "Only when you're around."

She rolled her eyes and met me at the front of the truck, easily slipping her hand into mine.

Once we were inside, I locked the door behind us, re-engaged my alarm system, and pushed her against the wall.

"What the—"

It was all she got out before my mouth descended on hers.

She instantly responded, curling her fingers into the front of my suit jacket, holding me to her.

"Fuck," I groaned. We had maybe thirty minutes and I needed this to be quick. "Turn around," I said, already guiding her where I wanted her.

"Beaux—"

"Need you. Want you here. So no matter where I am in this house, I can look right here and remember you letting me do what I want to do to you."

Her body shivered and she pressed her lips to mine before turning the rest of the way.

"Hands on the wall."

She complied. I ran my hands down her arms, and fuck there was nothing sexier than seeing her in a shirt bearing my number.

"I want to fuck you wearing nothing but this shirt," I groaned, reaching around to her front to undo her jeans.

"Jesus," she whispered. "What's gotten into you?"

"Have no fucking clue."

It was the truth. When I was around Paige, my brain malfunctioned. As soon as she was in my arms, animal instincts took over. The urge to claim, mark, make her mine in every possible way.

Doing it while she'd already marked herself as mine was hot as fuck, and my dick was punching against my zipper, searching for her heat.

I flicked open the button on her jeans, ripped down the zipper and while I shimmied her jeans and panties over her hips, I pressed my chest to her back. "This okay, though?"

My hand slid to her stomach, dipped to her folds. She mumbled something incoherent, but she was nodding.

Good.

"You're already wet." I kissed her throat, nipped at her ear. Jesus. I was turning into a damn animal and I didn't give two shits. My fingers slid through her wetness, spreading around her moisture.

She rocked back against me, shoved her ass right against my erection, and I tapped her feet with mine. "Open wider. This is going to be hard and fast, baby."

"Damn," she whispered. "I'm already close."

She always was. The girl went off like a rocket with a short fuse. Talk about boosting a guy's ego.

With my other hand, I reached beneath us, struggling with my zipper and undoing my pants. I shoved them down to my thighs and freed myself, pushing against her while driving her crazy with my fingers.

"Fuck," I groaned, pressing my forehead to my shoulder. "I don't have a condom."

"Pill," she gasped, rolling her body against me. One of her hands disappeared from the wall and she wrapped it around my cock, stroking it. "Please. I trust you."

Fucking hell.

Ungloved.

I didn't date women long enough to experience it and I was

always careful. I was never going to be the guy who knocked up a woman.

She must have sensed my hesitation because her hand stilled and she turned to look at me, question clear on her face. "Do you trust me?"

"I'm clean. I trust you, it's just I've never—"

"Yeah?" she asked, and her hand started moving again. "Never?"

God. She was going to make me come in her hand. I pulled back but she gripped me tighter, just the perfect amount of pain and pleasure, zinging straight to my balls. "Always careful. And I'm clean, Paige."

"I like the idea of you never having this before me."

Fucking hell. This girl.

I leaned in and kissed her, teased her clit more and slid two fingers deep inside her to make sure she was ready for me. Hell, I was nervous. This was intimacy at it's closest.

Funny I found it with the first woman not impressed by my money and willing to douse me with ice.

She gasped my name, rocking into me, increasing the speed and pressure until I feared we wouldn't make it to the final event.

I slapped her hand away.

No way was I missing out, and time was ticking down.

"Ready?" I asked.

"Yessss."

Her reply was needy, so damn greedy for me. I felt the same way.

Then I was pulling back, lining us up, gripping her hip with one hand and sliding inside her.

"Shit," I hissed.

Hot, wet heat surrounded me and holy shit condoms were the giant lying sack of shit things other guys had always said they were. Fucking heat surrounded my dick and I felt her walls, so damn tight around me. All of it minimized by rubber I was never.wearing.again when it came to Paige.

"Holy shit," I chanted curses. Sweat beaded at my temples. "This feels so fucking good."

"I know," she whimpered. "Move."

"I'm afraid I might come." I wasn't even ashamed to admit it. That's how damn good she felt. Like winning the Super Bowl, except hotter. Better. Sexier.

Her laugh was blissful, quiet but sweet, it made her cunt grip around me. I shoved balls deep inside her, rocking out. And damn...sex with Paige wasn't just hot or sexy.

It was fun.

She wasn't only different from other women, she was something special. Someone special who could grow to mean a hell of a lot to me, or she already did.

"Brace yourself, honey," I ordered, moving her hand back to the wall.

I moved, snapping my hips against her ass, my balls slamming against her. I took her hard. Rough. Fast.

She ate it up and demanded more, crying my name and digging at the walls with her hands.

I added my fingers, teased her, shoved a hand up her shirt to push her bra out of the way so I could wrap my hand around her breast, pinch her nipples.

I tugged and pulled, took her wildly against the wall, and when she came, throwing her head back to my shoulder, her entire body quivering and shaking with pleasure, her pussy gripped me tight like a vise. I followed her over the edge, slamming into her, releasing inside of her.

At the last second, I pulled out, shoved her shirt up her back, and wrapped my hand around my dick, tugged...and splashed the rest of me onto her ass.

"Fuck," I groaned.

I collapsed against her, careful of my cum and her body and pressed my fingers back to her pussy, fucking her with my fingers. I was inside of her, in more ways than one. She chanted my name and no more and please and yes, unable to make up her own damn mind on what she wanted, but she took what I was giving like such a good girl.

I took her mouth right as she lost herself in another climax. I wrapped my other hand around her waist, holding her up as I rubbed her clit, took her through her second orgasm until she was spent, panting into my mouth, hot and sweaty.

A perfect match for me.

"Goodness," she whispered, shaking her head back and forth. "That was insane. Did you...did you come on me?"

"Yeah." She looked surprised. I was, too. "Told you, you in my shirt, claiming me, I don't know what came over me but I had to do the same."

She laughed and shook her head like I was crazy. Which was fine. I felt crazy around her.

"I need to go clean up. Quickly."

"Hold on," I said.

She gave me a look. I was already tugging on my pants. "Honest, don't move. I'll get something."

I ran to my kitchen, grabbed a paper towel and came back to her, fighting the urge to laugh but unable to do anything but admire the curve of her ass, the summer tan lines that proved her swimsuit was fucking tiny.

I wiped me off her back and then held out her panties and jeans. "Shower if you need to," I said. "My sister and Powell are coming for dinner. They'll be here soon."

"What!?"

TWENTY-THREE
PAIGE

His sister. His freaking sister was coming. Nothing like throwing me into the fire. While I tried calming down as we took a quick shower, rinsing off our bodies and keeping my hair mostly dry, I still wanted to slaughter him.

What if they'd shown up early?

How would I face her knowing I'd just let her brother have sex with me against a wall?

I wasn't exactly a prude in bed. I liked variety. I liked changing it up now and then and like most girls in their mid-twenties, I survived dry spells with my handy-dandy operated helper.

But being thrown against a wall and taken like that, having someone finish on me and not in me...well, that was new.

It was also passionate, filled with a fire I couldn't stop burning whenever I was around Beaux. Since I had no intention of dousing those flames, I stopped being mad and started worrying about Shannon.

They were close. From everything Beaux had told me, and he always talked about Shannon, she'd not only pretty much raised him, she'd always protected him. She took care of him. She sacrificed what she wanted in order to help Beaux reach his dreams.

When he could, he repaid her by buying her a building for her own business, something I saw talked about constantly on local design blogs. Her jewelry was cool. Funky metal bangles and bracelets and necklaces and earrings, she hand-made everything herself. The woman must have been a sorceress, able to stop time with a blink of her eye or wiggle of her nose.

I had no idea how she worked so hard and managed to have a life.

Plus, she was engaged to Oliver Powell. One of the hottest and most famous tight ends in football. Hell, he'd even done some commercials and appeared on television shows over the last couple of years.

Together, they seemed like an unstoppable force. At least a couple I wanted to make a really great impression on.

I wasn't certain fucking her brother and still being wet from a shower when they arrived was the best way to handle that one.

I was fixing my mascara with Q-Tips and water because since Beaux hadn't warned me, I didn't have anything at his place. I hoped Shannon didn't think my flushed cheeks were after sex glow, but excitement over the win.

I needed a drink.

"Beaux!" I shouted. He'd already left the room, but I was still fussing with running makeup and frizzed out hair.

"What?" he shouted back. Seconds later, I heard pounding footsteps on his wood stairs as he rushed up to me. "What is it?

I held out my hand, trembling like I'd drank too much caffeine. Nerves and crazy sex adrenaline crash the causes for sure.

"Do you have wine? I need a drink. A big one. A box, maybe, not a bottle. Do you have anything?"

"Woah." He threw up both hands palms out. "Slow your roll, psycho. It's just Shannon."

"I need a drink." I leaned in, hissing. "You've freaked me out, I can barely stand up straight, thanks to you, and I didn't have time prepare to meet your only family. Plus," I circled my face with my finger, "I have this freshly-fucked look going on and I need to chill out."

He leaned against the doorframe during my rant and grinned. "You can barely stand up straight? Legs shaking too bad?"

I tossed the Q-tip into the trashcan. "I'm freaking out!"

"I know, crazy. It's funny. Seriously, it's Shannon. And as far as your freshly-fucked look, do you know how many times I've shown up at their place to see her looking the same? It's about time I got my payback."

I had no way to respond to that.

Nothing. This man was the biggest ninny I'd ever met.

"Beaux," I said, warning him.

He stepped back. Wise choice. "I have sauvignon blanc and pinot noir. What would you prefer?"

"Red, please." A rush of breath fell from my lips, shoving my shoulders down. "And thank you."

"No need. I grew up with Shannon. I know how to calm down psycho."

He skedaddled quickly, giving me no time to retort and by the time he returned, I was working on calming down.

I still drank half the glass in one large gulp.

~

I HAD nothing to worry about. Damn Beaux for not only being

a sexy beast in bed but for always being right. Well, mostly always right.

I was sure he'd been wrong a time or two at some point in his life.

Still, Shannon and Oliver showed up at Beaux's place approximately five seconds after I finished my first glass of wine and they came with three large plastic bags of carryout.

She'd dropped the bags in her hand to her feet when she saw me and threw herself at me so hard, I went back a step. "I'm so glad to meet you," she'd exclaimed. She shook me like a rag doll and pulled back, grinning. "I was going to come to your suite today but I didn't want to scare you. But I insisted we have dinner tonight since they're gone next week again. Oliver and Beaux have told me so much about you. Any girl who's willing to dump a bucket of ice on my brother is a-okay in my book."

"Uh," I 'd said, my gaze flying to Beaux.

"See?" he'd said. "I know how to deal with psycho."

"Shut your pie-hole," Shannon had snapped. "I'm being friendly."

"You're scaring the bejeezus out of her, babe," Oliver had said. He'd pulled his fiancée into his hold and with his free hand, held it out to me. "Nice to see you again, Paige. Your dad like the game today?"

"Well, you won, so yeah."

"Glad I could make that happen for him."

"You?" Beaux had cried out, aghast. "You made it happen?"

"Again," Oliver had said, ushering Shannon into the kitchen, not looking at Beaux. "I'm so glad you and I have come to an agreement on things."

"Smug little son of a bitch," he growled. His face was twisted with such confused aggravation I burst out laughing.

Like sheep, we followed them into the kitchen, Beaux

wrapping his arm around my lower back as he guided me there. Shannon had made herself at home, pulling out plates and silverware, while Oliver unloaded the carry out containers.

They lined everything up, we filled our plates, Beaux gave Shannon and me more wine while he and Oliver stuck to water, and then we sat down at his dining table and ate.

And talked.

And laughed.

It took me about twenty-two point two seconds to not only stop being nervous around Shannon but to absolutely fall in love with her.

She was a bit loud, a lot crazy, insanely in love with her fiancé, and fiercely protective of her brother. That came about when she started bitching about comments he'd already received on Instagram.

Oliver had turned to her and asked, "Why don't you get this worked up about people saying shit about me?"

"Please," she'd winked, "you're a grown man. You can handle yourself."

"And what the hell am I?" Beaux had asked.

"My little brother." Her expression showed she meant every word, and I knew we'd get along perfectly. Because I loved that Beaux, even if he was technically a grown man, had someone like that in his life.

They left shortly after dinner, claiming they didn't want to stay out too late and it was already closing in on ten, and they still had to drive back to their house outside Raleigh quite a distance.

As soon as Beaux had closed and locked the door behind them, engaged his security panel, he picked me up, flung me over his shoulder and carried me to bed.

Where we stayed for hours.

Not sleeping until much, much, later.

LIFE MOVED QUICKLY over the next few weeks.

The Rough Riders were leading the league, undefeated, surprising no one.

I saw Beaux when I could, sometimes going to his place, sometimes him hanging out at mine with my dad and me. He stayed the night with me, despite my quiet protests he shouldn't with my dad there.

He'd laughed at me and carried me to my room saying, "Your dad likes me, so I think we're past the concern of him shooting me. And it's not like he doesn't know we sleep together when you're at my place."

Still, I kept the physical contact to either the bathroom or above the waist in the bed.

No girl wanted to have her dad hear her having an orgasm. With as effectively and powerfully as Beaux delivered them, it would have happened.

One Saturday when Beaux had left for an out of state game, Dad, Melanie, and I went to eat dinner at Ride'Em Rough. As much as I had been enjoying the freedom of having a life again, I was also missing Hannah and my job there. Unfortunately, she wasn't working when we went in and I made a mental note to check in on her.

Sure the uniform sucked, getting ass-grabbed and propositioned every ten minutes wasn't my favorite thing in the world, but while things were going well at the garage, the looming hospital bills I knew were coming from Dad's surgery and recent hospital stay were already stressing me out.

We had decent insurance but even then, the bills were going to be astronomical.

I'd rested and spent time with Beaux like he'd wanted to have happen when he hired Melanie.

That didn't mean I didn't still have additional responsibilities.

And after our dinner the night at Ride'Em Rough, I talked to Paulie about returning in another week.

"About damn time," he scolded me. "You're lucky I haven't replaced you yet."

I leaned in and kissed his cheek. "You're a sweetheart, Paulie, you know that?"

He'd growled at me. "Get out of here before I change my mind."

I hurried away but grinned the entire time. He blustered and puffed out his chest, but deep down even if he wouldn't admit it, Paulie was a big ol' softie.

Dad wasn't only healing from his surgery and his leg, but his paralysis was continuing to improve. It was something we'd always known could happen, but with the additional therapy Melanie provided during the day, he was now spending more days out of his wheelchair than he ever had before.

Then he gained a different cast and crutches to use to hobble around the house, and Melanie was becoming less of a constant necessity. She took him to physical therapy appointments several days a week, but now that he was more mobile again and off his pain meds, she usually only stayed a few hours in the afternoon and overnights when I wasn't there.

I was beginning to feel guilty Beaux was basically paying for her to be our friend.

When I mentioned it to both of them, they told me to be quiet and enjoy the help.

So I stayed quiet.

The garage business was picking up.

I assumed that had something to do with customers who had several times spotted Beaux leaving there when he stopped by to see me either over lunch or after he was done with practice. Candid pics had hit the Internet after that and made the rounds on fan sites and Instagram and Facebook.

I wasn't aware of it until Mike shoved his phone into my face when I showed up to work one morning wondering why we had fifteen cars lined up for oil changes and maintenance. That particular morning, all our customers were beautiful women, around my age, wearing a lot less clothing than I ever did and who had clearly spent a lot more time on their makeup.

I tried to forget the bitchy comments about my ass being fat or being too ugly for him.

I never spent much time caring what people thought and I was trying not to let it bother me. The fact I could be found doing squats and lunges and eating salads after that meant nothing.

Overall, life was good. I had help. I had a guy I was falling ass over kettle for. I was in love with Beaux Hale, had been falling in love with him for weeks by the time I realized it but was too chickenshit to say anything.

My dad was healing not just from his broken leg but his stroke, regaining strength every day.

I had new friends. A social life. Even Shannon and I spent some time together occasionally and when the guys were gone, she would come and watch the game with Dad and me.

Life was better than good.

It was perfect.

But like so often when you were riding the top of the wave, enjoying the freedom and exhilaration of beautiful scenery, at some point, you had to crash into the dark water below.

TWENTY-FOUR

BEAUX

"Hey, Beaux. Do you have a couple minutes?"

I paused as Shelly, one of our main PR reps grabbed my attention. I was in the training facility where we practiced. I'd gone upstairs afterward to talk with our marketing department about scheduling a photo shoot.

"No problem, Shelly. What's up?" I slid my hands in the pockets of my jeans.

"Come into my office."

She backed up and I followed her in. Shelly was in her late forties, married to the same guy since she was eighteen. She had two grown children and already had three grandchildren. Typically, she was full of smiles and laughter and had a friendly attitude with everyone.

Her serious demeanor gave me pause.

I closed the door to her office. "What is it?"

"I'd debated sharing some things with you. It's probably nothing, but regardless, I think you should know. And, before you say anything, I've already spoken with security."

Security? A cold chill pricked the back of my neck. Only one reason for security in this life.

"What happened?" I demanded. "And who? Me? Shannon?"

"No. Paige." I fell into the chair behind me and Shelly pulled out three letters in plastic bags from an envelope. "As you know, we have our interns go through your fan mail. Don't get much of it anymore, not handwritten letters with technology the way it is, but these started coming in."

I ripped them out of her hands.

The first letter seemed like every other sort of weird fan I'd been getting messages about since I was in college.

I love you Beaux Hale. You're the best man in the entire world.

Your new girlfriend doesn't deserve you. She's ugly and broke and you can do so much better.

It went on. A bunch more nonsensical rambling, but it was the date that turned my blood cold.

Early September.

"This is one week after I met Paige," I said more to myself than Shelly.

"That's what made me worried enough to save the first one."

I scanned the other letters, fury and fear fighting in my brain giving me a headache. All my muscles tensed.

You will never be happy with her.

She will ruin you.

I will always be here for you.

I will always love you.

Get rid of her.

More threatening, more angry. It wasn't the typed letter that was the worst.

It was the photo she'd scanned into the last letter of Paige standing outside Halloway Motors. Hands on her hips, sunglasses covering her eyes. Her standard skinny jeans and work shirt.

Smiling at Mike, her head thrown back in laughter.

I had no idea when that photo was taken, but the letter was dated four days ago so it had to be recent.

"Holy shit." I rubbed my chest. The pain didn't go away. My heart was pounding.

"She's following her?"

"Like I said, Beaux, we've notified security. They're going to be here soon to look over these with local police. I think it needs to be looked into."

"Looked into? This crazed nut job is stalking my girl-friend." I waved the last letter in Shelly's face. "At her family's garage."

"I know you're worried, Beaux. But don't forget this happens all the time. It could be nothing."

My common sense fizzled. Visions of Paige spread out, sleeping on my bed, curling into me at night flashed in my mind. Her smiling and laughing over dinner. Drinks with her girlfriends, coming to me tipsy and dropping to her knees with that smile still in place. Taking care of her father with all the sweet patience I'd ever seen.

Could be nothing, my ass.

"I want someone on her. Even if I have to hire a security guard myself. She needs a driver and someone on her at all times."

Paige would kick me in the nuts for it. I didn't care.

I had athletic cups I could wear when I told her.

"How about we wait until we speak with the police and see what they recommend?"

"Oh. I'll be talking to them, but I want it anyway."

There were private security firms we'd used before. I

already had a couple of numbers. Jaxon Hayes was my next phone call.

"When are the police coming?"

"Any minute," she said, checking her watch. "Until they get here, I have something else to talk to you about."

"Jesus. Something good, please."

She laughed at my joke, but I didn't. I couldn't get the photo of Paige out of my head. It was one thing for a professional athlete to be photographed, even though it was rare. It was a completely different thing for my girlfriend to be noticed by a stalker within days of me being with her. Which meant the woman had been stalking me first, then moved on to Paige.

Terrifying freaking nut jobs in the world and all of it slammed against my brain, I barely paid attention to Shelly as she asked me to do an interview.

"Who?" I asked, even though I know she'd already said it.

"Curt Banner," she replied. Her eyes were soft, her faint smile even more so. She knew I wasn't listening to her and had no problems repeating herself.

Something about that guy always rubbed me the wrong way. He'd played defensive end for the Dolphins back when they were winning division championships. He'd also been a player in his day, three different marriages, rumors for decades about multiple women on the side.

His interviews didn't just stick to the sport or the game. He got personal. He was also the highest rated sportscaster on ESPN.

"Two weeks, right before you play Seattle."

"Hyping up the re-match?"

"Exactly."

"Fine." Banner was a jerk but I had other, more important things on my mind. I'd keep his questions to the game and that was it.

~

I WALKED out of the training facility feeling a thousand times worse than I had when I arrived.

Agent Joe Spellman, an investigator with the Raleigh PD, had come, talked to Shelly and I about the letters and he'd taken them with him for evidence. Although he'd also told me most people were smart enough not to leave fingerprints on things like this.

Which made me feel like pummeling my fist through a wall.

Stadium Security who came with him told me they'd provide additional security for Paige and myself when we were in the buildings or on Rough Rider property, but they couldn't watch her personally.

Which made me feel like throwing a chair across Shelly's office.

Basically, there was nothing we could do yet. Wait and see. Let the crazy lady keep following Paige or myself.

Which meant I was already on the phone with Jaxon Hayes by the time I reached my truck.

"Beaux Hale," I said as soon as his assistant Charlie answered the phone. "How are you, Charlie?"

"Better than you are probably."

"What have you heard?"

"Nothing," the feisty blonde replied. She'd worked for Jaxon for six years. I'd only known her for one but we'd met several times. "But no one calls for Jaxon on a good day."

"Right." My tone was clipped. "Need his help. Or someone else's but I'll make it worth his while to take this on for me. Does he have time to meet?"

Clicking sounds came through the phone line. "He's got a short opening at three. What's it about?"

"Some fan stalking me and my girlfriend."

Dead silence hit me and I looked at my screen to see if the call dropped.

"Charlie?"

"Uh, yeah." She cleared her throat. "I'm sorry. You said girlfriend? I'm talking to Beaux Hale, right?"

I laughed, despite the shitty day and my shittier mood. "Yeah. You heard me. We just had a meeting with Spellman with Raleigh PD and stadium security. Someone's following her. I think it started with me and now whoever this whacko is, has photos of Paige."

"Paige," she whispered. I rolled my eyes. "Pretty name."

"Pretty girl," I said. Because Charlie was good at her job and feisty but I had a feeling she could be a major pain in the ass, too. "I'll be there at three."

"I'll let Jaxon know."

I said goodbye and hung up. Leave it to Charlie to treat this more like a lunch date than a serious issue. Although, based on what she saw and heard on a weekly basis, this was probably nothing to her. Jaxon Hayes used to be a special agent with the FBI and before that he was special ops military. His client list was distinguished, at least the ones he was allowed to share he worked for. It was the fact he had a list of clients he couldn't talk about that made me confident he was the guy for this job.

I PULLED up to Paige's house and parked my truck in the street, hopping out before I'd barely had time to shut off the engine.

Jaxon had followed me and I waited while he stopped behind me and climbed out of his black Ford Explorer. He scanned the street, nothing casual in either his appearance or his intensity. He was on the job, taking it as a personal favor to me.

I'd owe him an arm and a leg but money didn't matter when it came to protecting Paige's safety.

After our meeting, we'd headed over to the police department where he'd gotten permission to photograph the letters already put into evidence. It was a pain, but Jaxon usually got what he wanted.

"You talk to Paige?" he asked, meeting me in the driveway.

"No. Didn't want to freak her out on the phone."

"Good idea. She won't be freaked out at all when she sees me with you." At a few inches shorter than me, Jaxon had buzzed black hair. It matched his black pants and black shirt perfectly. Not to mention all the treacherous looking ink covering both of his arms. Completing his badass look were a pair of black sunglasses and black combat boots.

He moved like a warrior and even though he might have been a bit smaller than me, no way would I ever fuck with the guy.

He could kill me in less than ten seconds, of that I had no doubt.

I jumped up the steps to the porch and knocked on the door. Melanie answered almost immediately.

"Hey, Beaux." She grinned at me and then caught sight of Jaxon. "Uh. What's going on?"

"Need to talk to Paige. Is Mike here yet?"

"Yeah." Her brow furrowed but she stepped back. "And he's being weird. Did you call him?"

"Yeah." I might not have warned Paige, but I did call Mike. He'd want to know everything and I didn't want to have this conversation more than once. Once was going to be hard enough.

All I'd wanted was to be there for Paige, date her, make her life easier, and being associated with me had made her life possibly, infinitely worse.

I loved the woman. Hadn't told her yet because we had time and we were still new, but there wasn't anything I wouldn't do for her. The fact she was going to be pissed as hell made me feel like shit.

She had enough on her plate without worrying about some psycho following her around, threatening to harm her.

"Hey, you," Paige said, walking out of the kitchen. It smelled like Italian food, rich with garlic and spices. She was wiping her hands on a towel as she greeted me, rolling to her toes to kiss my cheek. "What are you doing here?"

Like Melanie had done, Paige took in Jaxon behind me and her smile disappeared.

"What's going on?"

"Let's get to the living room. Is your dad awake?"

"Yeah, he's watching ESPN. Everything okay?"

I placed my hand on her lower back and murmured, "No. Let's sit."

She walked woodenly in front of me, glancing back at me, mostly at Jaxon behind me. A tremble ran down her spine.

Fuck. Fuck! I'd brought this to her. I'd never felt like a bigger pile of crap.

"Okay," she said, once she and Melanie were sitting down. Instinctively, they joined hands. Jaxon and I stood. Mike was at the fireplace, elbow on the mantle, showing none of his usually carefree demeanor. His eyes were narrowed and he didn't remove his gaze from Jaxon. "Tell me what this is about."

The temperature in the house dropped twenty degrees as I sat on the couch. I was telling myself not to freak out but it was pointless.

I was totally wigging out. The guy covered in tattoos and black standing next to Beaux looked menacing, like he could kill a guy in five seconds. Snap their neck before they saw it coming.

"This is Jaxon Hayes," Beaux said, pointing his thumb at the guy. "He's head of a security firm in Raleigh."

"Security?" Dad re-adjusted himself in his recliner and his eyes went alert. "What happened?"

"Nothing yet," Jaxon said. "And we're going to keep it that way."

"Jaxon, man," Beaux said, but Dad cut him off.

"No. No pussy footing around with this. You got something to say, spit it out."

I'd thought we were past the time frame when I had to worry about Dad aiming a gun at Beaux.

I might have been wrong.

"Go ahead," Jaxon said.

Damn. Beaux's look went forlorn and he flinched. He rubbed his chest like he was in pain and didn't look at me. Like he couldn't. His guilt was heavy and all of it sent a sinking weight to my stomach.

"I found out this morning that apparently, I have a stalker. A recent development."

"A what?" I jumped to my feet and rushed him. "Oh my God." My hands landed on his chest and he flinched again.

"Yeah." He gripped my forearms and pushed me back. He pushed me away. The heck? "But it's not me I'm worried about. It's you."

"Me?"

"Yeah." He looked at Dad. Then he explained.

And every single word he spoke shot that terror through me, chilling me straight to the bones.

Behind me, Mike shouted and paced back in forth in front of the fireplace.

Dad's face turned to stone.

Melanie had come and stood next to me, holding my hand, but I barely felt it.

The longer he talked, explaining the notes and photos, Dad and Mike cussed more and more, in volumes and in phrases I'd never heard my dad say around me.

When Beaux mentioned the police being involved, Melanie gasped.

I'd turned mute. I couldn't say or do a damn thing except absorb everything Beaux was explaining. I also knew by his flat expression and cold tone he was hiding more.

"So why are you here?" Dad said, looking at Jaxon, and interrupting Beaux for at least the tenth time with questions. Who could blame the guy for being worried and pissed the hell off?

"Beaux hired me. I'm Paige's new security guard."

"You don't go anywhere without him," Beaux said, his tone abrupt.

"What?"

"Miss Halloway," Jaxon said, his voice was firm. Warm, comforting, with a bite of viciousness. "I promise you, I'm the best there is. While the police do their job, mine is to keep you safe."

"Safe?" My head whipped to Beaux. "You think I need protection?"

Had I not been listening? I might have blocked it all out. This wasn't happening. Yesterday I was just a girl dating a guy who played football.

Today I had some crazed fan taking photos of me and sending threatening letters.

Of course I needed protecting. Or a safe house. Or a new name. A new life.

Maybe someone to slap some sense into me.

"I'm not about to risk anything happening to you, the fact she's followed you to work, or at least knows where you work, scares the shit out of me. I'm not going to lie, Paige. And there's no way in hell I'm playing this off. Not with you." Beaux's voice sounded broken, harsh and thick, filled with shards of glass. The effort it was taking him to explain all of this, was obvious.

I still couldn't move toward him. I couldn't comfort him. His eyes went glacial blue and he scanned the room. "Not with any of you. You're in this mess because of me and I will take care of it. Starting with a security system. Jaxon will have his team here first thing tomorrow to install it.

"Security," I murmured. "Security and safety and stalkers." Oh, my. I was losing my mind.

I'd been photographed in the last month. I'd noticed them. Traffic had picked up at the garage. All of it was an annoyance but it hadn't terrified me. This went beyond terrifying and I fell back a step, away from Beaux.

He reached for me but I held up my hands. "No. No, I just, I need a minute."

"Paige," he croaked. "I'm sorry."

"I know." He was. I knew it. I could feel it rolling off him along with his fury.

It didn't matter. I loved him. Had fallen in love with him. But I didn't realize in doing so, from what they were saying, my life could be at stake.

All I knew was I needed space. A place to think and organize my thoughts, lay everything out that he'd just told me, what it meant for me in the upcoming days or weeks.

Was Beaux worth it?

Of course he was. A thousand times yes.

Was I strong enough to handle it?

I had no answer for that one.

"Excuse me," I looked at my dad. "I'm sorry."

"Nothing to be sorry about, sweetheart. We just want you safe." He sounded as torn apart as I felt, as Beaux looked, as equally torn up as Mike was clearly fuming pissed.

I squeezed his hand and let him go. "I need some time alone," I said to Beaux. "To think."

"To think?"

"I'm sorry," I whispered, my fear clogging my throat and making the words bounce.

I WENT TO MY ROOM, pulled a pillow to my chest, curled up against my headboard and stared out my window.

Then I jumped off the bed, looked outside, and slammed the blinds shut.

Was she out there? Watching us now? Was she hiding in the trees? Behind my neighbor's fence? Was she using the garage? Did she know I worked at Ride'Em Rough? Was she doing anything other than turning my life and my safety upside down?

I didn't want to think about her, what she was doing, but until she was caught or stopped, it would be the only thing I did.

Knowing someone was threatening your life and following you didn't exactly scream comfort.

A knock tapped on my bedroom door and I ignored it. It wasn't locked, but I was still too stunned to speak or move.

It didn't matter how many times I rearranged what Beaux and Jaxon had said downstairs.

I didn't know how long I'd been in my room when the knock happened again.

I stared at the closed blinds.

The door creaked open and it was Melanie's sweet and concerned voice I heard. "I think you need a drink."

She only had her head and arms sticking in the doorway, but she was also holding two bottles in one, glasses in the other. A white wine and tequila.

We didn't have tequila in the house. She must have gone and got some.

I needed to chill out and calm down, but I didn't need to be puking in the toilet. "Wine, please."

She grinned, a sad and lopsided and understanding one, but she still skipped into my room, closing the door behind her.

"She could be out there," I whispered, going back to watching my closed window blinds.

Melanie poured the drinks and climbed on the bed next to me, handing me one.

"She won't hurt you."

"You can't know that."

"Pshh." She sipped her wine and bumped her shoulder into mine. "Yeah, I can. Did you even look at Rambo Sexy Pants down there? No way is some two-bit crazed chick getting past him."

Leave it to Melanie to lighten the mood. "Rambo Sexy Pants?"

"Yeah. Give the guy a mullet and a bandana and he's totally Sylvester Stallone circa early eighties."

"I have no idea what you're talking about."

"That's because you don't have a brother. Mine loves all those eighties, bad-ass guy movies. Anyway, Rambo. Green Beret. Vicious killer and sexy as hell. That's the dude downstairs."

"Hmmm." I sipped my wine. I couldn't lie and say Jaxon wasn't sexy. He just scared the crap out of me more. "Rambo Scary Pants."

She snorted. "Rambo I-wanna-get-in-his-pants."

I laughed. "You're a nut." Our giggles passed and we drank our wine. Melanie left me to my quiet, tormented thoughts and when my glass was empty, she refilled it. "I'm scared."

"I don't blame you. This is scary shit, but what are you thinking?"

"That I'm scared and it's Beaux's fault, and mine for dating him. And now I have to worry about my dad and Mike and the guys at the garage and wonder how insane or desperate this person is and is she following me all the time, or only at work, and does she know where I live? Has she followed me home? Does she know where Beaux is? What will she do to keep me out of his—"

A hand slammed over my mouth and silenced me. "Woah, woman. And you called me a nut?"

I flashed her wide eyes and shrugged. The fact I was a neurotic nutcase wasn't news to anyone.

"Biggest fear," Melanie said and with her hand holding her wine glass she held up a finger. "And you only get one."

Biggest? Most serious? There was only one.

I pulled her hand off my mouth. "Losing Beaux."

"And his greatest fear is losing you. So I'm not sure why you're up here hiding when you could be with him figuring out the best way to make sure neither of those two things happen."

She had a point.

I was a runner by nature. I didn't handle stress well, didn't like changes to routine.

The fact I had a nurse-turned-friend practically living with me now and was soon to have my life thrown into a crazy mess was enough to make me need some Xanax.

"I see your point," I admitted, and took a drink. It was warming, but still sweet. I would have drunk the tequila she brought at this point. I didn't care what alcohol burned my throat, I just needed it do its job and mellow me out. "Is he here?"

"No. He said he wanted to meet another dude of Jaxon's at the garage to go over security there. I'll tell you what though, your sexy guy is taking this incredibly seriously. He said he'll be back soon and you're not supposed to leave."

"Beaux said I can't leave?"

"Not without Rambo."

"Jaxon."

"Potato, po-tah-to."

We dissolved into a fit of giggles, and I hugged her. I needed this. Needed someone who could make me laugh when all I wanted to do was curl into a ball and ignore life around me.

But I had good friends.

Protectors.

Family.

I had Beaux.

And while we hadn't said that we loved each other, I knew I had Beaux's heart like he had mine. And I knew with how protective he was on a normal day, Melanie was right.

He'd do whatever he could; throw any cost and time and resources into keeping me safe.

And for the first time, without arguing about his help first, I decided to let him.

I needed him to do that for me, to be the guy who would do that for me.

TWENTY-SIX

BEAUX

I walked back into Paige's house expecting the eerie silence it'd been filled with when I left earlier.

Instead, laughter came from the dining room along with a manic shout of, "Bullshit!" A loud round of choruses echoed with Mike's voice the loudest at, "Screw you, Paige!"

The hell?

I hurried around the corner and came to an abrupt stop. At the dining table sat Mike, Melanie, Sam, Paige, and Jaxon. All of them with their hands full of cards, Mike pouting while he scooped up the massive pile in the middle.

"What's going on?" I asked, walking toward Paige like she was a wounded animal. When I left, she hadn't wanted anything to do with me. Now her eyes were a bit glassy, her smile lazy.

"I'm drunk," she drawled in her sweet Southern voice. "And we're playing bullshit."

"Bullshit?"

She wagged her finger at Jaxon. "It was his idea."

He glared at me. His sunglasses were gone, but his eyes

were just as black as them. His look told me this game was unequivocally, one hundred percent, not his idea.

Jaxon looked back at his cards and I moved to Paige's back. "It was Jaxon's idea?"

"No, that's bullshit." She giggled. Melanie joined her. "It was Melanie's idea and he's playing against his will because what else is he supposed to do?"

"Make sure you're safe?" I asked, hating I had to say it. My glare matched Jaxon's and he shook his head.

"I'm safe," she said, looking up at me. Her eyes were droopy, barely open and she swayed toward me. "I have you."

A bullet to the chest couldn't have caused a more heated ache in my chest. Except this was the best kind of pain.

She trusted me. She wasn't pushing me away and she wasn't screaming at me. Perhaps that would happen after she sobered up. I squatted down at her side so we were at eye level. "Yeah?"

She leaned into me, head bumping into my shoulder and stayed there. "Yeah."

"How drunk are you?"

She hiccupped. Trashed, obviously. Her brows furrowed and lips puckered while she took her time thinking. "My head is going to hurt in the morning but I won't be puking." She reached for a beer and I stopped her.

"How about we stay that way?"

She hiccupped again.

Melanie's giggles grew louder.

"That's probably a good idea," Paige said, her words stretching out over a yawn and she covered her mouth. "It just felt so good earlier, I couldn't stop."

If it'd been off-season, I probably would have done the same.

"Okay then, drunk girl." I pushed her chair back and pulled

her cards from her hand. "How about we get upstairs. I've got more things to talk to you about."

"No." She shook her head. "No more talking. I've had enough talky-talk today and I'm done talking."

"Then you can listen."

"I don't like doing that either today."

I glanced at Sam for support. There was more shit to figure out and there wasn't a lot of time. There was no damn way she was going to be working at the restaurant with the crowds it got until I knew she was safe. I hated to spoil it but if she were drunk when I told her I just paid her dad's hospital expenses so she didn't have to go back to waitressing, she'd take it better than sober.

Or she'd get even drunker, but I'd hold her head while she puked if she needed it.

"Not tonight, son," Sam said. He wasn't drinking, but he was sitting in a wheelchair. His hands were steady and his eyes were clear. "Let her do what she has to do."

My jaw went tight. "Sam—"

His eyes told me he understood. Maybe not what I had to say, but that things were more serious than we'd thought.

I didn't doubt Jaxon hadn't heard what we found at the garage, but he obviously hadn't said anything.

"She might be your girl, but she's mine, too. And tonight, give her this. You can smack her with reality first thing tomorrow, but she needs this."

"Come on," Paige slurred, pushing back from me. "Sit and play a hand with us."

"You can have mine," Jaxon said, already pushing back from the table. "I got calls to make anyway."

I stood from the table and brushed Paige's hair off her cheek. She wasn't wearing the clip in her hair like she usually did and her bangs covered one of her eyes, flopping back after I tucked it behind her ear. "You need another drink?"

"Absolutely."

"All right, then. Let's play some bullshit."

We did. For two more hours.

And the night ended with me doing exactly what I knew I would. Me holding Paige's hair back while she puked into the toilet.

But when she climbed into her bed next to me, rolled to her side, and clung to me, I didn't care I'd just held her hair while she puked.

She curled into me even though being with me put her in the line of fire of a psycho. Right before she passed out, her mouth at my throat, she whispered, "I love you."

And all of it, every fucking second of my shitastic day, was completely worth it to hear it, even if she wouldn't remember saying it.

PAIGE STIRRED in my arms and groaned. My hand was on the back of her head, holding her to my chest. I'd woken up but stayed in bed, wanting to be there for her when she woke up. She'd tossed and turned during the night, kicked off covers and moaned more than once, a pained sound that when she woke me, it didn't sound like it had anything to do with her alcohol intake the previous day, but her fear from earlier.

Every time she woke me up, I tucked her tight against me and she settled.

I waited to see if she'd fall back asleep but her body tensed.

"You okay?" I murmured.

She groaned again. "Stop shouting."

My chest shook while I tried to quell my laughter.

"Ugh," she groaned again and pushed off me. I let her go slowly as she rolled to her back and then her left side. "Shoot me and take my pain away."

After I'd brought her into the bedroom last night, she'd stripped out of her clothes and fell into bed, naked, passing out as soon as she curled into me. Now, her bare back was exposed to me and I reached out, tracing a fingertip down the length of her spine. She shivered, and curled into her pillow, hugging it to her side while I ran my finger up and down her back, goose bumps pebbling in my wake.

"Need me to get you some water and Advil?"

"Swallowing anything might make me throw up again."

"You tied one on pretty hard."

"I had a lot I wanted to forget." She moaned again and squeezed her eyes closed, turning her head before opening them. "I'm glad you came back. I thought you'd left."

"Never," I said and rested my hand on her back at the base of her spine. "I don't want to ever walk away from you."

Her lips lifted into a hint of a grin and then she turned a pale shade of green.

"Ugh." She groaned and covered her mouth. Before I could move, she jumped out of the bed and ran down the hallway. I hurried after her, grabbing a robe at the back of her door on my way.

Poor thing either didn't realize she was naked or didn't care. She would if her dad or Jaxon saw her. Although, he was most likely crashing in his SUV outside like he'd said he was going to do last night.

I didn't bother knocking on the bathroom door and I walked in as she was flushing the toilet, still leaning over it, and holding her hair with one hand at her shoulder.

"Better?"

I spent enough mornings in college to know that once you puked the next day, things typically improved.

"No," she croaked.

"I brought you your robe." I held it out to her and she took it, leaning back to her knees and looking down. "Oh crap. My dad—"

"Is sleeping downstairs. And I sent Melanie home last night so no one else is here or awake."

"Thank God." She sighed and tugged on her robe. "Why does drinking so much make your bones hurt?"

I doubted she really wanted a lesson in dehydration so I kept my mouth shut. "Take your time getting ready. I'm going to go downstairs and get coffee ready. Want me to bring you that Advil?"

"Yeah. In a minute. I might take a shower first."

"Okay." I kissed the top of her head and stood up. "We do have stuff to talk about today, though."

"Awesome," she muttered and closed her eyes, resting her head in her hands.

"Come on." I held out my hand and waited for her to take it. Gently, I pulled Paige to her feet and then tugged her into my arms. "It'll all be okay, I swear it. Neither Jaxon or his team or I will let anything happen to you or anyone else. I promise."

"Thanks, Beaux."

I held her, and slowly, she wrapped her arms around my back, holding on to me with the strength of a gnat. Chuckling, I let her go and reached into the shower and turned it on. "Let that warm up some," I said.

I needed to get out of there before she got naked again. I didn't care that she was hung over and feeling like shit, her body pressed to mine woke my dick up. If I didn't get out of there, her dad would receive a very loud wake-up call in the form of his daughter screaming my name.

Probably not the best thing.

"In you go," I said, pulling back the shower curtain. She dropped her robe and hobbled inside. I ignored the quick pulse of desire at seeing her naked body and when she was steady on her feet, I left the bathroom.

Sam was still sleeping in his recliner when I reached downstairs, but who could blame the guy? We'd all been up hours later than normal last night and the drunker his daughter became, the more concerned he grew.

Couldn't blame the guy for that, either.

I went to the kitchen and pulled out sausage and ingredients for gravy and biscuits and started cooking. After I heard the water running for a few minutes, I grabbed a glass of water and took some medicine up to Paige.

TWENTY-SEVEN
PAIGE

I rarely got drunk. I didn't enjoy the out of control feeling alcohol sent through my system. I wasn't a giggler by nature or someone who could toss inhibitions to the floor and dance on the tabletops or jump on stage and belt out a karaoke tune.

The fact I'd used alcohol to wash away my fears last night wasn't the worse thing I could do, but I still felt guilt on top of fear on top of an unceasing pounding inside my skull while I climbed into the shower.

I dropped my head in the shower spray, the water pounded against my neck and down my back. I closed my eyes against the onslaught of watery needles sluicing down my sensitive skin.

Last night's memories flickered through my brain like a slideshow. That horrible moment when you try to piece together missing bits of information, jamming wrong puzzle pieces into leftover holes.

Drinking wine with Melanie in my room.

Pulled downstairs when pizza that Mike ordered was delivered.

Waiting on pins and needles for Beaux to return so we could talk.

Melanie's ridiculous idea of playing the card game Bullshit. Jaxon's glare as we shoved him into a chair.

Laughing. The constant, crazy cackling as Melanie and I wiped the floor with Mike and my dad, and then later Beaux. Although as I replayed the memories, the looks Beaux and my dad gave each other, I pounded the shower wall with my fist.

Those freaking men didn't lose to us.

They threw the game to us, something I most likely would have noticed if I hadn't been seeing three of Beaux by the time the game ended.

"That little turd," I muttered and turned my back to the shower. Squeezing the shampoo into my hand, I worked up a lather and went at my hair, scrubbing my scalp and rubbing my temples as the memories continued.

Beaux carrying me upstairs.

Puking.

Good Lord the amount of liquid I expelled into the toilet was obscene.

A warm washcloth on my forehead and my neck. Water.

More puking. And through all of it, Beaux was there, my silent protector and supporter and encourager and comforter.

I finished my hair, washed my body, and picked up a razor, the memories dimming, but still coming.

Helping me brush my teeth, leaving me alone, stripping out of my clothes like a newly born giraffe, all long-leg and wobbly as I stumbled to the bed and then in it.

"Oh shit!" I cried out as I cut my knee. Blood rivulets formed immediately. I stared at it, blinked away the last memory of the night.

"I didn't," I whispered the phrase repeatedly, watching my knee bleed from a poor shave and set down the razor.

I didn't need a razor.

I needed a time machine.

"I did," I whispered. I swayed in the shower, threw out a hand to the wall to stop me from falling and closed my eyes.

"Go to bed drunk girl. I got you."

I curled into him, inhaled his cologne. God, how did he smell so good, cuddle me so hard when I probably reeked of vomit.

"Beaux—"

"We'll talk in the morning."

"K." I yawned, shoved my body to his, aligning us from shoulder to hip and threw a leg over his. "I love you."

"Ah, hell."

I did.

I totally told Beaux I loved him.

And worse?

I couldn't remember if he said it back.

"Damn it," I cursed again, slapped off the water and grabbed a towel I'd draped over the shower curtain. "He didn't say anything," I told the cloudy mirror as I dried off. "He didn't say a thing and he didn't bring it up this morning."

How utterly, horrifically embarrassing.

I could take it back. Blame it on being drunk, out of my mind, thinking of something else. Maybe someone else. Like my dad. Or Mike.

But I couldn't. I wouldn't.

Telling someone you love them wasn't the most embarrassing thing I'd ever experienced, even if it took me awhile to remember I said it in the first place, but I wouldn't take it back. I wouldn't diminish how I felt in that way.

I swiped the mirror again until my hazy reflection stared back at me.

"I'll just pretend it didn't happen," I told myself. Then I

nodded, needing the agreement from the woman in the mirror. "Yup. Pretend it didn't happen. Move on. Forget it."

Yup.

Brave, independent girl, I was. That was totally my game plan.

I finished drying off, moisturizing the crap out of my dehydrated body, and it wasn't until I was done I saw the Advil Beaux had dropped off on my small and cluttered vanity top.

Tossing them back, I pretended they were confidence pills. Forgetful pills. Time-rewind pills.

Those would be awesome.

But since I didn't have magic beans or special little red pills or a time machine, I hurried to my bedroom, feeling slightly more human and less zombie like, threw on a pair of pale blue cut-off sweat shorts and gray Tarheel's sweatshirt.

Then I headed downstairs. And saw a view that was eerily similar of last night.

Melanie, Beaux, and my dad were sitting around the table, but instead of playing cards in their hands, they were chowing down on eggs and toast ... and was that biscuits and gravy?

My stomach grumbled.

Yes. Grease, grease, and more grease. It was exactly what the doctor ordered.

"Hey," I mumbled to everyone. "Good morning."

"No it isn't," Melanie mumbled. She looked almost as bad as me and I winked at her as I passed.

"Feeling better?" Beaux asked, pushing back from his chair.

I stopped him with a hand. "Yeah. Need coffee though. You stay, I can get it."

He watched my every movement as I poured a cup of coffee, filled a plate with biscuits and gravy and halfway to the table, he reached out and took the plate from me.

"You're still tremoring," he said, grinning at me. "Let's not have this gravy all over your floor."

Not a bad idea. I took the seat next to him and dug into my breakfast fully aware everyone's eyes were on me. Well, except for maybe Melanie. But the way she was eating with her head propped up on one hand I figured she was just trying to stay awake.

"God, this sucks." She groaned and pushed away her food. "I'm so sick to my stomach, I can't even finish this. Now I'll never get to say I had Beaux Hale cook me breakfast."

"I cooked it for Paige and Sam, not you."

"Yeah, but I'm like family now, so I'm included."

"No." He grinned. "You're not."

"Says you," she grumbled playfully and stuck out her tongue.

Melanie moved from the table and refilled her coffee mug before re-joining us.

As she returned, I wiped my mouth with a napkin. "You made this?" I asked Beaux. "It's really good."

He pointed at my dad. "I had a good instructor."

"That Yankee wouldn't have known what to do without my help."

"I dunno," Beaux said. "I think maybe I was meant to be a southerner in my bones. Good people, no snow, all this deep fried food and BBQ. I was made for this place."

My dad laughed, and while they bickered about who was the Yankee and who could cook better, I focused on eating my food. Just enough to feel better, not too much my stomach would revolt again. It was always a tricky line and one I'd crossed in my early college days more than once.

Beaux refilled my coffee when it was empty and as he returned to the table, the front door opened and Jaxon appeared.

Once again, he was dressed in all black, his sunglasses tucked into the collar of his black T-shirt.

"Yum," Melanie whispered.

She wasn't talking about the food she was still trying to eat. I bumped her knee with mine and shushed her.

"Dear Lord, woman," she whisper-hissed back. "If I can't touch, at least let me look. Rambo Sexy Pants is the best cure for a hangover, even in visual form only."

"We can all hear you," Beaux said, his shoulders shaking with laughter. "You whisper as quietly as an elephant stomps."

At the head of the table, Jaxon didn't make any movement or give any indication he heard her. I was certain he was part robot.

Maybe more Terminator than Rambo.

Regardless, he arched a brow at Beaux. "You tell her yet?"

And...that was the sound of evading and pretending life wasn't a shitstorm coming to an abrupt halt.

"What is it?"

"Finish your food," Beaux said. "We'll talk then."

I wanted to argue, but I did what he said. What were a few more minutes to pretend we were just hanging out, enjoying a random morning of family and fun?

"WE FOUND cameras outside the garage of your work."

That came from Jaxon. He was now standing in my living room and all of us assembled gave a freaky deja-vu feeling to yesterday.

Unlike yesterday, Beaux was sitting next to me on the couch. Melanie was on my other side. Mike had shown up after breakfast and he'd pulled a chair up next to my dad's recliner.

Jaxon had taken the position at the front of the room like we were in some professional debriefing. I supposed we were.

Didn't mean I liked it. Especially once he crossed his bulging arms, biceps and ink popping all over the place, looked directly at me, and gave me that beautiful nugget of information.

"Cameras?"

"No audio and they were basic. Not top of the line and not live-streamed."

I'd had less than a day to process the fact someone was following me. Once Melanie and I started drinking, I'd done my best to avoid thinking about this at all.

But some woman had cameras on me? At our garage?

I shook my head as if to shake it free so what I'd heard would make sense. "Where else?"

"Nowhere we've found yet. But you need to know we left the cameras."

"What?" I gasped.

"Listen," Beaux said, holding me tight against him even as I tried to wiggle away. "Just listen."

I scanned the room, and my blood turned cold. Everyone was watching me like a wounded animal, afraid I'd jump and flee.

Yet none of them seemed surprised. "You all knew?"

"Jaxon told us last night," Dad said. "It's why I told Beaux to back off when he suggested you stop drinking. Figured you earned it whether you knew it or not."

"But, cameras...?"

"And we're going to keep them," Jaxon said.

My dad's jaw popped and Beaux tightened his grip on me. Still, none of them were surprised. Their faces were masks of frustration and anger, but not shock.

"Excuse me?"

"They're not streamed cameras. Means whoever put them up has to come collect them at some point. I've got two men on the building after hours. Don't know when they last collected them, but if Beaux's been getting a letter a week and that last photo she sent to him was a week ago, figure it'll happen any day."

"Unless she shows up and stalks me or the garage, and somehow she's already seen you."

Jaxon blinked twice. I was certain that was Rambo-man speak for "don't think I'm stupid and didn't think of that."

I flung my hands out. "So, what? That's the big plan? To sit around and wait? Hunker down behind a few hydrangea bushes and wait for some psycho to come get a video camera?"

"Unless Raleigh PD comes back with evidence, it's one of them, yeah."

"What's the other?" Because that first idea sucked. It meant waiting. Going to work and knowing I was being watched and followed and some psycho who's threatened my life could sit back and laugh at the absurdity of it all, all while plotting my death and clearing her path to Beaux.

"Draw her out," Jaxon said. "You two spend more time in public. We'll be watching. Figure you get enough attention, that'll set her off and she'll make her move."

"Which I'm still adamant about absolutely not doing," Beaux growled. His fingers dug into my shoulder, his arm vibrating with the same intensity as the tone of his voice.

My dad shook his head.

"I think I prefer the wait and see plan," I muttered.

I wasn't brave. I also wasn't stupid. Being watched on a camera seemed way safer than being a sitting duck in the middle of the open.

Jaxon dipped his chin, but somehow, it seemed like I'd disappointed him.

He might be Rambo, but I wasn't. I was just a silly, silly girl in love with the man next to me, hoping like hell we made it out of this, and this person was caught without anyone getting hurt.

So, no thank you, be disappointed all you want, Jaxon. No way was I putting myself in the line of fire so he could have more excitement to his job.

TWENTY-EIGHT
BEAUX

She didn't remember. Paige didn't remember telling me she loved me. I knew Paige. In the last two months I knew her so well I was certain I was beginning to know her better than she knew herself.

I'd firmly believed once she remembered telling me she loved me before she passed out, she'd blush when she saw me. Or she'd bring it up and brush it off.

She did neither. She came down for breakfast acting like nothing was wrong, and even when Jaxon was talking about what he'd found at the garage, reaffirming afterward he'd increased the security system there, was planning one installed in the house, and double-checking mine this afternoon, Paige had almost seemed calm.

Too calm. Eerily, spookily, quiet and serene, which wasn't an emotion I knew her to possess.

I was calm and laid back.

She was stressed and serious.

Type B versus Type A to the max.

While I was boiling with fury and anger and impatience,

the fact she'd settled into me like we're preparing for tea time, was more unsettling than if she'd been a nervous wreck.

There wasn't a lot I could do. Practice would go for hours, and I needed to get going, so I pulled her out to the front porch, noticing how she scanned her front yard before looking at me.

"Don't worry," I said, cupping her cheeks. "Everything will be fine."

"I know." She grinned up at me. "I have you."

Straight to the heart. Almost as beautiful as the other three words she said last night. The fact she obviously didn't remember, irked me, but I wasn't going to be a dick and bring it up. If she didn't mean it, didn't mean it to say it so early, I wasn't going to add stress to her life pointing it out.

I just really fucking hoped she meant it.

My eyes searched her, looking for clues and I saw nothing.

Damn. Pain and beauty at the same time stoked the fire in my chest. All the emotions I had for her, everything I felt, pounded against me to let it out. I would. A better moment, a different time, when fear wasn't lurking behind her hazel eyes.

"Have a good day. I'll call you later."

She glanced at the front door and back to me. "Sleepover at your house tonight?"

Which meant getting laid. Multiple times. Lots of places. "I'll have Jaxon bring you over once I'm home. You going to be okay?"

"Yeah. Eventually. It's scary, but Mike and Dad are telling me to stay home at least this week, so I'll just be here with Melanie. Hanging out."

"No wine," I teased.

She made a face. "No more wine."

"All right. I gotta get going. Kiss me."

She rolled her eyes, but she still moved to her toes, hands on my shoulders and she leaned in. I met her halfway and covered her mouth with mine, slid my tongue into her eager mouth and devoured her. Hot, hard, and quick, when I pulled back, it took her a moment to fall back to her heels and open her eyes.

And that was when I saw it.

Her love for me.

Shining so bright it almost blinded me.

I hurried down the stairs with that look on her face, Paige watching me, and then fucking slapped myself upside the head because I still hadn't told her about paying her dad's hospital bill. Or that there was no way she was going back to waitressing.

Fuck.

We had time, though. Plenty of it to get to that tonight after I gave her an orgasm or two.

"BEAUX—"

God. I hoped the way Paige gritted out my name when she was close to coming would always sound so hot to my ears like it did now.

She was on her back, my arms beneath her legs, spreading her wide at the knees. Her hands were wrapped around the wood slats on my headboard. I had half-dozen different, delicious, visions in my head of how we could use those slats.

They mostly involved her tied to them.

Paige's entire body was trembling as I pounded into her. There was nothing holding me back. Her hot heat tight around my dick felt like heaven. Every time I sank inside of Paige, I never wanted it to end.

She just felt so damn good.

"Please," she whimpered. Her eyes were on where we were

connected, my dick sliding in and out of her, and hell if I didn't love that. She always watched. Like she couldn't believe how glorious it felt to have me inside of her and she didn't want to miss a minute of it.

"Touch yourself," I told her. "Get yourself off with me inside you."

My hips ached from the movement. When she arrived at my house, I didn't give her much time to talk. She looked too damn beautiful, dressed in a wrap dress I hadn't yet seen.

Why she dressed up just to come to my house, I didn't know, but I damn well showed my appreciation by stalking to her, untying the belt at her waist, tossing her purse to the floor and sinking to my knees.

After I'd eaten her, I'd carried her to my room, where I'd played with her some before finally becoming undone with the overwhelming sensation to have her.

But now, I needed her to come again. I needed my release but hell if I was taking mine before giving her another one. There was nothing better than feeling her come around my tongue, and then around my dick.

Addicted. I was addicted to Paige and her cunt and I didn't give a shit.

"Come on, Paige." I could barely grunt the words, but she finally listened, slid one of her hands down to her center.

Her fingers went straight to her clit and then spread out, so I was sliding between her fingers.

"Damn."

Ecstasy. Who needed drugs to get high when making love to a woman was the best possible fucking adrenaline rush in the world.

"Beaux." Her thighs quivered, her pussy gripped me, and ripples shot through her body until she unraveled, flying high and tossing her head back. She quaked from her orgasm and while she was still in the thrall, I slammed inside of her, gripping her hips and pulling her against me.

"Damn," I said, "Fucking perfect. Every time."

She shivered as I held her still, releasing deep inside her.

I collapsed onto her, keeping most my weight off and she wrapped her legs and arms around me, kissing my shoulder, my throat, until I bent down and claimed her mouth.

We were slickened with sweat from exertion, her hair stuck to her cheeks and I brushed it back as I pulled away.

"Phenomenal," I whispered, peppering her cheek and her lips with kisses. "I love being inside you."

"I love having you there."

She grinned at me, that same love shining in her eyes I saw earlier.

Fuck, I wanted to tell her. Needed to tell her, and then was the perfect time.

"Paige—"

Her stomach growled and she laughed, squeezing my dick tight.

"I'm sorry." She laughed harder and I pulled out of her, rolling to the side. "I haven't eaten, like all day."

"We'll feed you then."

"We can order in. Pizza?"

"God, no. All that biscuits and gravy from breakfast this morning weighed me down at practice. More carbs tonight would kill me."

She rolled to her side and kissed my cheek. "You're such a health nut. Protein shakes and massive amounts of chicken. I've seen your fridge."

"And steak. I love a good steak."

"Funny." She winked. "I like a good chunk of meat too."

"Trust me, I know how much you like your meat."

She playfully slapped my arm and I grabbed her hand,

pulling her to her feet as I stood off the bed. "Let's get cleaned up and get food in you. You'll need more energy later."

~

I COULDN'T REMEMBER a time in my life when everything felt so damn easy. Sure, I had fun. I decided early on when my dream of hitting the NFL became closer to turning into a reality I was going to make sure I enjoyed every damn moment of it. From sponsors and free shoes and a whole host of shit I was given, life was going to be fun.

But it had never felt this enjoyable before, at least not that I could remember. Considering Shannon and I grew up with barely two pennies to rub together half the time, I'd always had to work my ass off for everything I earned.

Football was no different. Hard, grueling, muscle-aching and unending work.

Being with Paige wasn't work. It didn't even matter when she was pissed at me or that it'd taken time for her to see the guy I was. When Paige was around me, all the hard work, the grueling workouts, the bad practices, it all paled to how important she was to me.

She made all of it, every moment of the work and the training, worth it to have everything I had so I could give it all to her. She moved around my home like she was made to live there, comfortable in my space. Even though she'd been under a hell of a lot of stress this last year with her dad, then his surgery several weeks ago, and now the letters, when she was with me, it was as if all of that faded to background noise, too.

We clicked, in a way I never truly believed possible. So that even while we were standing in the kitchen, washing and drying dishes after dinner, all I could imagine and think of was her. In my home. Hopefully forever.

She fit there, and I wanted her there. I just knew I'd have to convince her of it. At least with the help of Melanie, she might not feel so guilty of moving out either, and it wasn't that we didn't have time to take things slow, we did.

I just preferred to go after what I wanted and not quit until I had it.

And I wanted Paige living with me.

"Last one," she said, rinsing off a plate, and handing it to me. "What should we do now?"

I dried the plate with a towel and set them down on the counter, blocking Paige in. "I know what I want to do." I cupped her cheek with my hand. "A little bit more of what we did earlier."

"Only a little bit?"

Good Lord, I loved her teasing banter.

"We'll see," I pressed my lips against hers. "It'll depend on how much of a good girl you could be."

"I—" She was cut off by her phone ringing, and even I knew by now it was her dad's ringtone.

"Get it." I stepped back and gave her space to reach for her phone. She'd checked it when we came downstairs for dinner and brought her purse I'd thrown to the floor earlier into the kitchen. "We can finish this later."

"Oh, we will." She winked at me, still smiling as she answered the phone. "Hey, Dad. What's up?"

Her happy look evaporated and her eyes shot to mine.

Cool pricks of ice cascaded down my spine. "What is it?"

"Yeah. Beaux's here," she said, ignoring me, but still watching me. "Why do you need—"

Worst-case possible scenarios flashed in my mind and her tone immediately went angry.

"Are you kidding me? No, you can't talk to him." She hung

up the phone and tossed her phone down. It skated across the counter, stopping precariously on the edge.

"What's going on? What happened?"

Her brows arched and her hands slammed to her hips. I'd seen that look before in a woman. Typically on Shannon—when she was PMSing and I'd stolen the last of the ice cream.

"What's wrong?" I asked again. Her chest rose and fell, long, measured movements.

Eventually, she rolled her lips together and then asked, "What's wrong?"

I was a man. There were questions women asked, in a certain tone, that we learned not to answer or we were a sinking chub in a school of sharks.

I was no fucking chub.

If she was pissed, it could only mean one thing. One thing I should have mentioned earlier but was too consumed with Paige to care to bring it up.

I leaned back against the counter and relaxed. "I take it you heard from the hospital?"

He paid our fucking medical bills.

He paid our medical bills.

In full.

With cash.

Heat singed my blood, making my entire body tremble. My hands shook, and I had to force them to my hips so I didn't wrap my hands around Beaux's sexy, corded throat.

I would take his home nurse because he spoke with my dad and my dad's medical care was still his decision.

I had to deal with that, even though I didn't like it, but it also gave me Melanie, and I was really beginning to love the crap out of her craziness.

But this? And God. It helped so much. I was trembling between fury and gratefulness, and I had no idea which one I should feel.

"Explain to me why you'd do this."

Each word was clipped. My throat already dry from the heat rushing through my veins. Beaux knew how important it was to take care of my dad.

He crossed his arms over his chest and shook his head. "It kills me you don't know why I'd do this for you. Because I care, maybe?"

"I didn't ask for this, Beaux. In fact, I remember very clearly I said I didn't want you helping me! This is my family, my dad, my responsibility." I threw my hands into my hair. Red was creeping in at the edges of my vision.

I might have been overreacting, but goddamn. I didn't want him to do this for me. I wanted to be the one who could take care of my dad. And now, every time I turned around, someone was making it so I didn't have to.

"That doesn't mean you can't take help when it's offered, Paige."

"But you didn't offer! You strong-armed me into accepting it without giving me a choice. How could you do this?"

"Because I care? Because I can."

"God. Stop!" Screw his millions and his ability to buy trucks with cash and throw equal amounts of money at my feet without blinking an eye. "Do you know how crappy that makes me feel when you say that, Beaux? That the only reason my dad is being taken care of is because of you, because you have boatloads of money and I have nothing? Have you once stopped to think how shitty that makes me feel? That you think I'm so incapable of doing something for the only family I have that you have to swoop in and save me? Save him?"

"Paige—" His voice softened and he stepped forward.

I threw up my hands. "Fuck you for pitying me, Beaux. I don't need this shit. You—"

"I'm not your damn mom, Paige. Shut up and listen to me, would you?"

I jerked back like he'd backhanded me. "What? My mom?"

"Yes." He shoved a finger at me. "You said after she left,

you hated that she sent you expensive things and money. You said she couldn't buy your love. That's now what I'm doing."

God. My head spun. He'd remembered that? Was that why I was so mad at him for this? I couldn't focus. Couldn't think. "I'm not pissed about my mom. I'm pissed you did this without asking me first."

"Bullshit. To you, it's all the same. I love that you don't care about my money, but I also have it and when I can, I'm going to spend it. Not to buy your love, but so I can help people I care about. It's different."

It was and it wasn't. And I was so thrown from all of it, how well he knew me, maybe better than I knew myself, I didn't have a comeback. Maybe he was right that I was thinking about my mom, throwing money at me once she got a new life, but it wasn't everything.

I wanted to be the one to take care of my dad, and not being able to made me feel so damn worthless some days I couldn't think straight. Dad was all I had, and I couldn't even take care of him the way he needed without needing someone else's wallet.

"I need to think." I turned and ran for the stairs. I needed a minute to process everything I was feeling and thinking without Beaux's inspection.

With my hands still trembling, I ripped off his shirt I'd tossed on earlier and grabbed my dress, flinging it over my head.

I was trying to knot the belt at my waist when Beaux's footsteps headed my way from down the hall. They were unhurried, but even from the thudded echo, I could tell he was determined.

And probably pissed, but too bad, so was I.

"I don't pity you," he said.

I snatched my panties up off the floor and turned toward his bathroom. "I don't want to talk right now."

He huffed and followed me.

I had just tugged on my underwear when I caught his reflection in the bathroom mirror, one shoulder resting against the doorframe. I did my best to ignore him, but after we'd gotten dressed earlier, he'd thrown on a pair of gray sweatpants and forgone a shirt.

All I saw were muscled biceps and the planes of his firm stomach. That sweet, sweet V-muscle that popped above his hipbones and the thick trail of his blonde hair above his waistband.

The man was dangerously sexy, and even upset, I wasn't immune.

"I care about you, Paige. I get you're pissed I paid your dad's bills without talking to you about it, but there's nothing wrong with taking someone's help, and I've got it to give."

"You should have asked."

"Would you have allowed it?"

"That's not the point." I slapped the counter and spun, putting my backside to the countertop and glaring at him. "It's my family. My responsibility. I get to decide how things are handled, not steamrolled just because you can. That's not fair. I don't need your glamour or your glitter. In some ways, this is no different than my mom."

"You're right."

"Pardon?"

"You're right, it's not fair. You know what else isn't fair? You're gearing up right now to run, cataloguing in your sweet little mind all the things that's wrong with us, why you don't need me, and downstairs, we were just doing the fucking dishes and all I was thinking of was how fucking perfect you looked in my house and how much I want you here."

Wave after wave of shock slapped at me, like brutal oceans crashing into shore with every word he spoke, with the volume of emotion behind them. I stared at him, completely breathless.

"What?"

"Yeah, so you want to walk out of here and be pissed at me for taking care of what's mine? You want to slam that door in my face again after all I've shown you about the man I am and how much you mean to me? Go right ahead." He flipped his hand out toward his bedroom.

Toward the door.

And I knew he meant his front door. Literally and figuratively.

It wasn't what I wanted. At all.

I shook my head. "Beaux—"

"But you gotta know one thing." He stepped in front of me, eating the space between us in one large stride, and glared down at me. "I love you, Paige. I'm so fucking in love with you I can't see straight half the time, and even when I'm on the field, I'm thinking of you. No one has ever distracted me from the game. I can stand in front of you, right now, flat out giving you everything I have, all of me." He punctuated his chest and his statement with his finger. "And I can tell you I don't give a shit. For the first time in my life, I've found something, someone, I want more than football. I know you feel it too. I see it in your eyes every time you look at me. I want to hear it."

I opened my mouth. Shut it.

"And don't lie to me," he said, leaning down and bracing himself on the counter next to me. He caged me in, the heat of his anger and frustration rolling off him. Good God. People shouldn't be this pissed off when they're admitting they love someone. And was that what he'd done? I was having trouble thinking straight.

"Beaux—"

"I know you love me." His gaze was knowing. Hot. Angry

and filled with something else that looked like a mixture of wanting to scoop me up and throw me on his bed or choke the breath out of me.

And God. He knew.

He had heard me last night.

All the fight left me in a forceful rush of breath. "I don't like not being able to take care of him. I hate it. Hate it with every fiber of my being and I hate having to lean on people for it."

"That's what people do when they love one another. It's not a list to keep track of, Paige. I give to you when I can, and you give to me when you can. It's us, leaning on each other, and trust me, babe, you don't give to me in money, but you give yourself and that's all I need."

His arms surrounded me tightly, no hesitation, he just pulled me into his body and held me while I whispered apologies.

He was so warm. So damn safe and strong.

And he was right. I loved him. Definitely. I'd still been keeping him at a distance, letting him close to me while keeping one hand out, firmly in place, so he didn't get too close.

I had to drop the hand and let him walk all the way in, or this was never going to work.

I could keep him out and lose him. Or let him in and have something better than anything I'd ever imagined.

Vulnerability sucked, but it was the only choice.

I sniffed, fought back tears and pushed against his stomach. His hand was at my head and he gave me space, but not much.

"You have my word, right now, I won't make decisions like that without your input, but you can't ask me not to help someone when I can, Paige. It's not in me to avoid that when I have so damn much to give."

"I know." I sniffed again. With tears blurring my vision, I gazed at him. So damn strong. "I wasn't thinking of running. I just like space when I'm upset so I don't say something stupid and regret it."

He arched a brow but stayed silent.

"And sometimes," I said, chuckling. "I still do. I would have gotten over it, I would have put all the pieces together you said, but sometimes I need to go through all the emotions before I get to the logic."

His steel blue eyes flickered back and forth between mine and then his hands slid to my cheeks. "Don't run from me when you're pissed. Let it out. I'd rather argue about it than watch you flee from me. Okay?"

"I'll try."

"Now tell me what I want to hear."

My heart stalled and everything inside me cooled. "Beaux—"

"Guarantee you right now, Paige, there's nowhere else, no other time when you'll ever be safer."

It didn't feel safe. It felt like standing on the edge of a bridge, staring down into stormy waters that were your doom.

But I'd opened the door. So with both feet, I jumped.

"I love you, B—"

It was all I got out before he stole the rest of his name from my breath with his mouth slamming down onto mine.

THIRTY

PAIGE

"What do you think of these flowers?" Shannon asked. She pointed to a photograph of a bouquet of beautiful and elegant white roses.

We were at a floral shop looking for flowers for her wedding. While she and Powell weren't getting married until spring when the season was done, Shannon was in full-planning mode.

"Aren't you getting married out at his farm?"

"Ranch."

Tomato, to-mah-to. When I learned Oliver Powell lived in a small house in the middle of nowhere with horses, you could have knocked me over with a feather.

"But it's in the spring, right, and small?"

"Yeah. Roses might be too formal."

I agreed. We flipped through the books the florist had provided and finally my finger landed on a beautiful spread. "What about these?"

Shannon looked to where I pointed and gasped. "Ooh."

"These large alliums are gorgeous. If you do the alliums

and a mixture of the roses or these lilies that could be really pretty, but still not so fancy."

She turned to me and grinned. "You and the other bridesmaid could carry the large alliums, and I could do the mixed bouquet."

Yeah, she'd asked me to a bridesmaid.

That made me get drunk. Beaux and I weren't just a pair, Shannon swept me into her family and included me in everything.

In the last two weeks, Shannon, Oliver, Beaux, and I had gotten together for a few more dinners. I'd stopped in repeatedly to Stamped, and she'd come to my house one night when the guys were in Detroit playing an away game against the Lions. That night, Jillian Rudolph, wife to another Rough Rider, Danny Rudolph, had joined her as well.

It'd seemed surreal. We watched an NFL game, in my childhood living room home, on a smaller than average flat screen television while my dad, who was now in a walking boot and flying through physical therapy, shouted at every play.

I was friends with people in the NFL. I was dating the best quarterback in the league.

And every time I met someone on the team, I was floored with how normal they were.

The season was half-over and they hadn't lost once. Every week, the hype over another Super Bowl appearance grew louder, and the louder the chatter, the more serious Beaux became.

It was sexy as hell. His intensity and focus and undying devotion to not only his job but his absolute love of the game, made me fall in love with him more and more every day.

I was in love with Beaux Hale. Beaux Hale was in love with me. I still couldn't even think the thoughts without blushing like a pre-teen with her first crush, but that's essentially what Beaux was to me...my first real love.

Today, Beaux had flown up to New York for an interview with some sportscaster named Curt Banner. He was coming home immediately afterward, arriving after midnight, and then early Saturday morning he was flying out again for a game in Tennessee.

Shannon and I were shopping for flowers and then heading to Ride'Em Rough for dinner and to watch Beaux's interview live. I hadn't been back since I called Paulie and told him I wouldn't be returning at all, and after he spewed off a small handful of half-meant insults, I'd felt like crap for not going in to at least see Hannah.

But in truth, I hardly went anywhere. Jaxon was my new shadow, usually following me everywhere I went, and sometimes it felt more like a hassle to go out than it did to stay in. I hadn't heard anything else about more photos. Nothing creepy, like a dead bird on my porch, had shown up. But there were days when Jaxon went more alert and Beaux hovered like a mama bird, and I knew they'd received more threats.

I was staying out of it. I wasn't burying my head in the sand. I was choosing to trust Beaux to take care of me like he promised. I trusted Jaxon to shoot anyone who looked at me funny, too.

His presence, while terrifying and nerve-wracking at first, was now more like a very hot, solid security blanket.

One Melanie was still trying to worm her way under to no effect.

Poor thing.

"Okay." Shannon slammed the design book closed and stood up. "That's done, then. Let's go eat. I'm starving."

"You're sure?" I asked. "I mean, this is only the first florist, and you don't even know if they can do what you're suggesting."

"I'll figure it out."

"You're like, the calmest bride-to-be I've ever come across. It's eerily scary."

"That's because my wedding doesn't matter. It's just a formality. I already know my marriage to Oliver is going to be beautiful. He shows it to me everyday."

Whatever insecurities, as small as they were, I had about Beaux fluttered away like butterfly wings as Shannon spoke. We were way too early to even discuss marriage.

But she was right. Beaux showed me every day and had since the night we met, how beautiful a life with him could be. It wasn't the money. It was everything else he brought with him. Security. Love. Laughter. An extended family who accepted my dad and I just as we were.

In short, Beaux gave me everything I'd ever dreamed of and much, much more.

I was one lucky girl.

"HEY, HANNAH!" I threw my arms around her as we reached the table in her section. We were close enough to the bar so we could watch the interview when Beaux came on, far enough away to have some privacy in a booth. "How are you?"

"Oh, you know me," she said, hugging me back. "Same, same. Good to see you. Who's this?"

She glanced at Shannon with a cool look in her eye and I frowned. "Hannah, this is Shannon, Beaux's sister. Shannon this is my friend, Hannah."

"It's lovely to meet you," Shannon said.

Hannah took her hand. "You too. Powell's fiancée, right?"

There was a tone in her voice that was friendly enough, but not the same excitement she usually had. "Hannah's a huge Rough Riders fan," I said to Shannon.

Shannon winked at her. "Aren't we all?"

"Yes, well, only the lucky ones get them, I suppose." She grinned at me. "I'll be right back with your waters. Y'all want anything else to drink?"

We gave our drink orders and she walked away. I slowly turned away from her and slid in the booth across from Shannon. "Weird. She's usually tickled pink when anyone connected to the Rough Riders come in. Plus, she didn't even give her typical googly eyes to Jaxon here."

I nudged him, which was the same as slamming into a brick wall. Like usual, Jaxon said very little, his eyes alert and focused as he scanned the restaurant.

"Chill, Rambo," I whispered. "There's no one dangerous here."

He shot me a look telling me how naive I was and opened his menu.

I shook off Hannah's coolness and looked around the restaurant. It was busy but not slammed, a pretty typical Thursday night. I set my menu to the side while Shannon looked at hers. I'd worked there long enough to know I'd be ordering the southwestern burger with an extra side of onion rings.

They were my favorite.

Hannah came back, chatting with us just enough to do her job, and the longer we sat there, having a couple beers and waiting for our food to arrive, I couldn't shake the strange feeling I'd seriously pissed her off.

And I felt like crap for it.

She wasn't a close friend, but until Melanie and Beaux and everyone who came with him fell into my lap, she'd pretty much been all I had.

Beaux's interview was just starting to come on, Curt Banner introducing him when she returned with our food.

Sliding everything onto the table, she looked at the television that held our focus. On it, was a split screen shot of Curt and Beaux.

"You know," Hannah said, "It's funny. You put their two faces next to each other like that and they look really similar. Don't you think?"

I was already looking at the images, but I was more focused on Beaux. Because how could you not be? The man wasn't just sexy as sin, he was all mine.

"I don't know," I said, at the same time Shannon did. "But their face shape, maybe."

"I think it's the eyes," Hannah said. "They both have the same blue eyes. And sexy lips."

That was the Hannah I knew.

"Yeah," I laughed. "He does have some sexy lips."

She rolled her eyes but lost her smile. Not even a comeback or innuendo to tease me. Strange. "Well, I should get moving. Just shout if y'all need anything."

She turned in a huff and I went back to the television screen.

We watched the interview, me mostly gazing at Beaux's smile as he talked about the team, the season, and everything in between. We sat through a few commercial breaks, and I was shoving an onion ring into my mouth when an image of Beaux and I outside their practice field popped onto the screen.

I'd met him there a few times when he was done working out or after practices so we could go out, and there were usually reporters there. It didn't surprise me they'd taken our photo at some point.

Curt smiled, asking Beaux a question, and Beaux's lips pulled into a thin line.

"Told you, Curt. My personal life is just that."

"Yeah, man, we all know. But come on. Give us something about this girl you've been with. Nobody's ever seen you tied to someone so many times."

"She's special to me," Beaux said, "And that's all you're getting."

The camera flashed back to Beaux. I was a mixture of nerves, glancing around the restaurant, seeing if anyone had recognized me, knew I was there, and cold needles pricked down my spine.

I turned and saw Hannah watching the television. Her eyes narrowed into a glare and then a little smirk as she turned and waved at me, flashing me a thumbs up.

I laughed and turned back to the table.

No one in the restaurant cared at all we were there. To make sure, I turned to Jaxon. "Everything okay?"

"Be better when you're out of this place. Something doesn't feel right."

"It's probably all that hot sauce you used."

He glared at me. I was used to it. "Eat your food."

"Aye-aye, Rambo."

He shook his head. He didn't think his nickname was nearly as cute as Melanie and I did.

Whatever.

We finished our dinner, Hannah still keeping her distance, and it only made me want to clear the air.

"Hey, girl," I said when she brought us our check. "Do you get off soon? I was hoping we could hang out and have a drink when you're off and catch up."

"Sure. That'd be great if you're not too busy."

"Never," I said, softening my voice. "Never for you, and I'm sorry if I've made you think that lately."

"Okay then. I'm off in twenty minutes."

Shannon took the check before I could protest and slid a credit card into the slot. "And I'm ready to pay for this, Hannah."

Hannah took the folder and went to ring us out. Once she returned, Shannon slid out of the booth and we said our good-byes. I was going to stay with Jaxon at the bar until Hannah was done, but there was no reason for Shannon to stick around.

"Thanks again for your help with my flowers today," she said. "And thanks for loving my brother."

"Both easy things to manage, Shannon. I'll see you soon."

She waved goodbye and once she was gone, I pointed at Jaxon. "You stay by the door, or the other side of the bar while I'm with Hannah. We have girl stuff to talk about."

"I'll be right there." He pointed to a spot by the front door where he could stand like a centurion guard. I already knew why he'd picked the spot. He could see almost the whole restaurant along with the hallway to the bathrooms, but he could keep an eye on me at the bar at the same time.

"Aye-aye, Rambo."

"Jesus Christ," he muttered. "Go, but don't get too drunk."

We were on drink number two, sitting at the bar with Joey serving us. For a few minutes, it'd felt like old times. Hannah came over as soon as she was done, changed out of her Ride'Em Rough uniform and into a slinky, sexy black tank top and scalloped pale pink shorts before she took a seat next to me.

Joey and Hannah and I talked. We giggled about Beaux and I answered all of her questions, even the ones like how he was in bed that made me slightly uncomfortable. It was girl talk, plain and simple, and if I had to step outside to mend the bridge, I'd do it.

When I asked how her life was, she waved me off. "Same old, same old. Struggling to pay for college. Guys all suck. You know how it is." She took a sip of her drink. "Or, at least you did."

"Yeah, but there are good guys out there. You'll find one."

"Sure." She didn't look like she believed me, but before I could pry into why she seemed more stressed than usual, she pointed at Jaxon. "What's with the scary guy staring at us?"

"That's Jaxon. He's my security. It's a long story."

"Security? What happened?"

The gleam in her eyes I'd been missing was back, so I started telling her everything I could, and when I was done, she was watching Jaxon.

"They don't know who it is?"

"Nope. And I've sort of stopped being concerned about it. I know letters still come but I don't see them anymore. And personally, I think if something was going to happen, it would have weeks ago when the letters started coming."

"Maybe whoever it is, didn't want to move too hard too fast."

"Geez, Hannah, thanks for the comforting thought."

"Sorry." She laughed and finished her drink. "You'll have sweet dreams tonight now, huh?"

I was sleeping next to Beaux tonight. Headed to his house and waiting for him when he arrived from New York. I didn't tell her I always had sweet dreams when I was in his bed.

I changed the subject, moved it back to her and the classes she was taking that semester. She was in college to become an elementary education teacher and with her usual, peppy personality; I could totally see her teaching a classroom of six-year-olds all day long. By the time we finished our third drink, we'd also devoured a plate of nachos and another order of onion rings when Hannah suggested she took me home. We'd been there for hours after her shift and I was certain Jaxon was about ready to blow his own head off having to stand in one spot for that long.

"Jaxon was going to take me to Beaux's place," I said.

She rolled her eyes. "So he can follow us if he has to. Come on, I'm having fun tonight and it's been so long since we've hung out like this. I miss you."

She pouted and it did me in. "Okay. I'll let Jaxon know. Come on."

We said our goodbyes to Joey, slid off our stools and when we reached Jaxon, he looked ready to bolt.

"Ready?"

"Yeah, but Hannah's going to drive me to Beaux's. Do you mind following?"

"Your wish, my command."

"Oh," Hannah said, laughing. "That sounds like fun."

He leveled her with a look, and Hannah looked away, hiding her laugh.

This was the girl I loved. Boy crazy and goofy.

"I'm parked out back, meet us there? It's the white Nissan," she said.

"Got it." He left the restaurant and I linked arms with Hannah, pulling her toward the rear entrance we used.

As we stepped outside, I immediately jumped back into the hallway. "Holy crap! It's pouring."

"Yeah, I didn't even realize it."

Rain was coming down in thick sheets and I cringed. Thunderstorms, crazy ones, and even the occasional hurricane, were totally normal in Raleigh, but I still never got used to them.

"Um."

"It's okay." Hannah reached for my hand. "I'll keep you safe."

She tugged me into the rain and we ran to her car only a few spots away, under a shining light and a quick scan proved the entire lot as now well-lit with replaced bulbs.

I thought of Beaux and smiled.

We were drenched by the time we got into the car, and Jaxon's lights were a pale blur behind us as Hannah pulled out of the parking lot, fishtailing through a puddle as she merged into traffic.

∾

WE WERE HALFWAY to Beaux's house, the rain still not letting up and only getting worse, when I realized that as we'd been driving, Hannah had already been prepared to follow my instructions before I ever gave them.

As soon as she yanked us into traffic, not bothering to wait for Jaxon even though she knew he was following us, I sensed something that told me I'd made a major mistake.

I didn't realize what it was, but something wasn't adding up.

Hannah's hands were tight on the steering wheel, but her fingers were constantly tapping like she was nervous. She was too jittery for enjoying a night out with a friend.

"Hey, Hannah," I asked, looking out the window. "Do you know where Beaux lives?"

Tap. Tap. Tappity. Tap. Her fingers were constantly jittering.

She laughed, but it was tight and strained. "Everyone who's a fan knows where he lives, silly."

"Okay."

That wasn't right, though.

Beaux had told me he'd never had fans outside his house. Never once been photographed out of it either. He said his house wasn't even in his name, something common with famous athletes and celebrities. I hadn't asked specifics, but he'd always assured me were safe at his place when we were there.

An alarm dinged in my mind, but I pushed it down.

This was Hannah. She was nutty.

A thick silence weighed down the car and I gripped the door handle as she flew through a puddle, giving that semi-weightless feeling.

"Hey, can you slow down a bit, sweetie?"

"Oh come on, Paige. Where's your sense of fun?"

"I don't like storms."

She huffed then and laughed. But it wasn't her laugh. My gaze went to my side mirror. Behind us, I knew Jaxon was there somewhere, but I couldn't see a darn thing through the rain.

Rain pelted the car, making it hard to hear the radio and I almost missed it when Hannah finally said, "You know, I don't know what's so special about you."

The heck? My head whipped in her direction. "What? Hannah—"

"No. I mean, sure you're nice and all, but you're not all that pretty. And you definitely don't have nice boobs like me. I'm just trying to figure out, why is it you get everything you want? Why is everything so easy for you? I mean, me? I've tried to get Beaux's attention for over a year now, and he's barely said hello to me. I've got great tits. I'm nice too, damn it. Plus, I give a blowjob that makes men mindless. Can you say the same?"

She'd lost me. Totally lost me. I had no idea where this animosity was coming from, but it chilled my blood quicker than the storm had.

It wasn't until she brought up Beaux my warning siren blared in my head, but it was on full force as she took another curve too fast.

"Hey, let's slow down. We'll talk about what's upsetting you." I grabbed the oh-shit handle above the door. "Hannah! Slow down!"

Another burst of thunder and lightning lit up the sky. The storm was heavy, late in the season for such a storm but they'd been warning us about it all week.

She flew through another puddle, not bothering to brake.

"I'm not upset." Her eyes flashed to me, wild and green, and wide open. "Tell me, Paige. What is so damn special about you that suddenly, Beaux Hale gets one good look at you and it's game over for me?"

There was nothing I could do. We were driving too fast. The roads were wet. I couldn't jump out going seventy miles an hour. That'd kill me for sure.

I tried to calm her down. "It's not a competition, Hannah. You'll find someone."

"I don't want anyone!" she shouted and slammed her hand on the steering wheel.

Behind me, Jaxon's headlights were now visible in the rearview mirror. Somehow, he'd closed the distance.

I sent up flares into the karmic air, screaming for help.

"Okay," I said, my voice calm. I quieted my tone, ignored the rush of adrenaline roaring through my system. "Okay, Hannah. Please, though, pull over. We'll talk. Maybe there's someone else on the team I can set you up with."

Her head whipped to me. "You'd do that?"

Her smile was manic. Green eyes were glassy like she was drugged.

Maybe she was. I thought I knew Hannah pretty well, and I never would have guessed she was a drug addict.

I also never knew she would have been the stalker I had to worried about but all her freaking out was making that glaringly obvious.

"Of course I would. Just please, you're scaring me. We'll get home, have a drink, and we'll think of someone. Anyone."

"I want Beaux."

It was like she hadn't heard me. Perhaps she hadn't. The thunder was rolling constantly. Lightning flashed all around us. Rain hit her window so viciously I couldn't see through it, and her wipers were on full blast.

Every time she splashed through a puddle in her two-door Nissan, we did a mini-fishtail.

"Hannah, Beaux and I are in love."

"You're not!" she screamed, and I jumped back into my

seat. So much for calming her down. "He can't love someone like you. You're plain, and you have your stupid dad to take care of. He only pities you, Paige. He doesn't love you."

Two weeks ago, definitely a month ago, her accusations could have made me doubt what we had.

I had the recent benefit of spending time with Shannon. Of practically living with Beaux.

Hannah was hopped up on crazy pills and on her way to psycho town. Every word she spoke was a lie.

"That's not true, Hannah. I wish you would have talked to me about this, earlier, but I don't understand. You told me to go for him."

"Yeah, because I knew you'd toss him away and then I could be there to make him feel better. I'm better for him."

"You're not. I love him, Hannah, and I'm not giving him up."

She whipped her head toward mine and sneered. "You will if I don't give you a choice."

We hit another curve, a steep incline ahead and she didn't turn the wheel.

"I told you and him. If I can't have him, you don't get him either."

"Hannah! Slow down!" I shouted, but it was no use. I was frozen in the car, watching as she hit the curve. Rain splashed as she flew through a puddle and she didn't care one shit about the iron railing at the side of the road.

She drove right through it.

I screamed.

Metal scrunched.

The car took flight and all I saw was trees before the screechiest, eeriest sound slammed into my ears and then everything went black.

THIRTY-TWO

BEAUX

It took hours to get back to Raleigh, a flight delay due to the weather, but I kept in constant contact with Jaxon.

He'd pulled Paige from a fucking smashed car driven by Hannah.

As soon as I got his phone call, one he made while Paige was in his arms on the side of the road while he waited for an ambulance, I'd leaned over and threw up.

From the way Jaxon said everything happened, he said it wasn't an accident either. Said the girls had been drinking, but not too much.

It didn't matter.

All that mattered was seeing Paige. Holding her. *Fuck!*

I slammed my hands on the counter to the nurse in the main waiting room of the emergency room.

"Paige Halloway," I panted, breathless from worry and fear rotting my stomach. "Where is she?"

"Are you family?" the nurse asked. "Only family can be back there." She didn't look at me while she clicked on the computer screen.

"I'm family," I said. "Husband."

The word came out before I could stop it. Fuck it. I'd say or do anything, give this woman my millions to let me through those double doors.

She shot me a look. It obviously wasn't the first time she heard the lie. "Have a seat, we'll send someone out."

I didn't sit. I texted Jaxon, asking where in the hell they were.

He answered back. "Room 415 dumbass. I already told you."

"Fuck," I groaned and flipped up through my texts.

I hurried out of the emergency room to a hallway that led to the main entrance. Repeatedly pushing the button to the elevator, I willed it to show the fuck up.

I had to see her.

Needed to see she was going to be okay.

The elevators opened, waited for fucking ever to shut again despite me pounding the "door close" button and then it took another million and half fucking hours to reach the fourth floor.

I didn't bother to stop at the reception desk on the floor, I just moved like I knew where I was going, following the signs, until I saw Jaxon outside a room that had to be hers.

"How is she?"

"Sleeping. She'll be okay."

"Fuck," I knew that. He'd already said she only had minor injuries, maybe a concussion and a broken arm from where the car smashed against her when it hit a tree.

Good Lord. Not the texts I ever wanted to see in my life again.

"Didn't want to tell you this on the phone," Jaxon said. "But you should know. When I pulled her out of the car, she opened her eyes for just a second and all she said was 'It was Hannah.'"

"What was Hannah?"

"Either she meant it was Hannah who crashed the car or Hannah who was stalking you. I've got people looking into it."

"What happened to Hannah?"

"Wasn't wearing a belt. Flew through the glass. Didn't make it."

Fuck. That would kill Paige. I couldn't wrap my head around the information he was giving me, I also didn't give a shit.

If someone hurt Paige intentionally, I was glad they were dead. If that made me a heartless bastard, I didn't care.

"Her dad's in with her. He doesn't know what I told you."

"Thanks."

I walked around him and entered her room, steeling myself for the damage I was sure to see, but all I saw was Paige.

Her brown hair matted with some dried blood at her temple, but it'd been mostly cleaned up. She was lying on the bed, head tilted to her side, eyes barely open and on her dad.

She was smiling.

He was holding her hand.

Crying.

God. Pain slashed my chest and I walked to the end of the bed. "Hey, you're awake."

"You're here," she said, turning to look at me. She flinched and reached up to touch the brace around her neck. "You're finally here."

"Always."

Sam rolled his wheelchair back and gestured for me to take the empty chair. "You two talk. I'll be outside with Jaxon."

"Thanks, Sam."

"Dad, I love you," Paige croaked. Her voice was dry and scratchy and I cringed at the noise. God. But she looked okay. Better than dead, which didn't make me feel better.

"Love you too, baby girl. I'll be back tomorrow but promise you'll get some rest tonight, okay?"

"In this damn place with all the crappy food?"

"Funny." He grinned. "That's what I said last time I was here."

She smiled. He shook his head and I held the door for him while he wheeled himself out. He'd been getting better on his crutches and with a walking cast, but he must have been exhausted to be in his wheelchair.

"Can you get him home?" I asked Jaxon.

"I've got Melanie," Sam said. "She ran to get coffee but she'll be here."

"I've got work to do," Jaxon said. "Calls are coming in."

Both of us stared at him, and at the same time, said, "Call me when you know something."

He turned back to his phone, Sam wheeled himself back to the floor's waiting area, and I went back to the room.

"I saw your interview," Paige said as I pulled the chair close to her bed and collapsed into it. "You looked sexy."

I'd already forgotten about the interview.

I grabbed her hand and brought it to my mouth, kissing her, smelling her, tasting her.

"What happened?" I asked. "And are you okay?"

I'd heard it. She looked like she would be. Scratches at her temple, goose size egg in the middle of them. Her right arm was in a brace, not a cast, but over all, she looked damn lucky.

"I might have a concussion, and I hurt, but honestly, I'm okay."

"Your arm—"

"Is fine. Not broken, just sprained from when it smashed against the glass."

"God. Fuck, Paige, I'm so sorry. So damn sorry."

"It's not your fault," she said, reaching for my head but she pulled back, gasping. "My back hurts too, I guess."

"Don't move, then. Tell me what happened."

"I don't know. But Hannah, she just, I don't know how to say it, snapped? We were having drinks, having fun and she said she'd take me to your place. Then I realized she already knew where to go, and when I asked her about it, she totally freaked out."

"Hannah? It was Hannah. That's what you told Jaxon. Do you remember?"

She shook her head, closed her eyes as if thinking hurt her. "No. The car crashed and I woke up in the ambulance, that's all I know. But I think she was the stalker. She started ranting about how I didn't deserve you, how she did, and the last thing she said after I told her I loved you, was that if she couldn't have you, I didn't get to either. Then she turned the wheel and she flew off the road. She meant to do it."

Her chin wobbled and tears fell from her eyes before I even realized she'd started crying.

"Shit." I climbed into the tiny bed next to her and lay on my side, holding her, careful not to hurt her, but comforting her.

"I was so scared," she said through her tears, shoulders shaking. "It came out of nowhere, and it was storming, and I hate it when it rains that hard, and then she was yelling at me, and the sounds..."

"Shhh. We'll talk later."

The sound of stormy waters rushed through my ears as I held her, willing her to calm down while trying to settle myself. It didn't work for me, but eventually, her cries dwindled, her sniffling stopped, and she relaxed into me.

"I love you," I whispered. "Love you so damn much. I was so fucking scared when Jaxon called me."

"I love you, too. I was so scared."

"I know, but I got you. I promise."

Not that they were worth much. Jaxon and I had promised her she'd stay safe and wouldn't get hurt. We both failed her. But there was another day to wallow in guilt, now she needed me to be strong for her.

I held her while she slept, not sleeping a fucking wink well into the middle of the night when a nurse came in to check her vitals.

She glared at me until I climbed out of the bed and settled in the chair next to Paige's bed. "How is she?"

"Vitals look good," the nurse said. "We'll know more in the morning."

She left the room quietly, and I didn't know if it was the exhaustion, the adrenaline coursing through my system finally evaporating, or the nurse's reassurance Paige was doing well, but I rested my arms on the bed, dropped my head, and I was asleep as soon as my eyes closed.

THIRTY-THREE
PAIGE

I ached everywhere. Every minuscule movement sent shocks of pain rippling through my entire body.

I'd never been in a car accident before last night. I'd never so much as fallen out of a tree, and I wasn't athletic enough to play sports when I was growing up.

This was the absolute worst pain I could imagine, and even then, I knew I was still, really freaking lucky.

All last night I'd been battered with nightmares. Hannah's face floated through my visions, screaming at me, and even as I was drifting awake, already knowing Beaux was right next to me because I could sense him anywhere, I still had no clue why she'd done what she did.

What was she thinking?

I couldn't reconcile the sweet, playful girl I'd worked with for months with the psychotic and shitty racecar driver she'd been last night.

I'd always thought I was a decent judge of character, but damn, I was way off with her.

I shivered as I remembered the last thing she'd yelled at me, and jerked away, my eyes meeting Beaux's concerned one.

"You okay?"

"I was thinking of Hannah," I said, wiping the sleep from my eyes and yawning. "How is she?"

A muscle jumped in Beaux's cheek and his jaw went tight.

"Beaux?"

"We'll talk about it later. When you're better."

I was sore and in pain, but I was damn lucky. Nothing was broken, nothing permanently damaged. The doctor had said I'd been lucky, might have a few scars where my head crashed into the glass, but my hair could hide them. The possible concussion had concerned him the most, which was the reason they admitted me overnight. Otherwise, I could have been sent home.

"I'm fine, Beaux. Tell me."

He rolled his lips and heaved a breath. "She wasn't wearing a seat belt, Paige."

"What?"

It took me a moment, but I slowly understood. I shook my head, trying to shake away the tears already flooding my eyes. The girl had literally tried to kill me. I knew that even if I didn't want to admit it. And she was obviously sick, needed some help.

"What happened?" I asked when Beaux didn't say anything further.

"Babe, she didn't make it."

He reached for me, grabbed my hand and held it tight. "She went through the windshield and into a tree."

"She..." I tried to picture her. Laughing. Smiling. Teasing me. She was so young. Had everything in front of her. The world. Sweet parents. I couldn't see any of that. All I saw were green eyes as she shouted at me. Her manic screams once she got me in the car. "She died?"

Beaux nodded. A shudder rolled through me and I braced myself for the onslaught of emotion, of tears, or pain, or sadness or whatever.

None of it came.

"You okay with that?"

"No," I whispered. "I'm not okay with any of this. And I can't believe it happened. But God, does it make me a bitch to feel relieved she can't hurt anyone anymore? I wouldn't want that for her though."

"Yeah, I know." His voice was cold as steel and thick as molasses. I looked back at Beaux, jaw tight, muscle popping his jaw, one throbbing at the side of his neck and I reached for him, placed my hand at the muscle on his neck and held him tight.

"I want to go home."

"Nurse said the doctor would be in here soon, and we'll talk about it."

Good. I was still exhausted. Not even sure what time it was or how many times I'd been woken up during the night to have my vitals checked, but I closed my eyes and laid back down.

"When I mean home, I mean yours."

My voice was slow, thick with exhaustion, and as sleep pulled me back under, I barely heard him reply. "Good. Because that's exactly where you're going."

WHEN I WOKE UP AGAIN, a nurse was pulling her stethoscope away from my inner elbow and my dad and Beaux were whispering to each other at the side of my bed.

I looked at the nurse first. "All good?"

"Seems that way. Doctor's making his rounds so he should be in in a few moments. Need anything?"

"Ice water, please."

"I'll get it," Beaux said, stepping from my dad to grab the large plastic cup next to my bed. "I need to stretch my legs."

I didn't want him to go. I liked him next to me. I liked hearing him tell me he loved me. That I was going to his place as home. I wanted him to be next to me.

"Maybe—"

"Hush," he whispered, bending down and gently kissing me. "Your dad wants to talk to you. I'll be back before the doctor gets here."

"Dad?"

"Yeah, darlin'," he said.

He wheeled himself over to me and Beaux gave me another kiss. "Be right back."

"We need to talk," Dad said, taking my hand with his good one. It struck me then how frail he was, and I didn't think all of it was his strokes or being worried about me. He was just getting old.

I bit my lip and nodded. "Okay."

"First, I need you to know how much I love you and how damn glad I am that you're okay. When I got that call last night," he paused, shook his head. My chest burned with emotion but I held it back, staying strong for him. "No dad should ever get that call, scared the hell out of me, sweetheart."

"I'm going to be okay, Dad."

"Yeah. And I'm thankful. But thinking of you, how much you've given up for me by giving up your job in Charlotte and moving home, taking over the garage, working two jobs, that's not right."

"I don't regret it for a second."

"Don't care," he said, and his voice was thick. Stern. My

dad was rarely grouchy, and I pushed up as best I could on my hospital bed and took notice. "Talked to Melanie last night on the way home, and she and I, along with Beaux this morning, made some decisions."

None of that sounded good. My pulse raced, the beeping of my monitors increased. My dad looked at them and back to me.

"Don't get mad. But some things need to change and I needed Beaux's help with some of it."

"Okay." I swallowed a thick mass in my throat and squeezed his hand. "Hit me with it."

"Melanie found me a place at Crossroads Townhomes."

"What?" I knew the development. It was a fifty-five and older community on a golf course. He was barely eligible. "Why? You've always said those places were for old people."

"I know what I said, but I've changed my mind. It'll be good for me," he said. "Lots of people around and things to do in the clubhouse. The places are all one-level and only two bedrooms. It'll be easier for me to manage."

Nothing was computing. I shook my head. "But you're doing better."

"Yeah, and I don't need Melanie hovering over me at home, and I don't need you pausing your life to take care of me."

"I wasn't—"

"You were. But now you got a man who loves you and a life to lead with him, and you, doing whatever you want. I've already talked to Mike. I'm handing over the garage to both of you. He can lead the mechanics and you can handle the garage." He waved a hand in the air. "Or figure it out for yourselves or walk away. That's your choice."

"I like the garage." I didn't necessarily want to own it, but it was my family's. For that reason alone, I didn't want to let it go. He'd talked before about leaving it to Mike and me, but I had still thought that was years down the road, decades, even.

Emotion gripped me, lodging in my throat. My chin trembled as I stared at my dad. "Everything's changing so quickly."

"And it's about damn time it does. All of this needed to happen. It's time we move forward."

"What about when you're better?"

His brown eyes softened, and he held my hand to his mouth, kissing it. "I ain't ever gonna get one hundred percent better, Paige, sweetie. And even if I do, I'm still getting old. I'm tired of being alone. I don't want to be a burden to you, and I need to live my life the best I can. It's not living in that house, unable to take care of it, unable to take care of myself. This development gives me that freedom, plus, they have an on-site medical facility so I can continue getting help if I need it."

"So it's all decided, then." This was a lot of information thrown at me at once, and Beaux had promised he'd talk to me about these decisions.

Yet, for once, I couldn't summon the energy to become angry.

Everything my dad said was right, as much I despised change and thinking of him getting older. And Beaux had already proven all he wanted to do was be there for me, to help make my life better.

"Where will I live?" I asked, trying to follow everything my dad was saying.

"In the house, but to be honest, I think you got yourself a man who for a long time, isn't going to let you out of his sight again, honey. Worried I wouldn't see the day you found a man who would love you and take care of you the way you needed it, but Beaux's got that for you in spades."

Before I could say anything, the door opened and the doctor walked in, Beaux right behind him carrying my water.

THIRTY-FOUR

PAIGE

"You have to go," I whispered to Beaux. Even though I'd told him I wanted to go to his house when I left the hospital, I'd then remembered it was Saturday.

He was supposed to be getting on a plane for an away game.

He scowled at me. "I'm not going. And I'm not playing. You're nuts if you think I'm leaving you right now."

I scanned the room. Jaxon had followed us home from the hospital. Melanie and my dad were there. Mike and two other mechanics, Lance and Killian, had come over to welcome me home.

People who cared about me and would protect me, surrounded me.

Nothing would happen, especially with Hannah not being alive, which was still something I was trying not to think about.

"You have to," I said, my voice firmer. "I'm not having you miss a game when it's not necessary." He opened his mouth but I held up my hand. "Please. Do this for me. I'll be here resting all weekend, just like the doctor ordered, and when you get back tomorrow, I'll be waiting for you at your place."

He lost his scowl and grinned mischievously. "Our place."

"What?"

"Our place. You said my house was your home, so if I agree to go play this game, you agree to move in with me."

A rush of warmth flooded my veins and it had nothing to do with the blanket covering me or his body so close to mine. We were on the couch, but there were a half-dozen people in the room. A quick scan told me none of them were even pretending not to be listening to this.

"You're blackmailing me into moving in with you? Now?" My brows rose.

"No. I'm using all the plays at my disposal." His grin died and his face went serious. "I love you, Paige. I want you there. Everything feels right when you're in my home. Move in with me."

Tears blurred my vision and I didn't bother blinking them away.

He was right. When Beaux showed up at the hospital, all I'd wanted was him. I wanted to be surrounded by him. And with everything my dad had already shared with me about his future plans, there was nothing holding me back.

Not anymore.

"Okay," I whispered. My fingers slid to his neck, back into his hair. His head fell forward until our lips brushed against each other's. "I'll move in with you."

"And I'll kiss you properly when your dad isn't staring us down and we don't have an audience."

I laughed against his mouth and he kissed me anyway. It was short and sweet, given the audience, but it still left my breathless. I forgot anyone else was in the room until Melanie whooped and hollered, "Woo-hoo! This calls for champagne!"

~

THE ROUGH RIDER'S LOST.

I watched the game from my living room in Beaux's town-home with Dad, Melanie, Shannon, and Mike.

When I agreed to move in with him Saturday, he demanded I pack up and get moved in so he could come home to me, to our home, after he returned from the game. The men from the garage came and moved everything over as I packed my clothes and personal things. But I stayed the night at my dad's house.

Sunday morning, Jaxon came over and loaded me into his Explorer while everyone else followed us to Beaux's or met us there.

He was still hanging close even though when he showed up early Sunday morning, he'd said he had one of his men go to Hannah's apartment. They'd found dozens more photos of Beaux and I together and apart. He said they also found three DVDs, the same kind that had been in the garage. I suspected it wasn't all they found, but I didn't ask more questions.

I knew all I needed to know.

They turned around and called Raleigh PD, gave them all the evidence, and Agent Spellman had stopped by shortly after to talk with me about the events that occurred.

Beaux hadn't been there to hold me while I cried through the story, reliving the fear I'd felt when I realized Hannah wanted to hurt lyme. But my dad held one hand, Melanie held the other, and even though Beaux wasn't there, I was still thinking of him, getting through it. When I was done, Agent Spellman handed me his card and told me to call him if I remembered or thought of anything else. The PD would continue investigating but considering it seemed pretty cut and dry that Hannah had been the person sending the notes, I doubted anything would come of it.

I tried, again, to push it all out of my mind. I didn't know what to think of Hannah, how she'd tried not just to hurt me, but kill me, and willing to take her own life in the process.

I'd deal with it someday when I wasn't still wearing a brace on my arm, and hearing the screeching of a car slamming through metal in my dreams.

Then the game started, and with each passing quarter, Shannon and I grew exponentially more frustrated. The offense struggled to move the ball. The defense couldn't stop Seattle's running game.

In the end, Seattle won twenty-one to six, our only points coming from two, fifty-yard field goals. Beaux left the game looking dejected and I started planning how to help him feel better.

"Well, that sucked," Shannon said, slumping into the couch next to me. "Oliver's going to be one grumpy man when he gets home tonight."

She didn't sound that upset about Oliver's grumpiness. From the time I'd spent with them, I figured even if Oliver was upset about the game, one look at his fiancée and he'd turn into a sweetheart.

"How does Beaux take losses?" I asked. It was their first loss of the season. I hadn't been around him after one and even after a win he always finds a way he or the team can improve.

"Like he takes everything else."

Figured. Nothing ruffled the guy, except for me.

"Well, that was fun," my dad said. "But I need to head back home. Lots to do and lots to start packing up."

Over the weekend, Dad and I had talked more about his decisions and while they still made me uncomfortable, I now understood them.

This was what he wanted for me. A life with friends and a guy who adored me. I not only wanted it, I'd do whatever I had to keep it.

"I'll see you soon," Melanie said, coming to where I was resting on the couch. My back was sore, and while I didn't have a concussion, my head occasionally throbbed. The worst injury was my sprained wrist, and I was able to handle all of the injuries with Advil. She kissed me on the cheek and stood up. "Call me if you need me."

"I'll be fine."

"Yeah," she grinned and winked. "Once that hunk of yours gets home, I'm sure you'll be just fine."

My cheeks burned. My dad was in the room for crying out loud. "Go away." I mock glared, and even that was pointless. When Melanie was around, I was almost always laughing and that time was no different.

"I'm going, I'm going. Ready Sam?" She waited until he hobbled over to her, blowing me a kiss so he didn't have to maneuver around the coffee table with his crutches. "Ready Freddy. Love you, darling."

"Love you, too, Dad."

Everyone said their goodbyes, clearing out, and leaving me alone with Jaxon. He turned the television station to another football game and I flipped my phone in my hand, debating whether or not to text Beaux.

I always congratulated him after a game, but I didn't want to say anything to upset him.

I settled on the one thing I knew would make him smile.

I love you.

"You can take off," I said to Jaxon after I sent the text.

"Not until Beaux's here." He'd crossed his arms over his chest on the chair at the other end of the couch, kicked up his feet on the coffee table. Despite his relaxed posture, I knew he was still alert.

It wasn't necessary. Hannah was gone as gone could get.

Jaxon's presence still comforted me like a thick blanket.

"Thanks, Jaxon. You're the best."

He arched a brow. "No Rambo?"

"I thought you hated it."

He shrugged a shoulder. "It was starting to grow on me."

My phone buzzed in my hand and I smiled at Beaux's response. Love you too. Heading to plane now. Be home late.

Home. I couldn't stop the smile from splitting my cheeks so wide they ached.

They'd played an early game but with the time change, he still wouldn't get home until after eleven.

That meant eight more hours alone with only Jaxon.

My fingers flew across the keypad. I'll be here, in OUR bed. Naked and ready for you.

His response was almost instant. Jesus. Now I have a fucking hard-on and I'm sitting next to Quinten.

A laugh burst from my throat. Better not let him touch what's mine.

Woman.

I could practically hear his sexy growl.

Still laughing, I turned to Jaxon. "So, Rambo. What do you think of Melanie?"

That growl, I definitely heard.

THIRTY-FIVE
BEAUX

"Damn it," I groaned, and tightened my grip on Paige's head.

When I arrived back to my place—or, our place, rather—after the game, she'd practically attacked me as soon as Jaxon left.

It was fitting, I suppose, considering how many times I attacked her as soon as she walked in the door.

Now, my back was against the wall, and she was on her knees. She had her good hand wrapped around my cock and her mouth doing most of the delicious work.

My balls were pulled tight, ready to blow, but no way was I letting that happen.

The first night we spent together, living together, I was having her slowly, taking my time with her body, drawing out our orgasms until our echoes came close to shattering the windows.

"Paige," I groaned, trying to pull her off.

She responded by taking me deeper and opening her throat until I hit the back of her.

"Fuck."

Screw it. If I got off now, it gave me more time to play with her later.

She hummed around my dick like she knew what I was thinking and liked the idea, so I tossed my head back, locked my knees so I didn't collapse, and I let her take me there, her hot, wet mouth clamped around my cock, her hand working in tandem on my shaft. I let Paige set the pace of the world's best damn blow job.

"Yeah, honey. Just like that." I pushed her hair off her face and watched every damn moment. Her eyes met mine and that was my ending.

Because every damn time she looked at me since I knew she loved me, she could never hide it in her eyes.

Brimming with love, her gaze locked with mine, and my orgasms soared through me.

"Gonna come, honey," I warned her.

She hummed her response, tightened her hand on my shaft.

I thrust into her, felt my dick swell, and then I held her gently while she took everything I gave her, swallowing it down and making me feel like the luckiest damn man alive.

She slowed her hand and slowly pulled off me, leaning back to her knees with a noticeable grimace. "Welcome home," she whispered.

"You're hurt." The rush of my climax quickly evaporated. I yanked up my pants and zipped them. "Come here." I held out my hand and helped to her feet. When she was standing, I gently pulled her into my arms, picking her up.

"I'm not that hurt," she said, tucking her head into my shoulder. "But I did want to make you feel better after the loss today."

I kissed her forehead. Her temple was still swollen, an ugly purple bruise rimmed with jagged cuts that made me almost fucking happy Hannah was dead every time I looked at her.

"I appreciate the gesture, and I'll take them whenever you want to give them, but I don't need help feeling better. You win some, you lose some."

I walked up the stairs and she tightened her hold on me.

"Really?"

"No. I'm frustrated." I kissed her head again. "Losing sucks and I hate it, but we played a shit game, couldn't find our groove regardless of what we changed, and I wasn't entirely in game mode this weekend."

"Beaux." Her voice went sad but I kissed her, gently setting her on my bed and following her until I was on top of her.

"Not your fault, Paige, but you can't expect me to go out there and not be worried about you."

"I'm fine. Or I will be."

"I know, which is why I only got sacked once tonight instead of the six times I should have been. You're strong, you'll heal, and we'll move on, but someone important in my life was hurt and because of that, my mind was on you and that not only made me play like shit, the other players not only felt it, but they were worried too. It was just a crap day, one I want to forget."

I brushed her hair off her shoulder, fanned it out on the bed and came closer, pressing my lips to her jaw, her throat, her collarbone.

She shivered beneath me, dug her fingers into my shoulders.

"You need to get out of your suit then."

I laughed against her skin and then thought of how she'd flinched downstairs. "Are you too hurt? We can wait."

"I don't want to." Her hands were on my shoulders, pushing under my suit coat and shoving it off. I leaned off her, straddling her waist, and shucked off my suit and then unbuttoned my shirt enough so I could pull that off, too.

"I want you," Paige said, her gaze roaming my bare chest.

She looked at me like I was her hero. I still felt like shit. Jaxon did too. It'd take awhile to wash that away. Which was the main reason why I played like such shit. To my coaches' and team's credit, as pissed off as they were, and as frustrated as they'd been with me, they also understood. We'd come back. Seattle was a damn good team, anyway, and on the best days, it would have been a hard fought battle.

Sitting in this bed, now belonging to both Paige and I, and watching as she wiggled out of her T-shirt beneath me, none of it mattered.

She wasn't holding our faults and failures against us.

She was now living with me.

Soon, when the time was right, I'd get a ring on her finger and plant a baby in her and then we'd have everything we ever wanted.

I couldn't tie her like I wanted, like she enjoyed, and I couldn't hold her hands like I fucking loved doing while I was inside of her, but I could still make this night exceptional.

I stood from the bed and kicked off my pants and boxers, ripped off my dress socks, and moved to the end of the bed. Leaning over her, I kissed her ankle, up to the back of her knee, grinning as she spread her legs.

"Beaux."

Her voice was already breathy and needy little gasps fell from her lips as I teased her knee, her inner thighs with my lips and my tongue. My touch was gentle, reverent.

I wanted to pour everything I felt for this crazy, strong woman, into this night, into this moment, so she would know down to the marrow of her bones how much she meant to me.

Tugging down her shorts and underwear, I pressed kisses just above her center, adding teasing flicks of my tongue to her already swollen clit.

God, she was gorgeous. Everywhere.

She arched into me and I pressed a hand to her hipbone, holding her still.

"What do you want, honey?"

"You," she gasped as I slid a finger inside her and twisted. "You. Only you."

I love you didn't even the same impact as those words did. She meant all of them, but that admission struck me hard and fast in the chest. She was being truthful. I could have been a mechanic, a bartender. I could have sold cars or taught school, or been the world's richest tech giant. She didn't care about money or fame or expensive shit, if anything, I'd learned me having it made it harder to get through to her.

But I'd busted down those walls weeks ago, and now, there was just us.

Her. Me. Only us and who we were at our cores.

"Fuck, I love you," I whispered.

"Please, Beaux," she gasped.

I quit teasing. I bent down, slid my tongue through her folds and then I ate her.

She writhed as soon as I groaned against her hot and slickened flesh, and with my finger inside her, I added a second, stretching and twisting until I reached the rigid flesh inside. I rubbed against her, continued sliding my tongue over her clit until she bucked wildly.

She came, screaming my name, pulling on my hair, grabbing for me like she always did when I made her come.

It was fucking wild. It was heaven.

I wanted to flip her over, take her hard and fast, but with her back, I didn't want to risk hurting her.

As she was still coming, I slid my fingers out of her, running them through her slit until I reached a barrier I hadn't yet gone past.

Her eyes flew open as I pressed against her. "What are you—"

"Ever been taken here?" I asked.

She shook her head, and I went back to her pussy and gathered more moisture. "Would you?"

She shivered, goose bumps popped all over her as I teased her again, pressing against her with the tip of my finger.

I had this insane need to take her everywhere, having every single inch of her body known to me.

I pressed inside and a shudder racked her entire body. "Okay?"

She flinched and I paused. Then her hand came out of my hair and she lifted up, wrapping that hand around my wrist. "I'll give you anything you want, Beaux, anytime you ask."

"Fuck, but I love you." I pressed further inside.

She fell back to the bed and moaned. I followed over her, bending back down and went back to her pussy. Her clit.

I teased her everywhere while I began pressing and pulling my finger in and out of her ass, going slow, taking my time, and it wasn't long before she was fucking drenched.

Panting. Writhing. She gripped my arm, pleaded for more and she came again, louder than before. Her legs shook while she came and I slid my finger out of her, moving up her body, kissing everywhere I could touch. Her stomach, her breasts, her nipples.

I was hard as a rock, ready to blow again, but I held back, giving her time to come down and when she opened her eyes, she looked at me and smiled.

"I love you, too."

"Good. Then show me how much by making love to me."

She wrapped her body around me, arms and legs at my shoulders and hips, and I slid inside her.

We made love slowly, lazily, kissing and giggling, and it wasn't just the best sex of my entire life.

When we came together, me holding out long enough to give her a third orgasm, we came with our hearts beating against each other's. Our mouths fused together, and our bodies joined as one.

It was the only way I wanted us to be, for the rest of our lives. If life had taught me anything, especially in the last forty-eight hours, it was that everything could change in the blink of an eye.

I wasn't waiting, taking anything slow with Paige. We had the rest of our lives to live together, but we were starting them now.

EPILOGUE

Paige

LOUD CHEERS ERUPTED as soon as Oliver pressed his lips
to Shannon.

The minister had just pronounced them man and wife, and
they kissed. He held her flushed to him, bending over and
tipping her back. Oliver kissed Shannon like it was the best
damn kiss of his life and he ended it to another loud round of
hoots and hollers.

I stood to the side as a bridesmaid, Shannon's best friend
from Iowa, Melissa was her maid of honor. She grinned at me
and I laughed, shaking my head while they continued practically having sex with each other on the small stage they'd
constructed on their property for their wedding.

Finally, Oliver pulled back, and he spun Shannon to the
crowd and they raised their hands in the air.

Music blared, escorting them down the aisle, and I quickly

followed Melissa. She took Danny Rudolph's arm, Oliver's best man, and I waited for Beaux to reach me.

When he did, he kissed my cheek and whispered, "Our wedding kiss will be better than that."

I playfully slapped his arm. "Too bad we don't have much time to practice."

He'd just proposed last week.

"We don't need practice. We already are perfect."

He was absolutely right.

Beaux walked me down the aisle, and we headed straight for the dance floor and reception area set up at the back of Oliver and Shannon's house. Bethany Carlson was there with her band. A famous country singer, she was also a good friend of Oliver's and now Shannon's. She'd volunteered to provide entertainment for the night as her wedding gift to them.

There was also a full bar, an enormous catered buffet of seafood and steak and more piles of meat and vegetables than I'd ever seen anywhere, but most of the team was in attendance and those guys ate.

Six weeks ago, the Rough Riders won their second Super Bowl in a row, filling the new stadium in Minnesota while they took on the Green Bay Packers.

Beaux had said it held an extra special moment of love for him since he'd started his NFL Career in Minnesota.

After the parade Raleigh had for the team and the media craze died down, we immediately went on a two-week long vacation to Fiji.

We were going back next month for our wedding. My dad, Melanie, Mike, Shannon, and Oliver were going to be our only guests.

It was an easy decision. My dad's broken leg had long since healed and over the last several months, he'd regained even more movement in his right side. He used a walker or a cane now, his wheelchair rarely pulled out of the corner. He spent his nights playing poker at the clubhouse and while he couldn't golf, he'd go out with a group of a guys and drive the golf cart. He came to the garage occasionally and hung out when Mike or I would bring him. He always had company and had made dozens of new friends.

We ate together at least once a week, usually at our house. When Beaux traveled, I went to Dad's place and watched his game in the clubhouse. Most of the men and many of their wives would join us for a potluck dinner while we screamed and shouted and cheered at the ninety-seven inch projector screen television.

Melanie was no longer his nurse, but instead, she'd become my best friend, and we got together at least once a week for dinner or lunch.

Our lives were settling. The pain of my accident and Hannah was a memory neither of us talked about much. She was laid to rest days after the accident, and when I knew that was happening, I'd cried in Beaux's arms, falling apart in our living room, so damn thankful I was okay, that Beaux and I were together, but so utterly devastated at everything that had happened. It was the last time I cried over it, but when I continued having nightmares for weeks, Melanie talked me into seeing a therapist.

That had helped, and after a few months, the nightmares went away and so did my therapist.

By the time the Super Bowl came around, Beaux and I were more in love, my dad was happy, and I had absolutely everything I could have ever wanted.

Life was perfect.

Or it would be in four weeks when we flew to Fiji and exchanged our own vows.

Overall, I couldn't complain. Had nothing to complain

about.

So, I let Beaux sweep me into his arms, pull me onto the dance floor.

We celebrated the entire night with our family of football players and their wives or girlfriends.

I drank champagne with my new sister-in-law and brother-in-law.

We laughed.

We partied.

And when we went to bed that night, after making me come three times, Beaux pulled me into his arms.

I threw my leg over his like I always did and rested my head on his shoulder, my arm draped over his stomach.

Playing with his thin trail of hair beneath his belly button, I kissed his chest.

"I love you, Beaux. You've given me more than anything I ever wanted, ever dreamed possible."

"Jesus," he gasped and tightened his hold around my back. "I love you too, Paige."

"There's just one more thing I want from you," I said, still kissing him and sliding my hand down.

He was already hard and I wrapped my hand around him, sliding up and down his shaft.

"Shit," he gasped. "What is it?"

I tilted my head up. "I want a baby, a boy with your blue—"

It was all I got out before I was tossed to my back, and he was on top of me. He kissed me, stealing my words.

"Tomorrow you go off the pill. We start trying right away." He pressed the tip of him to my center and slid inside.

I kissed his throat as he began moving. "I threw them away tonight," I admitted.

Beaux would give me anything I ever wanted, and I had no doubt when I knew we were ready to have kids, he'd want to start trying as soon as possible.

"You're crazy," he said, laughing and kissing me. "And I fucking love you."

"Fucking love me? Or love fucking me."

"Yes."

I laughed and pressed my mouth to his. "I love you too. Forever."

We moved, joined together, touching everywhere. His hands clasped around mine and he held me down, pinned me in place, and as we made love, both of us crying out our climaxes at the same time, I'd never felt so utterly, completely, free.

THANK **you for reading Filthy Player! Keep reading more Rough Riders and fall in love with Gage Bryant in Wicked Player. Check it out today by clicking on the title.**

CLICK HERE to sign up for my newsletter and receive information about all upcoming releases as well as sales and other exclusive content. Plus, as a thank you, you'll receive a FREE E-Book of mine.

WANT to be the first to know about upcoming sales?
Follow me on BookBub!

. . .

WANT to ensure you never miss a new release? Follow me on Amazon.

THANK YOU

I have the best team! Thank you so much to Shannon, Hilary, Ellie, and Virginia. You ladies make my world go around. Thank you for all your hard work with helping me promote Filthy Player as well as your creative abilities and design and editing. You're all amazing.

The Rough Riders was supposed to be a standalone, beginning and ending with Dirty Player. It was supposed to be a break from more emotional stories I was writing with The Fireside Series and lighten up my mind a bit. Instead, due to the constant messages I received from my readers, I began thinking..."What if?" And Filthy Player was born. Now, these guys are burrowing deep, and while I don't know whose story is next, there will definitely be more Rough Riders in the future, so stay tuned!

To my readers and all the bloggers who are excited about my books, and tirelessly promote authors, thank you from the bottom of my heart! I couldn't do what I love without your help and I'm so eternally thankful.

And last...but definitely not least. My family. You're the best parts about my day and my life. I love you always.

ABOUT THE AUTHOR

Stacey Lynn currently lives in North Carolina with her husband and four children. When she's not conquering mountains of laundry and fighting a war against dust bunnies and cracker crumbs, you can find her playing with her children, curled up on the couch with a good book, or hanging out with her friends.

She lives off her daily pot of coffee, can only write with a bowlful of Skittles nearby, and has been in love with romance novels since before she could drive herself to the library.

If you would like to know more about Stacey Lynn, follow her here:

Website: www.staceylynnbooks.com
    Facebook: www.facebook.com/staceylynnbooks
    Twitter: www.twitter.com/staceylynnbooks
    Instagram: www.instagram.staceylynn.author

If you enjoyed this book, please leave a review on the site where it was purchased.

ALSO BY STACEY LYNN

The Rough Riders Series

Dirty Player

Filthy Player

Wicked Player

Love In The Heartland Series

Captivated By You

This Time Around

Long Road Home

Before We Fell

Perfect Match Series

Fake Wife

Knocked Up

28 Dates

Weekend Fling – coming soon

The Luminous Series

Dominate Me

Crave Me

Long For Me

The Fireside Series

His to Love

His to Protect

His to Cherish

His to Seduce

Tangled Love Series

Entice

Embrace

Enflame

Just One Series

Just One Song

Just One Week

Just One Regret

Just One Moment

The Nordic Lords MC Series

Point of Return

Point of Redemption

Point of Freedom

Point of Surrender

Standalones

Remembering Us

Don't Lie To Me

Try Me – A Don't Lie To Me Novella